'Two Steps Over Intrigue'
By
Neal Hardin

Featuring, the stories,

'The Go-To Guy'

And

'The Lady Below'

© Neal Hardin 2023

All rights reserved.

Third Edition

Neal Hardin has asserted his rights under the Copyright, Designs and patents act 1988 to be identified as the author of this book.

No part of this book may be reproduced or used, or transmitted in any form, without the prior written permission of the author. For permissions requests, contact the author.

This is a work of fiction. Names, characters, businesses, places, events, and incidents are either the products of the author's imagination or used in a fictitious manner. Any resemblance to actual persons, living or dead, or actual events is purely coincidental.

ISBN 9798865642046

Acknowledgement

I will be forever grateful to Rose Drew and Alan Gillott of Stairwell Books, who first published my novel 'The Go-to Guy' in March 2018. On the ending of that agreement in March 2023, the author now wishes to independently publish the story, in this book, along with some new material.

With thanks to my good friend Alison Henesey, for her corrections, suggestions and ability to spot the typos.

The Go-To Guy

Chapter 1

Not many would deny murder is a gruesome business. But for some, it's not quite as black and white. There are some who use murder for personal gain, assassins, hitmen, mercenaries, and the like. These people will kill if the price is right. Hired killers are a breed apart: they don't advertise their services and they don't brag about their conquests, or they wouldn't be in business for long.

Then there are the arrangers: the people who act as the go-to guy. Tom Masson was such a guy. Masson was born into a family of villains, but had gone straight for most of his life. He had gone into business at twenty-two, putting his time and energy into a chain of market stalls throughout North-West London. Five years later he set up a chain of strip joints. When the stripping business went 'tits-up', he converted the premises into eateries and did okay. When the market place became saturated with eateries, he diversified and turned them into wine bars. As the licensing laws relaxed, he hit the jackpot and did well by turning the venues into go-to places. The only thing he did that was not legit was to become a go-to between those who wanted a service and the guy who would carry out the task.

Masson lived in the west London area of Bedford Park, a little known enclave between Chiswick to the south and Acton to the north. He liked it. He liked being connected to the City, but not being so close that it pressed down on him. At forty-two he was hitting the sweet spot in his life. He was not old enough to fear the future and not yet old enough to regret the past. A number of relationships had come and gone. He wasn't looking for someone special. At five-ten and lithe, he came across as the kind of guy who looked after himself, but wasn't obsessed by the way he looked. He wasn't God's gift to women, but considered himself a reasonably good looking forty-something with a decent dress sense, a good sense of humour, who wasn't too bad in the sack.

It all started with Divorty.

Liam Divorty wasn't a hoodlum and he wasn't a villain. He was a killer for hire. If you had the need, the money and the contacts, you could hire his services for a fee of £80,000. He could rub out a rival, an errant business partner, a relative, or a spouse. He wasn't choosy about who he killed. As long as you paid him he couldn't care less.

He was a part-time killer because he could hardly be full-time: murder was a big deal. His services were rarely required. As well as being a killer for hire, he was the owner of a large used-car business in the north London area of Islington. His murder record went back a few years to the time he'd been hired by Earl Carter to rub out business rival Harry Ronson. Carter had asked Tom Masson if he could do it, or if he knew someone who could carry out the hit. Masson knew Divorty and knew that he was strapped for cash, so he asked him.

The prospect of becoming a killer for hire had never surfaced in Divorty's mind until the night Masson put the question to him. Divorty had asked him why he didn't want to do it himself. Masson, forever the pragmatist, had said that it was simple: he didn't need the money. Whereas Divorty's business was suffering from a cash-flow crisis. In reality, Divorty needed money to fund his lavish lifestyle. So agreed, said he would seriously consider it for £80,000, half now and half when the job was complete. Masson contacted Carter and told him he had a killer for the job, without naming him. From then on, his go-to role was established.

Harry Ronson was dead two weeks later. Divorty, had donned a full-face balaclava to prevent anyone from recognising him, then he ambushed Ronson in a dark alley, as he walked home from an East End pub. He attacked him with a baseball bat and smashed his head in. Brutal, but job done. Divorty's reputation as a killer was born, though it was hardly broadcast around the neighbourhood. Naturally there wasn't a high demand for such a service. He had only carried out three other jobs in the four years since the murder of Harry Ronson. His favourite method was with his bare hands. He found that first night he couldn't stand the sight of blood. Cold, calculating, and unstable summed up Liam Divorty.

Whilst Divorty and Masson were not exactly buddies, they were partners of a sort. A few knew that if the service was needed, the 'go-to' guy was Tom Masson. First, they had to put it to Masson and if he thought it was doable, he would inform Divorty. If Masson agreed, it was extremely likely that Divorty would agree. Masson received twenty per cent of each payoff: it was a symbiotic relationship. Divorty had little remorse when it came to killing. It paid well and he had a sadistic streak.

Chapter 2

It had been two weeks since Masson had first met the woman who said she was Mrs Charles Croft. He had had little doubt that she was who she said she was. Now, two weeks later, he was not so sure. He recalled how the meeting had come about. First, he had heard rumours that someone had a job. Then, one Thursday morning he received the word from a contact in south London. There was no formal structure to these things. Masson didn't have a set method, as each enquiry tended to be different in its own way.

On this occasion, the contact had been someone by the name of Peter Smetham, a man associated with some criminal-types who were involved in forgery. He had revealed that someone's wife had expressed a wish to become a widow. The reasons were not clear. The client had left a mobile phone number with Smetham which he gave to Tom Masson.

Tom had only the number, and the scant information supplied. As always, he was in doubt as to whether it was genuine, or was in fact a sting to bust him. He had to be cautious.

He decided to wait for a few hours to make the call from a telephone box not too far from his home. The call was answered by a posh-sounding female, who didn't give her name. Masson didn't introduce himself either. He simply said, "I understand you may have a problem that you want an answer to."

The woman on the other end of the line didn't reply for a few moments. Perhaps she had her own doubts that this was the optimal way to go. It was a few seconds before she answered in a clear and determined voice.

"Yes. Yes. That is in fact the case." Immediately, he had the impression of someone who knew what she wanted and could also be careful and shrewd. However, it was too early to be sure about that.

"Would you like to meet me?" he asked.

Again, she didn't answer straight away, but waited to compose her response. When she did she was unequivocal. "Yes. That would be a good thing to do."

Masson sensed that he was under starter's orders. The only difference was that the tape was still down and the horses were agitated as they milled around the box, excited by the roar of the crowd in the distance.

"Do you know the entrance to Green Park tube station on Piccadilly?" he asked.

"Yes?"

"Meet me outside of the entrance at two o'clock tomorrow afternoon. Can you make it?"

"Yes. I'll be there."

He noticed that definite tone in her voice. "How will I know you?" she asked.

"Stand at the second bus stop. The number two-five-six to Shepherds Bush."

"A bus stop?" she asked, as if she'd never used one before.

"Yes. A bus stop. Two o'clock tomorrow?"

"All right," she said.

Masson ended the call. He replayed the conversation in his mind and summarised it. There was a sort of mild hostility to the bus stop which told him she could be moneyed and the real deal.

Friday 11th September

The next day, Masson made his way into town and walked along Piccadilly. It was a changeable, fairly mild mid-September afternoon. He walked up Piccadilly from the Hyde Park end, on the path facing the traffic. Despite the move into early autumn, the streets of the capital were still busy with tourists. A tour bus, only half full, came by. The Union Jacks attached to the front of a nearby department store were still in the listless breeze. Tom liked the feel of the city at this time of the year. The heat of summer had gone, to be replaced by a fresher, more manageable, atmosphere and the traffic, though not exactly quiet, wasn't as busy as it had been. He looked up at the entrance to the Tube and the canopy hanging over the path. There were a small number of people milling about the entrance and the bus stops. He unconsciously raised the collar of his coat and slipped a pair of shades over his eyes.

There were three people standing at the second bus stop: two men and a woman, who had joined the queue in the last few seconds. Was she the client? The potential client, he corrected himself. He glanced at his watch as the hands moved to two o'clock exactly. The woman was white and was dressed in a sky-blue ski-jacket and dark blue jeans. On her head she wore a navy-blue baseball cap, which sported a rowing club motif. A long ponytail tied by a pink scrunchy was poking out through the opening at the back of the cap. She was carrying a handbag on a gold chain strap over her right shoulder. A cool, sophisticated look in keeping with the image of the person he had spoken to on the telephone.

On reaching the queue for the two-five-six to Shepherds Bush, he slid across the path and stood a few feet behind her. She was almost as tall as him, five-ten. She turned her head to look to the side. As she did so, he caught the profile of a woman he estimated to be thirty years of age. A very beautiful woman with an exquisitely sculptured face, and full, rose coloured lips. Her figure under the jacket and jeans suggested a slim body full of curves.

On sensing that someone was behind her she turned and looked at him. Tom had his first view of her delicate nose, her turquoise eyes, and narrow, thin eyebrows, shaded by the brim of her baseball cap. If she was indeed the client, then she looked like someone who had money. He glanced down at the diamond-encrusted gold band on her wedding finger.

"Are you waiting for the two-five-six to Shepherds Bush?" he asked and looked into her eyes.

"Yes," she replied reservedly.

"So am I. But I don't think it's coming. Perhaps we should walk some of the way."

She observed him through eyes that could melt icebergs. Her cheek bones were to die for. Her lips cried out to be kissed. Nevertheless, he knew he had to stay focused and not to allow any distractions to get the better of him. That could be costly.

"Are you…him?" she asked in a semi-whisper.

"Depends on who *he* is," he replied, though he didn't know if she would appreciate this, so he quickly changed tack. "Yes, I am."

"Perhaps we should walk, then," she replied.

Even from this snippet he knew it was the same person he had spoken to on the telephone yesterday. They moved away together and stepped along the path, walked towards Hyde Park, then turned through a gate, and down one of the paths that dissect Green Park lawn. He noticed the running shoes on her feet and the gold bangles around her left wrist.

There were a number of people sitting on the grass and on the park benches along the path. They walked in silence towards Constitution Hill. He could feel his cheeks reddening in the warmth of the sun. After a further twenty yards they came to an unoccupied park bench. He motioned to the bench and they sat down with a gap between them. She sat back and crossed her long legs. She was wearing white ankle socks. He glanced from side to side, then discreetly over his shoulder. They were alone; the bench at the other side of the path was unoccupied. Over his right shoulder he could see the Ritz Hotel on Piccadilly looming high above the park. He looked at her and she returned his gaze.

"I'm Tom," he said.

She averted her eyes from his then looked down at her feet. He got another look at her profile. There was always an uneasy start to these things so he decided to move on.

"What can I do for you?" he asked, leaving a pause at the end of the sentence to see if she would fill the gap.

"Call me Sara if you wish."

"What can I do for you, Sara?" he asked.

She slowly rolled her eyes to meet his. "It's my husband," she said, then flicked her view from side to side in much the same way he had done. She hitched around to face him. He noticed her fingernails were perfectly manicured. He had a thing about hands and fingers. She could be a perfect hand model. He put his mind back to the task.

"Fine. I can help with that I suppose. And I don't want to know the reasons why. That's none of my business. I just need…" He paused as a group of people came along the path. He smiled at them. A police car came hurtling along Piccadilly, the sound of its siren bouncing off the wall. He waited until the people were well out of earshot. He continued, "I just need to know some basic details…"

"I want it doing next week," she said quickly.

"Next week?" he asked in a surprised tone, then lowered his voice. "The fee will be £80,000. Half now. Half later." He turned and looked at her. "Is that acceptable?"

She nodded her head.

"What's his name?" She looked at him in silence. "The name of the other party?" She stared, expression unreadable. It still didn't register. "The name of the person you want killing," he said finally in a sotto voce voice.

He asked the question like that in order to gauge her reaction. If she was serious about killing her husband, then 'killing' was a key word. After all, this is what they were talking about – murder. This was serious stuff. It would give her the opportunity to back out if she wished.

"Charles Ernest Croft," she said. "My husband." She had already told him it was her husband, but she seemed keen to emphasise the point.

"Charles Croft?"

"Yes. Charles Croft. He'll be at home next Saturday evening. You'll break in and make it look like a burglary. There's a safe in the main bedroom behind a long wall mirror. Kill him. Break into the safe. Inside there's money and jewellery." She had obviously given this some consideration. She slipped her hand into her handbag and extracted a folded sheet of white paper. She handed it to him.

"This is the address where the murder is to take place." He looked at it. It was printed in a bold type face. "He won't put up much of a struggle," she added. "He's old and already ill."

Masson didn't ask her why she wanted him dead. There was no rhyme or reason for some of these things. The 'whys' had nothing to do with him. He was the 'go-to' man. But he had no reason to tell her he was only the go-between.

"How will you do it?" she asked.

"Why? Do you want it done in a certain way?"

"No blood."

"No blood?"

"Do it by strangling him," she said, in a nonchalant way, as if she had dreamed of doing it herself. Masson didn't reply. He waited for a few moments then said, "If that's the way you want it doing."

He was gauging her state of mind. He was no expert on the human psyche, but she appeared to be sane, or as rational as the next person; yet also cunning and street-wise. She was beautiful on the outside, but there was a coldness in her manner that suggested to him that she was genuine in her desire. The real deal.

He looked at the note again, then he sat up and slipped it into his back trouser-pocket. Overhead the sun had broken through the clouds to bathe the park in its glow. It was so incongruous: the beauty of the park, her beauty, and then…the topic they were discussing. His immediate impression was that she was a trophy wife who had become tired of life with an older man. She had married for money and now wanted rid of him, but had no desire to lose the cash. As the heat of the sun hit the top of her head, she whipped the cap off and ran a hand over her blonde hair before placing the cap back on her head. Masson realised she was no bottle blonde.

"Can you do it?" she asked.

"Yes."

"Next Saturday?"

"Today is the eleventh. Next Saturday is the nineteenth. It's tight, but it can be done. I'll need to know a lot more about the house and the surroundings. This is the first meeting. We'll need to meet again in the next few days. In that time can you draw me a plan of the house, indicating where he'll be. Let me know about any alarm system or cameras. The local roads. Neighbours. That kind of thing. Is there a neighbourhood watch scheme?"

"We live on a secluded lane," she said. "The next property is a hundred yards away beyond a screen of high trees."

"What about an alarm?"

"He always turns it off. Says it's a waste of time. He's a tight bastard."

She had a bit of the street in her. Like a poor girl from the wrong side of the tracks who had married up. It seemed she'd been schooled into becoming an elegant, sophisticated woman, and now the old teacher had outlived his usefulness. She wanted him gone, so she could have his money, the house, the lifestyle, everything.

"Can you get me a photograph of your husband?" he asked.

"Yes."

"Good. We're done for the time-being. Half in a few days. Half after the job. Can you get £40,000 in a few days?"

"Yes."

"Good. I need…I would appreciate," he corrected, "as discussed, a hand-drawn plan of the house to scale. The room layout. Then some directions to the house would help. And the roads clearly marked. Can you do that? What time will he go to bed?"

"Around midnight," she replied.

"Are there any weapons in the house? A gun in the safe, perhaps? Anything like that?"

"No."

"Can you get the £40,000 by Tuesday?" he asked again.

She nodded. "Yes. Yes. Where will we meet again?"

Masson looked around the park. "Here at the same time on Tuesday. Bring the money."

"In cash," she said.

"In cash. Buy a brand-name string cord sports bag. Put it in there. Put the drawings into an envelope. A4 size. Can you do that?" he asked.

"Yes," she replied.

"Give me his name again."

"Charles Ernest Croft," she replied.
"Okay. I'll see you here at two o'clock on Tuesday. You go that way." He cut his eyes towards Piccadilly. With that he didn't say another word, stood, and walked away towards Constitution Hill.

He didn't want to come to an early conclusion, but he thought she was genuine. Still, he couldn't be certain. After all, sending Divorty to the house to kill a man he didn't know was no simple thing to do. If she came up with the money and the information he wanted then that would be a clear signal of intent. Either she would or she wouldn't deliver. He was still open minded, despite leaning towards her being genuine. He now had to carry out several checks, but knew the tight time-frame might mean he may not get them all done in time.

Over the course of that Friday evening, Masson carried out his investigations. He looked online. There was nothing in 'Who's Who' for a Charles Ernest Croft. There was a basic entry in LinkedIn, but it didn't amount to much. His best hit was a simple name search in Google. He found a few articles about Charles Ernest Croft – a Surrey-based former stockbroker, which tied in with the information she had given him. He was a self-made man who had made a large amount of money from trading, then he had turned his hand to providing information to other investors. This had resulted in making a substantial amount of money over the past thirty years. He was on his third marriage. The first had lasted for thirty years and resulted in two children, a girl and a boy. The second marriage lasted for three years. His third marriage was to Suzanna. He was sixty-five by then, she was thirty. Though the search was not exhaustive he was now pretty sure that the woman he'd met in Piccadilly either was, or was pretending to be, his third wife, Suzanna Croft, though she had called herself Sara. Unfortunately, what he was not able to find were any photographs of the couple together. Armed with the background information he had, he would now contact Divorty to put him in the picture and tell him that a job might be in the pipeline.

Masson reached Divorty by their usual method, a quick phone call. He told him about the enquiry. It was a young wife who wanted to get rid of her much older, much richer husband.

"Can't she wait for him to die?" Divorty remarked.

"It doesn't look that way. It looks genuine. All the dominos stack up. She's young and beautiful. He's old and rich."

It was a common enough scenario, but that didn't mean to say that every trophy wife wanted to get rid of her rich, ailing husband. From the information she had given she appeared to be who she said she was. The usual escape route would have been a divorce. But old man Croft sounded like a careful guy, who protected his millions. He had probably insisted on a pre-nuptial agreement that prevented her from obtaining a large settlement should she seek to leave the marriage. If he divorced her, of course, she would be quids in. But with a shrewd beauty like her to show off, a divorce on his part seemed unlikely.

The only problem Masson could see was the swift turnaround. She wanted it doing a week on Saturday. Why so soon? When he put this to Divorty, he didn't seem concerned by the timescale.

"Look," said Divorty, "If you've done the numbers and you're happy to go along with it, then so am I. I don't care too much. £80,000, man! She's in a hurry. So one of the dominos doesn't fall into place. So what?"

Masson said, "OK. I'll push ahead."

Over the course of that weekend, Masson didn't do a lot. He searched online for any peripheral information on Charles and Suzanne Croft, but still did not locate any photographs. Charles Croft was clearly a private person. What he did discover, however, confirmed previous information. A self-made millionaire, a successful stockbroker, who had used knowledge, skill, luck, and other people, to make a lot of money. Over the past thirty years he'd gained a reputation as a skilled operator. He'd certainly proved himself on the marriage front – the third Mrs Croft was a stunner. Masson was looking forward to seeing her on Tuesday, if she turned up.

Chapter 3

Tuesday 15th September

Tuesday was far warmer than the previous Friday. The middle of September was producing some pleasant days. Masson took the tube to Green Park, came out onto Piccadilly and sauntered into the park. The fine weather had coaxed sunbathers onto the grass: tourists, shop workers and people from the nearby offices. Nannies pushing strollers along.

As he approached the bench along the path, he could see Suzanna Croft already sitting there. She was wearing a tailored dark jacket, matching knee-length skirt, and black stockings. With no hat, her long blond hair was flowing down her back; she was power-dressing. He wasn't sure who it was for. Maybe she had an appointment in Bond Street or wherever. The simple gold chain around her neck added to the image of a beautiful young woman with an elegant manner and burning sex appeal. He noticed that her legs in the stockings and high heeled shoes were shapely and toned as if she had been a dancer or a gymnast. The bag she was carrying on her shoulder looked like a Louis Vuitton. He doubted it was fake. She looked as if she was on route to Christie's to attend an up-market auction.

As he approached her, she looked up and met his eyes. He casually surveyed the park, taking in some of the people nearby. Like the couple eating lunch on the bench at the other side on the path just a few yards further on. Suddenly it didn't feel like the ideal venue anymore, but as he looked, no one appeared out of place. As he sat she gave him a half-smile. It was the first time she had done this. It seemed genuine rather than forced. He inched a little towards her and breathed in her fragrance, which smelled expensive.

"Have you brought it?" he asked. She dipped into her shoulder bag as if she was going to bring out the money. "Not yet," he said. "How about the photograph? Did you get one?"

"Yes."

"And the plan of the house and roads."

"Yes."

"Pass them to me," he said and held his hand out.

He glanced around at the young couple at the other side who were smiling at each other and laughing out loud. They looked very much in love. She dipped her hand back into the bag and withdrew a manila envelope which she placed into his hand. The flap was sealed. He could feel a thin pad of documents inside. He peeled the flap open and extracted several sheets of paper. One was a glossy, A4 sheet with a black and white photograph of the intended victim. The other was an A4 plain sheet on which she'd drawn a plan of the house with a sharp pencil. It was an adept drawing, with the placement of the internal doors and windows inserted.

"You did this?" he asked.

"Yes," she replied. She ran the tip of her tongue over her lips.

He took the photograph and studied it. It looked like a promotional photograph of a man who was trying to smile under orders from the photographer. It was a face and shoulders shot that had been taken at an angle, so it didn't reveal the excess flesh under the chin. He was in his mid-sixties and his face was lined and podgy whilst his head possessed plenty of thick, grey hair. A good quantity for someone of that age. He was wearing a dark jacket, white shirt and tie. Altogether not a bad looking chap for his age, though hardly a Richard Gere look alike.

"When was it taken?"

"Last year. I think."

"A year ago?"

"Yes."

Her terse answers suggested she had little emotional attachment to him. He looked into those gorgeous eyes. He paused for a moment. "No second thoughts?"

"None."

"Okay."

"When can you do it?" she asked.

"Saturday night. As you suggested, it'll be staged as a bungled burglary. A chance break-in. I'll look around the house. Go upstairs. Find him in bed. Get him out of bed, so it'll look like he confronted the intruder."

She seemed very disconnected and didn't utter a word before saying, "Good."

It was the first time he had heard anyone say 'good' about something like this. He assured himself there was a first time for everything.

"What about the alarm system?" he asked.

"The control box is in an alcove as you enter the house through the front door. But don't worry; I doubt he'll turn it on. He never does."

"And the house will be empty, but for him?"

"Yes."

"Where will you be?" he asked.

"We have a home on the outskirts of Paris. We go there at this time of the year. I'm spending the weekend there. He's planning to join me on Sunday. He's booked onto a mid-day flight from Gatwick."

Masson nodded his head. Someone came along the path so he slipped the photograph and the sheets back into the envelope.

"What about any maids. Or cleaners. Anything you may have forgotten."

"The maid and cleaner only work on weekdays. Not at the weekend."

He nodded, then looked around the park and took in the moment. "Final thing. The money."

She reached into the bag and withdrew a draw-string sports kit bag and handed it to him. "How much?" he asked.

"£40,000 in cash," she replied. He felt the bag and could feel the thick wads of cash, at least six inches thick, inside. "You'll receive the other £40,000 when he's dead."

She had no heart, but this murder was just business. There was little time for sentiment. He noticed the glint of the diamond ring on her finger. There would be more of these to come and perhaps a new husband. She must be the sole heir to his multi-million-pound fortune.

Masson took the kit bag and held it tight. "Where did you get this?" he asked.

"From out of the safe."

"And he won't miss it?"

"No."

"Are you sure?"

"Positive."

If she was certain then he had no need to question her.

"What time will you do it?" she asked.

"Why do you ask?"

"He's planning to call me from the house at around eleven o'clock to ask if I arrived in Paris safely. I'd appreciate it if you do it after that."

Masson pondered for a moment. His eyes went to her thigh as the hem had ridden up a couple of inches.

"I can't guarantee a time," he said. "Maybe around midnight."

She didn't reply. He took the envelope and the bag containing the cash, got up from the bench, smiled at her, then walked away without saying another word. He never looked back to her, though he was tempted to. Only when he reached the end of the path did he peek back to watch her step onto Piccadilly. That was that. Deal done. Now to deliver on it.

Chapter 4

It was five o'clock on that Tuesday evening when Masson put in a call to Liam Divorty to inform him that the light had changed from amber to green. The job was very much on. The client had handed over the first payment of £40,000. Divorty's cut was £32,000. Masson would retain £8,000. On a successful outcome, the other thirty-two would be given to Divorty. He said he would be at the Emirates Stadium this evening to watch an Arsenal game. He suggested they meet outside of the stadium at around seven o'clock that evening.

Masson said: "Fine. See you there."

As a north Londoner, born and bred in Finsbury, Liam Divorty was a devoted Arsenal fan. He followed the Gunners home and away. Tonight was no exception. Arsenal were at home to Italian side Lazio in the second leg of the qualifying round of the Champions League. Not even planning a murder could keep him from watching his beloved Arsenal. A home win tonight would see them qualify for the group stages of the competition.

Masson wasn't into football or any other game. He couldn't get his head around the tribalism attached to team sport. At seven o'clock, he ventured along Holloway Road and into the area around the Emirates stadium. Football fans were making their way into the stadium in their thousands. In a jacket pocket Masson had a packet that contained £32,000. He ascended the stairs in front of the stadium, with its montage of former Arsenal stars linked arm-in-arm across the wall of the huge stand. He stepped onto the wide concourse. Kick-off was in forty-five minutes. Masson became lost in the throng making their way towards the turnstiles, the majority of whom were buzzing in anticipation of seeing a good game and an Arsenal victory.

Up ahead Divorty was standing by himself next to a barrier looking down onto the street below. Liam Divorty was a big guy. He had a shaven head, though he wasn't bald. He was the kind of guy who could grow a full head of hair in weeks. He shaved it so he didn't have to worry about keeping it manageable. It made him look much fiercer. He was wearing a red Arsenal jacket with the club emblem attached to the front, and the word 'Arsenal' written on the back. Surprisingly, Masson thought, there was something quite ordinary about him. Who would suspect that they were not mates meeting up before the game to chew the cud and talk about the match? The smell of hot dogs cooking in a mobile vending unit reached Masson's nostrils and made his mouth water. A roar went up inside the stadium as the line-up for the home team was announced over the public address. Through the glass panels on the wall of the stand the floodlights shining onto the pitch were visible. Masson didn't understand the fanaticism of people like Divorty and the other 60,000 other disciples congregating in their stadium of worship. To him it was madness to pay through the nose to watch twenty-two millionaires kicking a football around?

Divorty looked like a beacon in a red jacket against a pink head. He was okay to look at. Strong features, though maybe he was beginning to get excess fat around the chin. His teeth were pearly white and his eyes were slate grey.

He observed Masson coming towards him and stepped off the barrier. He had a pair of earbuds plugged into his ears. He took them out, moving along the railing for a few yards. Masson joined him and looked down onto the street which was full of fans making their way up a set of stairs onto the concourse. Another roar went up from inside the stadium as the players emerged from out of the tunnel and ran onto the pitch for the pre-match warm up. Masson slipped his hand inside his jacket pocket, extracted the packet containing the cash and gave it to him. Divorty felt the weight of the money, then he stuffed it inside his jacket. He didn't say anything. Masson gave him the envelope containing the photograph of the intended victim, the drawing of the house and the other information. He looked down onto the street as the more fans streamed up the steps. The time was seven-fifteen and there was still thirty minutes to kick-off, but these people wanted to be inside the stadium to soak up the pre-match atmosphere or have a pre-match pint.

 Masson fixed his eyes on Divorty. "How's it going?" he asked. "Ready for the game?"

 "Okay," he replied. "When we going to check out the place?"

 "Tomorrow. I'll pick you up at half six from outside the usual place."

 "Okay. What's the score?" Divorty asked.

 "Make it look like a botched burglary. According to the client, the victim should be in the master bedroom. Top floor. Front of the house. No cameras. There's an alarm control box in an alcove around the corner from the front door. According to her he doesn't even use it."

 Divorty nodded his head. "Half six tomorrow," he said. Then he zipped his jacket to the top, said nothing more and walked away from Masson to join a line of fans queuing at the turnstiles. Masson watched as he approached the turnstiles. A security guard asked him if he had anything he shouldn't have. He shook his head and was waved into the stadium without being searched.

 After leaving the stadium, Masson returned home and spent an hour looking on Google Earth at the address the client had given him. The best thing was to see the location in real time, in natural light and to assess the conditions in the early part of the evening when residents would be home.

Before he turned in, he caught the late news at midnight. Arsenal had won the game: two-one. Which he guessed meant they had advanced to the group stages of the competition. Divorty would be in a good mood, this evening.

Wednesday 16th September

As planned, Masson collected Divorty from outside of the 'Green Man' pub on Essex Road in Islington. Divorty was in a quiet, reflective frame of mind. Though Masson knew him, he didn't know every intimate detail of his life. Divorty had been married and had a son who would be eight years old. He didn't know a great detail about his friends or who he associated with, which in some ways was dangerous, but on the other hand was perhaps no bad thing. Their relationship was one of business rather than friendship, and depended on a healthy wariness for each other.

Masson knew that Divorty associated with some hard-arsed underworld types, such as James Malloy and a couple of other guys he had met before, but it was perhaps better he didn't know too many details. They were in many way opposites. Masson was Ying, Divorty was Yang. He was maybe a couple of years younger than Masson. He lived in Islington, close to where he had his used-car business. It was known that he liked a drink. The evidence was starting to show on his stomach. He wasn't drunk tonight, but Masson could smell beer on his breath. He must have had a couple in the pub before meeting up. It didn't bode well for his judgement on a job, truth be told.

Masson drove in a south-westerly direction into the southern extremes of the built-up area, into Surrey and into stockbroker country. It was an area of Esher dominated by big houses in even bigger parcels of real estate; along leafy tree-lined lanes that were a million miles from the grime of densely-packed urban south London. The Croft house was on a lane on the western edge of the town. It was down a long lane maybe a quarter of a mile long from one end to the other. The lane was lined with splendid houses all set back from the road and bordered by first a grass verge, then fences or walls marking the boundary.

The target house was on the left-hand side about three quarters of the way down the lane. It was the British equivalent of a chateau or about as much chateau as you could get in south-west London. A pair of stout gates were set into a brick wall, then a pebble forecourt in front of the house. Topiary trees in fancy clay pots lined the front. Six shuttered windows were evenly set across the upper floor. The front was an eye-catching effect of red stone cladding. There was a central doorway set in a colonnade storm porch. Two alarm boxes were attached to the rim of the roof and provided a warning to any potential burglar that the place was wired for sound, but no sign of any security cameras. There was nothing in the way of cars on the forecourt. A double garage was down a short driveway leading into the garden. There were no cars parked along the lane. A line of tall sycamore trees formed the boundary between the Croft property and the property next door. The trees were beginning to lose their leaves as the first sign of autumn made itself felt. At the back of the house would be a large garden, according to the client's drawing, then a fence, which formed the boundary of the property across the other side. There was no obvious suggestion that anyone was in the house. What was visible was a line of spotlights attached to the eves where the facade met the roof. If the alarm did sound then the entire property would be lit up like the Trafalgar Square Christmas tree.

Divorty didn't say much, other than to ask him about the alarm system. Masson repeated what the client had told him. The alarm control box was in an alcove around the corner from the front door. The four-digit code was one-five-eight-nine, used to arm the system, and disable it. But in all likelihood it wouldn't be on. They looked at the plan of the house. It showed the ground floor layout and the staircase to the upper floor, then the upper floor and the bedroom where he would be sleeping. If he was not asleep he might be watching television in the lounge or in the bedroom.

Masson drove by the house to the next junction, made a U turn and came back in the opposite direction. As they passed the Croft house again, Divorty said he would drive to the end of the lane and place his car in front of a house that was being renovated. He would back track to the house on foot, break in and do the job. Masson said 'okay'. The operational aspect was not his concern. Divorty was doing the hit, not him.

Masson kept going. He was keen to get out of the area in case they were observed prowling in the location. A car passing at low speed was a dead giveaway.

"You sure this is real? Is this woman genuine?" Divorty asked.

"As much as I can be," Masson replied. "She's parted with the first payment. And she's arranged to be on the other side of the channel, doing whatever she does across there. At least that's what she said."

Masson thought it was ninety-nine per cent kosher. She had to be genuine. She knew a lot about the target. Only someone close to him would know the information. Divorty didn't say anything about how he was going to do the B&E. A cleaner would find the body when she arrived for work on Monday morning. That was that. Masson drove back to North London. He dropped Divorty outside of the 'Green Man' pub at ten to nine, and watched him go inside.

That was the last time he saw Divorty for two weeks. The next time he would see him, he would be wearing a different type of jacket. Only this time it wouldn't be Arsenal red. It would be stone grey with a yellow patch: Property of 'HMP Belmarsh'.

Chapter 5

Sunday 20th September

The first inkling Masson had that the job had not gone to plan was when he tried to contact Divorty. He didn't get an answer on the mobile. Then he went to Divorty's used car business in Islington. He wasn't there either. The guy working there said he hadn't seen Divorty or even heard from him, unusual on a weekend.

At one in the afternoon Masson turned his television on and tuned into the local news. The police were reporting that a prominent Esher resident had been murdered in his home on Sandy Lane. The police had a suspect in custody. Something had gone badly wrong. He had killed the target, but managed to get himself caught in the process.

Monday 21st September

On Monday, around lunch-time, a report on the local news said that a forty-year-old man by the name of Liam Divorty had been charged with the murder of Charles Croft and remanded in custody after a brief hearing at South-West magistrate court on Lavender Hill. He would be transferred to HMP Belmarsh later in the day. It wasn't until later that night that Masson heard anything. He received a call from a man called James Malloy, who was indeed Divorty's pal. Malloy told him that Divorty wanted him to visit Belmarsh and see an inmate called Eric Rose, who had a message for him.

And so, two weeks after first meeting Suzanna Croft, Tom Masson was to visit Belmarsh prison to meet with Eric Rose. A meeting with Divorty would be too dangerous. The prison authorities would be keeping a record of everyone who visited him. If Divorty had requested a face-to-face meeting in the prison, Masson would have turned him down flat. After the instruction from Malloy, Masson got online immediately and found the telephone number for the prison.

The next morning he rang the switchboard and asked to be put through to visitor administration. He said he was Tom Masson and requested a visit to see Eric Rose. He told the person he spoke to that Rose was his partner's brother and that he needed to discuss an urgent family matter with him. The prison administrator told Masson he couldn't visit Rose until Thursday at two in the afternoon. Masson was told he had to produce some identification on arrival, such as a driving licence, or a passport and recent post with his address.

Thursday 24th September
The visiting room in HMP Belmarsh was hardly an attractive place; a square area of no more than fifty feet with single tables set out in a nine-by-nine grid. As Masson entered the room he let his eyes drift around the interior to take in the drabness. He felt the cold air, and heard tinny echoes of movement and conversation.

The overhead lights were on, though daylight was pouring in through heavily frosted windows set high, near the ceiling. Several notices on the plain, grey walls advised visitors that only one visitor was allowed at a table at one time. Other notices asked visitors and inmates not to embrace. A number of prison guards were watching the floor and observing the people sitting at the tables. A prison guard would occasionally walk up and down the aisles to ensure that no one was passing contraband and whatnot.

It was a mixed prison, catering for two sets of inmates: those on remand and waiting for the trial that would determine their guilt, and Category A prisoners, those already proven guilty. Divorty and Rose were grouped with the former in here. Masson found it suffocating, even on the visiting side of the tables.

He had been given a description of Rose so he knew who he was looking for. He looked round the faces and recognised him. Eric Rose was the guy sitting at the table in the second column from the right and the third to last row. It was the first time in his life that Masson had seen him. Rose was wearing a grey inmate's jacket with a yellow patch down the back, to indicate that he was a prisoner on remand. He was on remand for several burglaries of business premises in north London. His large arms rested on the table. A number of inmates looked up at Masson as he made his way to the table where Rose was sitting. He put his eyes on Rose, took the chair at the other side of the table, pulled it out and sat down. From the other tables the cackle and hum of voices increased. He edged close to the middle of the table.

"How's he doing?" Masson asked quietly.

Rose gave him a neutral look. "Not great," he replied.

"What happened in the house?" Masson asked.

Rose glanced left, then right. "Liam said the guy was already dead…"

"Already dead?" Masson asked incredulously.

"Yeah. Already dead. According to Liam, someone must have got there first and did him and he's not fucking happy about it. Someone set him up."

Tom could only suck in air between his clenched teeth. "Let me get my head around this. Liam broke into the house, finds the guy, but he's already dead."

"Yeah. The guy's already been dispatched. The house, the bedroom, was in a right fucking mess like someone'd ransacked it. Liam backs out and he's about to go down the stairs and get the fuck out of there when the friggin' alarm goes off. Next thing, the fucking cops are there in no time and coming in from all directions. He said someone'd tipped 'em off."

Masson could only say 'shit' under his breath. He looked at Rose. "He doesn't suspect me, does he?" he asked.

"Don't know who he suspects. But what I do know is he didn't kill that guy. Someone else did it."

"What about the code for the alarm system?"

"What about it?

"Did he turn it off?"

"He tried to. The control unit wasn't in the place it was supposed to be." Rose edged forward. "There's something he wants you to do."

"Yeah. Anything I can do."

"Find out who set him up. Someone has. And he wants answers. From you. He's starting to wonder about you."

Masson shook his head. "Tell him from me that I wouldn't have messed him about. He knows that." They were keeping their voices low, but anyone observing them would know that they were involved in a heated conversation. "I'll see what I can find," he said.

"No," said Rose. He sucked on his front teeth. His voice dropped to a whisper. "You find out, period. And if you don't, he knows some boys who owe him a few favours. Get my drift?"

It was a threat delivered from Divorty by a proxy. Masson leaned back in his chair. He put on his best dumfounded face and looked Rose square in the eye.

"Tell Liam from me that I didn't set him up. We go back a long while, see? Whoever set him up, it wasn't me."

Rose pulled back. "I'll tell him."

Masson leaned forward. "If he was already dead, how was it done?" he asked.

Rose shrugged his shoulders. "Divorty said he didn't hang about to check. He smelled a massive fucking rat. As he got to the stairs the alarm sounded, all the lights came on and the friggin' place lit up like the friggin' London Eye on New Year's night. Then the cops come storming into the place before he'd the chance to get the fuck out. Someone definitely knew he was there and they did him over." He moved close to Masson. "There are some guys outside who owe him and they'll be in contact with you in a few days."

"Okay," said Masson. He had an inkling who he was getting at. People like James Malloy.

"He wants answers. Else he won't be a happy bunny."

There was the threat again. Masson knew he had to get answers to satisfy Divorty. Just then a prison officer came down the aisle. Rose quickly changed the subject and asked him if he'd seen the Arsenal game last night. Masson said, "Yeah, on TV." He said he had watched the highlights and Arsenal had beaten Newcastle three-one. And so on. They made some small talk for the next twenty minutes until a bell rang to signal that the visiting period was over.

Several of the other prison guards went along the aisles to encourage the visitors to get up and leave. The sound of chairs scraping over the hard slippery floor competed with the sound of people saying 'goodbye' and wishing their loved ones 'farewell' until the next time. Masson doubted there would be a next time for him.

Two weeks on from that first phone call, Masson pondered his dealings with Suzanna Croft, Divorty and Rose. He needed to understand recent events. Clearly, he must have failed in some respects to fully research the Croft assignment. He could put that down to a lack of time. However, that shouldn't be an excuse. Yes, he might have been slipshod and perhaps Divorty did suspect that he had set him up. Of course he was upset he was behind bars – that was only to be expected – but also, adamant that he hadn't murdered Croft. There was something undeniably wrong here. Someone had ensured Divorty would take the fall for this. Someone had put Divorty in the frame, and left themselves in the clear.

This set Masson thinking. Who, apart from his wife, wanted Croft dead? If the woman really was his wife. Maybe she wasn't. Maybe someone else wanted Croft dead and had used the excuse of his wife wanting him dead as the method to achieve the objective. This woman 'Sara' wouldn't know he wasn't the killer, therefore, someone who knew her was still alive. And she wouldn't know. He was only the go-between. They wouldn't know that the job had been given to someone else. This could allow Masson to discover who was behind it.

He had to find out because an angry Divorty had friends who could easily turn on him if he asked them to do so. That worried Masson. If Divorty got it into his head that he'd been stabbed in the back, he would never let it rest. With Divorty threatening him, and probably implicating him if he went down for murder, Masson had to convince Divorty that he hadn't been framed. He had to discover who was behind it. To achieve the first objective, he had to achieve the second, and get himself off the hook.

Though Divorty had been caught five days ago, he hadn't wanted to do anything, for three reasons. The first was a reluctance to even contemplate that Divorty had been arrested; the second was a need to let the dust settle; the third was a period of reflection in order to get his head into gear.

Chapter 6

As soon as Masson arrived home from the visit to the prison, he began the task ahead. Someone had set up both him and Divorty. Plus, Masson was in potential danger: Rose had passed on a none-too-subtle warning about Divorty's friends on the outside. He considered the best way of finding out what had happened.

    He began the investigation by going online. He pulled up the local Esher paper in order to scroll though the headlines. Not surprisingly, the murder of Charles Ernest Croft was still front-page news. There was a photograph of Croft and an account of what information the local police had released. Croft had been home alone last Saturday evening when someone, a would-be burglar, had broken into his house at around midnight and killed him. Conveniently, the cause of death was asphyxiation by strangulation: Divorty's preferred method. The suspect was a forty-year-old North London man by the name of Liam Divorty. He had been charged with murder. It couldn't get any more serious than that, not to mention the murder of a rich prominent citizen would guarantee a lot of media coverage.

    Following a search of the local news, Masson trawled through the BBC News to the BBC South London page. The Croft story was still prominent, but had been knocked off the top spot by political upheaval in the local council. He read the Croft report. It stated that Charles Croft, a former City of London stock broker, aged sixty-seven, had been in his house on the outskirts of Esher when someone had entered at around midnight. His wife of two years, thirty-two-year-old Suzanna, was away at the couple's Paris home. She had returned to England the next day to formally identify the body.

Unfortunately for Masson, there was no photograph of them in any marriage announcements. He typed 'Charles Ernest Croft' into the search engine and hit the search button. He sifted through the list of references that popped up. On the third item he got lucky. He found an obituary. It supplied a photograph of him and his third wife. She was very young and pretty, but it wasn't the same young, pretty woman he had met in Green Park on Piccadilly, nine days before his murder.

He saved the article to his hard drive, isolated the image and converted it to a jpeg. This allowed him to increase it in size, though it was a bit pixelated. It had been taken at a banquet of some prominence; one of those black-tie events. She was in a long black dress. The caption declared it was a photograph of Mister and Missus Croft at an event earlier in the year. Masson examined the photograph. No way was she the woman who had told him her name was Sara Croft. They were similar in many respects. The same long, blonde hair. The same trim figure and height. She must have been a good inch taller than her elderly husband. But she definitely wasn't the person he had met in Green Park.

Masson leaned back in his chair and put his fingers to his chin in a reflective pose. Someone had gone to a lot of effort to find a woman to pose as Suzanna Croft in order to kill Croft and frame Divorty for the murder. As cool and determined as she had seemed, he doubted the woman who said she was 'Sara' Croft had planned it on her own. Someone else had plotted to kill him, possibly someone close to Croft, or maybe someone in dispute with him. He considered the possibility that two women, the real Mrs Croft and the impersonator, were working together. The real wife had given the pretend wife the details of the house and also had the perfect alibi. But who did the killing? If it wasn't

Divorty, who was it? He doubted that the woman he had met in Green Park had killed Croft, but of course he couldn't be certain of that.

He recalled the conversation he had had with the pretend Mrs Croft when she had asked him about the timing. The question had seemed odd at the time. Maybe someone was tipped off on the time Divorty would arrive. Masson mapped out a possible scenario. Whoever had murdered Croft had broken into the house or entered through the front door, gone up the stairs to the bedroom, killed Croft, then set the alarm as he or she departed. When Divorty broke in and entered the bedroom Croft was already dead. As he got out the alarm went off. Then right on cue the coppers arrived on the scene. He remembered what Rose had said: 'The fucking cops are there in no time and coming in from all directions'. Had someone observed Divorty entering the house, then contacted the police? It could have been the killer. Five minutes before Divorty had arrived, the killer could have called the police to say he had seen someone breaking in. The police were on their way even before the alarm went off. That's what could have happened. But how was he going to find out for sure?

Later, Masson tuned into the six o'clock news and watched a report about the murder of the ex-stockbroker in Esher. They showed the same photograph he had found on-line. The reporter who was standing outside of the Croft house said Mrs Croft had been in Paris for the weekend attending a fashion event. She had returned to England on Sunday evening to identify the body of her husband. It was the same report he had read on-line. There would be no further statement from the police or the family that evening. A forty-year-old man had been remanded to Belmarsh prison and would appear in court in the next few days: Divorty. The only thing Tom Masson could do now was to try and find the woman who had said she was Mrs Croft. In a city of ten million people that was going to be a difficult task.

    Masson wondered what to do next. The only thing he knew about the pretend Mrs Croft was her appearance. By the shape of her legs she may have been a dancer or gymnast. Then there was the real Suzanna Croft. She was young and pretty, but not as attractive as the other Mrs Croft. Maybe she had set up the job. It was a possibility of course, but that was all it was.

    Would the police suspect her? Probably not. Why? Because they had the man who had done it in custody. They had the man who had entered the house on a B&E job. The safe had been emptied and the contents were all over the floor. It was an open and shut case. But Divorty hadn't come equipped to break into the safe. And where were the stolen items? Maybe the police hadn't considered that. They had arrested the intruder at the scene. The consensus would be that Croft had disturbed Divorty in the act of breaking in. A struggle had taken place, but there would be no marks on Divorty. No scratches or anything like that. His clothing was not ripped. But that could be easily explained away. He had simply overpowered the older man and strangled him with his bare hands. But why? It didn't add up. If he was a B&E man, he would have just subdued him and tied him up using the sash cord from around the curtains or the cord around his dressing gown. But he didn't. He murdered the man. Maybe it was what it looked like – a contract killing, but not a very efficient one.

    Masson had an idea. He searched online for the funeral director handling the service. It gave details of the location and timings. The funeral would take place at Esher crematorium five days from now, on Tuesday 29th of September at 3 p.m. Nothing indicated that attendance at the funeral was going to be family only, or a private affair. Maybe the pretend Mrs Croft would be there. She would assume Masson was the killer for hire. She had hired him to do it, not someone she had never met. If he could make it to the funeral and observe who was attending, it might be his chance to discover a snippet of information or some clue that could piece it all together. He needed to do something to discover who was behind it. He had little to go on, so he had to try and bluff his way into the ceremony.

Chapter 7

Tuesday 29th September

The day of the funeral was dark and overcast. He felt like a fake intruding on someone else's private grief. It wasn't the done thing, but neither was murder, particularly if arranged by the so-called grieving widow. It was with an open mind that he set out for the crematorium in Esher dressed appropriately in a dark suit, white shirt and black tie, with his patent black shoes shining like glass. He arrived at the crematorium thirty minutes before the ceremony was due to commence and parked nearby. He waited.

It wasn't long before parking spaces at the crematorium began to fill with cars, most of them new and expensive models. This was the funeral of a retired stockbroker who had made a lot of money for other people, and so Masson assumed that there were going to be a lot of sad, but grateful, former clients in attendance.

The funeral notice had talked about a 'joyful celebration' of Charles Croft's life. But by the look of the faces of the people emerging out of the cars there wasn't going to be much in the way of joy. The mourners were from a cross section of age ranges and gender. The mourners looked middle to lower upper-class. These were well-to-do people. They were dressed appropriately and appeared respectably mournful.

By the time the cortège, led by the hearse, came down the lane towards the crematorium, the sun had broken through the clouds and through an arch of yellowing trees and wilting rose patches to splash across the damp, leaf covered grass. The hearse was followed by six long black limousines, and then a line of other plush cars edging their way to the side entrance of the red-brick building.

After observing the cortèges' approach, Masson slipped out of his car and followed a group of four, two males and two females, towards the building housing the Chapel of Remembrance where the service was due to take place. One of the men in the group glanced back to frown at Masson, perhaps wondering who he was. Masson acknowledged him with a nod of his head. The group were each holding a programme of the service in their hands. Masson increased his pace and drew level with the chap who had glanced at him. The man, who was around sixty, was arm-in-arm with a rather buxom woman in her fifties and two thirty-somethings – a male and a female.

"Sad occasion," Masson remarked, as if making conversation.

The chap looked at him with a blank face and could only nod his head. He looked at Masson's hands. "Do you have one?" he asked.

"Excuse me?" replied Masson.

"A programme."

"No. I left mine at home."

"Have mine," he said. "I have a spare." He passed the programme to Masson before taking another from his jacket pocket.

"Thank you very much," Masson said.

"Did you know Charles well?" the chap asked as they walked across the forecourt towards the entrance.

"Only through a business set-up," he replied.

"He managed your stock portfolio?" the man asked.

"Er…Yes. That's right," he replied.

"A shocking business," the man said. "The murder," he qualified.

"Yes," replied Masson. He looked at the chap then fixed his eyes on his female partner. "I do hope Suzanna is coping."

The woman's face dropped and the chap gave Masson a withering look. The couple shared a grin, as if to say, *You certainly don't know her!*

After that brief exchange, the couple walked ahead with the other two, never looked back and seemed content to ignore his presence. Masson gazed ahead at the entrance to the chapel, where a number of people were either entering or milling about close to the steps. It didn't seem as if anyone was checking who was who as they entered. He thought he might just succeed in blagging his way into the chapel. He ventured across the forecourt, stepped around those in the archway and entered the vestibule. He kept his head low and used the act of reading the programme to keep his face turned away from the gaze of those who were gathered in the area.

There was a gentle hush of chit-chat coming from the chapel, with the sound of soulful, melodic organ music playing over the sound system. There were at least thirty to forty people in the area in front of the door to the chapel, making it virtually impossible to check who was who. Masson was beginning to think that he might just get in without being challenged. However, just inside the door leading into the chapel, two beefy looking men, dressed as ushers, were asking the attendees a question as they entered. As Masson came forward one of the men looked him up and down through a pair of beady, inquisitive eyes. They could see the programme in his hand and that he was dressed appropriately. Still, Masson assumed he was heading for a swift exit, but the question he was asked was simple in the extreme: "Friend or family?"

"More business related," Masson replied. The usher looked at him, glanced at the programme in his hand once again, then gestured to the left-hand side of the chapel.

"Take a seat on the back row will you please," he asked.

"Of course," he replied. He had blagged his way inside. Anyone now would assume he was an acquaintance of some description here to pay his respects. It then dawned on him that the programme in his hand must have been the ticket to get into the ceremony.

He turned into the chapel, wended his way to the back, went along a bench of pews and took a seat on the bench at the far end of the row. The Chapel of Remembrance displayed the familiar symbolism. A white-metal cross was sitting on an altar and next to it was a raised marble slab where the coffin would be placed. A podium from where the vicar or the father or whoever was going to deliver the address was to one side. A melancholy sonata was now playing over the sound system. On such a dull, drab day the house lights were on.

Several minutes passed and the line of mourners trickling into the chapel became a flow. Most of them were glum and unsmiling. A man in his mid-thirties, who was wearing a dark, three-piece suit, and accompanied by a pretty flame-haired woman, came along the bench towards Masson. The chap made eye contact with Masson and smiled. Masson smiled back. Then the chap held his hand out. He introduced himself: "Tony Delmonte," he said.

"Barry Manston," Masson replied. He took the man's hand and they exchanged a short handshake.

"Nasty business," Delmonte said.

"Yes. Shocking."

"Symptomatic of the times we live in," Delmonte said, as if he was some kind of social commentator. Masson had to agree with him. Delmonte took a seat, made a comment to the woman he was with, then opened his programme and looked at the schedule.

A further ten minutes passed before the service began. The music faded away, then a voice came over the public address and said, 'Please stand'. There was an audible creak of stiffened joints as everyone rose. In the next moment, a vicar appeared and the coffin, which was carried high by a team of six burly pallbearers, entered the chapel. The vicar began reading the 'Lord's Prayer' out loud. The coffin was followed by members of the immediate family, including a lady dressed in a long black coat, black hat and with a black veil over her face. The young Mrs Croft was on the arm of an older woman. Other members of the family filed in behind the young wife. There was a stony silence. The coffin was carried down the central aisle to the altar where it was placed on the marble slab. Masson could just about see the proceedings over the heads of the congregation. There must have been about one hundred and fifty people in attendance; all tightly packed into twelve or so rows of pews on both sides of the chapel. When the coffin was safely on the altar, the pallbearers departed, the vicar approached the podium and the service got underway.

First the vicar read a psalm, then two hymns were sung with gusto. A friend of the deceased read a poem by Tennyson, and then Charles Croft's younger brother, Ronald Croft, read the eulogy. It was all very tasteful and poignant. From the back of the chapel Masson couldn't see anything of those sitting on the front row, but he had seen enough of Mrs Croft to know that although she was an attractive woman, she wasn't the woman he had met in Green Park.

The service lasted for forty minutes, precisely to the timings in the programme. When it was over the two men who had been acting as ushers came in, went to the front and asked those seated at the front, the close family members, to begin filing out into the foyer.

It was a few moments before the family members came down the central aisle escorted by the ushers. Masson observed the proceedings. The regal young wife was first to depart, followed by the deceased's son and daughter, who were keeping their distance from their younger stepmother. She was *persona non grata*. She looked like a glamorous Hollywood actress in the black coat, rounded brim hat, dark gloves and the pearl necklace. Very elegant and refined in her grief, but not as attractive as the other woman who had claimed to be the real Mrs Croft.

Over the next couple of minutes or so, everyone else began to file out of the chapel until only those at the back were left. As Masson was stepping along the bench to the end of the pew, the chap who had introduced himself as Tony Delmonte paused to turn and look back at Masson. "Who did you say you are?" he asked.

"Barry Manston."

Delmonte gave him a slightly curious look. Masson decided to try and get him off the scent. "How did you know Charles Croft?" he asked.

"Well, it's a long story," Delmonte said.

Masson smiled. "Perhaps another time then?"

"Are you going to the after…" Delmonte asked, then he hesitated as if he was searching for the right word, "…drinks?" he offered.

"I don't know. Where are they?" Masson queried.

"They're in the hall next to the church over the road. Over there." He pointed in a vague direction. "It's in the programme."

"Oh. Okay. I missed that," replied Masson. "Yes. I'll see you in there."

He watched Delmonte and his partner step outside, then he paused near the exit as if he was waiting for someone to emerge out of the chapel. He looked at the programme. Indeed, there was a paragraph asking all those in attendance to attend a brief after-service lunch.

Chapter 8

Inside the hall a team of caterers had erected tables, which held a wide range of foods and beverages. It was difficult to be absolutely precise, but it looked as if the majority of those in the chapel had made it into the hall. The atmosphere was more relaxed. Over the course of the next few minutes the volume of chit-chat increased five-fold and there was even some laughter. The lovely, young Mrs Croft was sitting with a woman who could have been her mother. Not surprisingly, Masson felt a bit out on a limb. No one had asked him for a clear explanation of just who he was. Although Delmonte had been on the verge of asking him he had beat him to it. It was human nature to assume he was somehow connected to the family or even the funeral directors and no one wanted the embarrassment of asking him who he was.

He stepped over to a table and helped himself to a glass of juice and a sandwich from a plate, then he spotted the man he knew as Tony Delmonte. He moved towards him. Delmonte was chatting to an elderly chap. Masson caught his eye. Delmonte broke off his chat with the other man and turned towards Masson. Delmonte had the look of a keen sportsman. He was a slim and athletic looking guy, with fair, shoulder-length hair that was neatly groomed. He spoke in a well-to-do accent and looked to be someone who was comfortably well off.

"Barry, isn't it?" he asked. "Tell me, how did you know Charles?"

Masson smiled. "It was quite a few years ago. I was looking to invest some money in the stock market so I sought his advice."

"Where did you meet him?"

"At my golf club."

"I didn't know Charles played golf. Always said it was a good walk spoiled."

Masson chuckled. He had to think on his feet. "I didn't say he was playing. He was there at a function. We chatted and he invited me to meet him. That's how we met."

"Oh, I see."

"I seem to remember it was a golf club charity function. Charles was very kind to me."

Delmonte grinned. "How much commission did he ask for?" he asked, and gave a kind of chuckle of his own. Masson did not reply. "I bet it was twenty per cent," Delmonte added.

"Twenty-two if you must know. But whisper it, will you?" Masson replied. Delmonte forced another grin. Masson continued, "I had to pay my respects to him today, so I came along, but didn't expect to be invited to the drinks." Masson looked past Delmonte's shoulder and clapped his eyes on the young widow.

"I say, Tony. Maybe this isn't the right occasion to say it, but I didn't realise Charles's wife was a bit of all right."

Delmonte glanced at her, then refocused his eyes back on Masson and moved his head closer to him as if he was about to tell him a state secret. "Charles had an eye for beautiful women. His only vice. Suzanna. A gold digger by all accounts. I ask you! The age difference! Married for two years. Now she stands to inherit forty million at least."

Masson's jaw dropped. "Oh my word. You don't say?"

Delmonte must have had a glass of strong wine in his hand because his mouth began to run away from him. "Actually, between you and me, she's a bit of a scrubber," he said. "His body's not yet cold and she'll be hopping into bed with her lover."

Masson gave a tuneless whistle. "What! She's already got a bloke on the side?"

"Well, as a matter of fact, there *are* rumours she's been seeing another chap for some time. Marcus Ward. They say."

"What's his background?" Masson asked.

"You mean, who's Marcus Ward?" Delmonte asked as if Masson should know him.

"Yes."

"He's the same Marcus Ward who owns the string of estate agents in the south of England. 'Wards of Esher', 'Wards of Epsom' or whatever. His specialty is finding homes for wealthy people."

"Is he rich?" Masson asked.

"Depends on what you term rich. He's wealthy, alright. He's also got a number of travel agents. 'Ward International Travel' or some such. He creates bespoke travel packages for those who prefer the finer things."

"So the widow and this Ward chap are an item?" Masson asked.

"Surprised you don't know. Everyone around here does," he said in a whisper. "Just so happens that the person who killed Charles did their dirty work for them."

"You don't say," Masson said. "Tell me. Where does this Ward fellow live?" he asked.

"Right here in Esher." He thought about it for a brief moment. "Not a million miles from the Croft home." Masson refrained from saying *'you don't say'*. Delmonte had the bit between his teeth. "When the will is read, she'll stand to inherit a lot of money."

"I bet!" Masson said.

"The prenuptial agreement would only pay out if he divorced her. If it was the other way around nothing… *Nada.*" He took a long sip of the wine in his hand. "I mean, have you ever seen such a fine pair of jugs on a flirty wench?"

Masson chuckled. "Oh yeah. I see what you mean."

"Thing is, though, Ward's married. If you think Missus Croft is a lovely bit of stuff you want to see *his* wife."

"You don't say."

"Blonde. Legs up to her armpits."

Masson looked at him with a serious face. "Is she about five-ten, slim, elegant looking? Early thirties at a guess. A dancer's physique."

"Have you met her?" Delmonte asked.

"Yeah. I think I may have, but I can't recall her name."

Delmonte screwed his face as he tried to recall her name. "Er…Rachel…or, something like that." He clicked his fingers as it came to him. "Rebecca. That's it! Rebecca Ward."

"Yeah. Yeah. Now I remember – Rebecca Ward. Very beautiful woman."

Delmonte looked him in the eye. "You've met her then?"

"Think so. Perhaps I have," Masson replied. In the next second he put the plate and glass down onto the table, glanced at his watch and held his hand out. "Well, very nice meeting you, Tony. I have to go now, I'm afraid. See you around maybe." Delmonte was surprised by the sudden haste. He took Masson's hand and they exchanged a brief handshake. With that Masson was out of there.

As soon as Masson got home he went online and searched for the name Rebecca Ward. There were several people with that name. Then he searched for 'Wards Estate Agency'. He found a string of outlets throughout North-West Surrey and beyond. He searched for 'Ward International Travel' and got a similar result. Then he looked for Marcus Ward. There was someone of that name on the electoral roll for Esher, no address or telephone number, but he had the same postcode as Charles Croft. He considered his options. If Rebecca Ward was the wife of Suzanna Croft's lover then it opened up a new front and a whole new can of worms. He felt he was getting warm. He wondered how best to discover where the Wards lived. His sole intention was to discover if Rebecca Ward was the lady he had met in Green Park.

The next thing he did was to contact 'Ward's Estate Agent' at the Esher office on the telephone. He spoke to a pleasant lady who introduced herself as Maria. When he asked her if Marcus Ward was there she told him that Marcus Ward had been the owner of the business a few years ago before selling up to a larger national company who kept the name 'Ward's'. Marcus Ward no longer had any connection or involvement with Ward's Estate Agents. He asked Maria if she knew if he still had the travel business. She said she didn't know. He asked her if he still lived in the Esher area. She started to hesitate and he could sense that she was becoming suspicious.

"Well, I think so. But who is this, please?" she asked. He swiftly thanked her for her help and hung up before she could hang up on him.

If this Marcus Ward chap was playing away with Mrs Croft, the question was, did Missus Ward know anything about it? If she did, surely she would have elected to get rid of Mrs Croft, not Mr Croft. Something didn't quite fit. Maybe they were in it together. Ward had persuaded his wife to impersonate Mrs Croft, then pay for a hit man to kill him in order that they could gain... What? Was this even a possibility?

That evening at six o'clock Masson received the phone call he'd been dreading. It was James Malloy, the associate of Divorty's he had spoken to the other day. Malloy demanded a face-to-face meeting with Masson that evening. He didn't ask him. Masson was to meet him in a bar called 'O'Flynn's' on Holloway Road in Islington at eight o'clock. They had business to discuss. The meeting would take place in a back room of the pub. Two other associates of Divorty's would be in attendance: Dave Toshack and Matt Royce.

    Masson had met Malloy on a previous occasion, but only fleetingly, so he didn't know him well. Divorty had introduced them. He remembered that Malloy had been okay. Masson had come to the conclusion that Divorty was far more embroiled in the London crime scene then he had assumed or Divorty had admitted. The used car business could have been a front for another operation, such as supplying criminals with vehicles for their enterprises.

Chapter 9

'O'Flynn's' was situated on the corner of the junction of Holloway Road and Liverpool Road in Highbury and Islington. The entrance was up a couple of steps, through a doorway, passing a water feature before a turn into the bar area. Masson stepped through to the bar. The smell of spicy food simmering, probably in a big pot, made his mouth water. An Irish ballad was playing over the sound system, and a wide screen television behind the bar was showing the recording of a recent Hurling game from the Emerald Isle. At eight on a Tuesday evening there weren't many customers.

    A thick-set guy in a black leather button-up jacket and blue jeans was standing at the bar talking to another guy who was sitting on a high stool. Up ahead, a couple of guys were playing pool on a blue baize table. Masson thought he recognised the thick-set guy as James Malloy. He assumed the other chap was Dave Toshack. Malloy glanced at Masson and nodded his head. Toshack seemed to know him, though Masson couldn't recall ever seeing him before. Toshack was the older and the shorter of the two. He had a round, acne-punctured face, and a thick neck. Fair to ginger hair was thinning on the dome of his skull. As the sound of the ballad faded the volume on the television took over and the commentator raised his level of excitement as a monstrous shot went between the goalposts and County Clare took the lead over County Cork.

    Toshack took a long pull on his beer. The way he was necking the contents of the bottle seemed to suggest a love of drink. Masson stepped towards the bar. The guy behind came to serve him and asked him what he wanted.

    "I'll get his," Malloy said.

    "Right y'are, then," said the barman, in a distinct Southern Irish accent. "What is it y'd be havin'?

"What he's having," Masson replied.

"Make that four, Danny," Toshack said before downing the remaining contents in the bottle. "And bring them through to the back room will yer?" Danny, the barman, nodded his head but said nothing.

Malloy led the way across the floor to a closed door at the far side, opened it and they all entered into a dark, windowless, stuffy room. Toshack turned on an overhead light. There was a sink on one side laden with dirty glasses and other utensils. A smell of stale chilli lingered in the air, and there were various boxes of snacks stacked upright against one side. A square table in the middle of the room had four straight-backed chairs around it, illuminated by a naked bulb on the end of a long flex that hung from the ceiling. A fourth guy, one of the pool players, also came in and closed the door behind him. Malloy introduced him as Matt Royce. Royce was an average-looking young guy, but tall and beefy. He didn't acknowledge Masson and retained a cold hard expression on his face. They all sat down at the table and it was Malloy who introduced everyone to everyone else. Before they got down to business there was a knock at the door and Danny entered carrying four bottles of lager on a tray. He placed the tray on the table then got out of there sharpish. Before starting the discussion, Malloy dipped a hand in a jacket pocket, extracted a packet of cigarettes and a lighter which he placed on the table.

"We all know why we're here. Right?"

No one replied to the question. Masson didn't know precisely why he was there, but elected to say nothing.

"Liam is banged up in Belmarsh. It's our job to spring him." He opened the packet of cigarettes, extracted one, put it into his lips and lit it. He sucked on it, then let the fumes stream out if his nostrils before he continued to speak. "We got a tip-off that Liam is to be taken to see the peek on

Monday at South West magistrate's court on Lavender Hill. The hearing is due to start at two o'clock. It's about a forty minute drive to the court. Inside information tells us they'll be leaving Belmarsh at eleven o'clock. We'll need to be in a position to spring him. There'll be three of 'em in the van: the driver, his mate and a guard in the back. We don't think there'll be a police car following, or anything like that."

Masson detected that they were deadly serious about springing Liam from out of the prison van. Malloy killed the half-smoked cigarette in an ashtray. Toshack and Matt Royce took deep swigs from the bottles in their hands. A haze of cigarette smoke floated around the bulb and swirled like a fog. Malloy cleared his throat.

"We'll have three vehicles for the job. A truck to take out the prison van. A following car and a getaway vehicle. Any questions?"

Why am I here? Masson was dying to ask. But he said nothing.

"Who's supplying the transport?" asked Matt Royce.

"Sorted. Not a problem," said Malloy. "The truck will be a ten-ton tipper lorry. It will take out the front of the van. I'll be driving the following vehicle with Tosh and you, Tom. Matt, you'll be driving the truck. We've got a couple more guys in on it. I'll let you know who they are in good time. As soon as the lorry hits, three of us will run to the back door of the van and snap open the door using crow bars. Matt, you'll be in the truck with a couple of other guys. You'll join us at the back of the van and you'll be responsible for crowd control."

"Who's driving the getaway car?" Royce asked.

"To be decided. There'll be seven of us. Maybe eight. Any more questions?"

"What about a safe house?" Royce asked.

"That's sorted," Toshack said. "We're renting a house out in the sticks. Barnet way." He lifted the bottle to his lips and downed most of the contents in one.

This was how Tom Masson found himself embroiled in a plot to spring Divorty from out of a prison van on its way to court. It was risky to say the least. But they were as serious as a heart attack. There was no way Divorty would be in court next week.

The team chatted for the next twenty minutes about various aspects of the task. The exact spot where they would attempt to stop the van. Inside information, no doubt secured from an employee of the security company responsible for taking prisoners to the courts in the London area, had given them details of the route and the timings. Once the truck hit the front of the van to stop it, everyone would pile forward, open the door, get inside and release Divorty from one of the eight tiny cells inside the vehicle. Divorty certainly had friends. It sounded simple, but these things are rarely that straight forward. Masson was involved and there wasn't a great deal he could do about it. He couldn't say no. Asking questions would only irritate the others. Malloy, who might still wonder about him, would become more suspicious. That would be like signing his own death warrant.

Chapter 10

Wednesday 30th September

The next day, Masson drove into Esher. His first task was to discover where Marcus Ward resided. He knew from Tony Delmonte that it was close to the Croft home. He needed to know where exactly, in order to observe him coming and going. It was just after one in the afternoon when he drove along Esher High Street. His old-style BMW Boxster didn't look out of place in this vicinity, but make no mistake, this was stockbroker country. The line of fine restaurants and expensive stores of every kind bore testament to that. As an ironic gesture perhaps, there were a couple of charity shops, but the higher-end sort, ones that housed unwanted designer coats and unused crystal glasses. And no Pound Shops. Nobody bought anything for a quid around here.

  He managed to find a space in a car park, then walked the short distance into the town centre. He didn't have a plan as such, but thought he would be able to obtain the information he wanted by simply asking the right people the right questions. During the morning he had used Google Earth to re-familiarise himself with the streets of Esher. He knew there was a 'Ward's Estate' agent on the main street. After ambling along the pavement for a couple of hundred yards, he came across it.

  Before going inside, he peered into the window so he could see into the interior. A young man was sitting behind a desk, probably staffing the office telephone. Without further ado he opened the door and stepped inside. A bell sounded as he entered. It was nothing out of the ordinary. Just an everyday estate agency. A good looking, tall and slim guy with thick dark hair, not much older than twenty-five, was sitting in a black leather armchair at a desk. As Masson strode to the display boards in the side panel, the young man looked him up and down. Masson looked at the properties for sale. Three quarters of a million pounds wouldn't buy you much in this neck of the woods. You would be lucky to buy a one-horse shack with that kind of money. The guy got up from behind the desk and stepped towards the customer.

"Can I assist you with anything today?" he asked in a pleasant manner.

Masson lifted the sunshades off his eyes and looked at him. The badge attached to the fellow's jacket said his name was Andre.

"Just thinking of moving into the area," Masson replied.

"Are you looking to rent or buy freehold?" Andre asked efficiently.

"To buy. Freehold."

"Do you have your ideal price range?"

"About a million and a half," Masson replied. The properties he was looking at were in excess of three million.

"Perhaps you may wish to view the boards on this side," the young man advised. Then he went into a salesman mode. "We have an excellent range of properties in the town with good commuter links to the city," he said. "Where are you now, if you don't mind me asking?"

"North London," he replied.

"How many bedrooms do you require?"

"Four."

"En-suites?"

"One."

"Kitchens?"

"Just the one."

"Perhaps this property may interest you. It's just come onto the market at one point four million. Only ten years old. Detached. Good school location. Double garage. All the modern conveniences."

Masson looked at the photograph. "Looks ideal," he said.

"Care to arrange a viewing?" he asked.

"Yeah. Why not?"

"I'll just check the details." Andre went back to his desk and sat in the armchair. Masson watched him tap into a computer and pull up the details. "By appointment only. I can contact the vendor right now if you wish."

Masson stepped towards the desk and slipped into the seat opposite him. "To tell you the truth, I don't know this area all that well. An ex-school pal of mine lives in the area. His name is Marcus Ward."

Andre looked at him with interest on his face. "The chap who used to own this chain of estates agents. Do you know him?"

"Yes. He's an old school chum. A friend called Toby Harrismore told me Marcus is still in the area. I haven't seen Wardie in what…ten years, but understand that he's still in the town. Amazing. Wouldn't you say?"

"He lives in Esher. Beautiful house. A five-bedroom property. Swimming pool in the garden and a tennis court."

Masson raised his eyebrows. "Well I say it sounds as if Wardie's done very well for himself. Good for him. We all knew he would. What's it called? Where is it? Toby did tell me, but I can't for the life of me remember what he said."

"The Vicarage on Esher Lane," Andre volunteered.

"That's it. The Vicarage. Lovely name. On Esher Lane."

Andre nodded his head. "The Vicarage. It's been in the Ward family for many years."

Masson leaned back into the chair, threaded his hands together and put them in his lap. "Now what's the name of his wife? Let me think." He looked at the ceiling. "No, don't tell me. I'll get it. Rachel, isn't it?"

"I think it's Rebecca," said the young man.

"Rebecca. That's it."

Andre was suddenly interrupted by the sound of a ringing telephone. He asked to be excused for a moment. Masson got up from the seat, stepped to the display board and listened to the telephone conversation. Andre was taking an email address and promising to send someone the details of a property. As Masson looked at the property board he reflected on what he had learned. He now knew where Marcus Ward lived and that his wife's name was definitely Rebecca. Andre quickly finished the conversation and put the telephone down. He looked at Masson.

"Sorry about that."

"Is there a florist in town?" Masson asked.

Andre looked puzzled. "What?" he asked.

"A florist," he repeated, "a shop that sells flowers?"

"Yes. Just down the high street to the left, two hundred yards. Would you like to make an appointment to take a look at the property?" he asked. The prospect of earning some commission from the sale must have been percolating in his head. "I can make an appointment immediately."

Masson turned back towards the desk, but stopped after a couple of steps. He ran the tip of his tongue over his lips. "Tell you what," he said. "Let's leave it for a couple of days. I want to have a good look around the town before I decide. I might even raise my budget closer to three mil. Be seeing you, and thanks for your help. You've been very kind." He opened the door to the shop and stepped out onto the street, leaving Andre to reflect on one that had slipped away.

Masson found the florist just along the street. He opened the door and stepped inside. As he entered the proprietor appeared behind the counter. She was a nice-looking thirty-year-old. She had a trim figure, a pleasant smile and wore a chest hugging short sleeve T-shirt.

"Can I help you?" she asked.

Masson smiled. "I hope so. Can you deliver six red roses to an address in the town?"

"Well. Yes. Who are they for?" she asked.

"Mrs Rebecca Ward of The Vicarage, Esher Lane," he replied.

She looked at him with a blank expression. "I don't think she lives there's anymore." She edged closer to him and tilted her head slightly to one side. "I was told they've been apart for at least a year. Separated."

"Separated?! Who, Marcus and Rebecca?! No, surely not?"

"Yes. Such a shame," she said, and made a disparaging face.

"You don't say? What a disappointment. I had no idea about that...er, well, in that case I won't be needing the roses. Sorry."

She didn't reply. He left the shop and walked back up the street, past the estate agent and into the car park. His next task was to locate Esher Lane and find the 'Vicarage'.

He drove to the end of the road, took a couple of turns, and within minutes he was on Esher Lane. Tony Delmonte was correct. The two houses were close by. Esher Lane ran parallel to Sandy Lane where the Croft property was located. The properties were probably less than five hundred yards apart as the crow flies. The Croft house faced west, whereas the Ward home faced east. Each of the homes was set in their own parcel of land, bordered by trees and a boundary of either wooden fencing or brick walling.

The Vicarage looked to be exactly what it was called: an old vicarage. It had a slightly crumbling, stress-effect, green pebble-dash finish. Five windows across the top floor.

A central doorway with a porch roofing over the entrance. It was nice and secluded, though not as impressive as the Croft chateau. No doubt it had a large area of land to the rear. It had a double garage to the side and a spacious stone-chip forecourt that could have easily accommodated a dozen cars. A metallic red Porsche 911 turbo, the latest model, was parked on the forecourt and glinting like a new penny.

After passing the house at a relatively low pace he picked up the speed and drove on for another five hundred yards, turned right, then right again and drove by the Croft house. The distance from house to house was – at a guess – an eight hundred-yard walk. Much quicker if a short cut was taken through the back gardens. Assuming Ward was relatively fit, he could have done the walk in less than three minutes. At the top of the lane, Masson took a right turn, then another right and came back along Esher Lane.

The time was now two-thirty. He considered heading back into central London, but something told him to hang around for a while. The sight of the Porsche on the forecourt could possibly mean that Marcus Ward was at home. He wouldn't try to break in. He just wanted to observe. For one thing, he didn't have any hard evidence that Ward was guilty of anything. Right now it was just a hunch.

He cruised back close to the Ward residence, pulled onto the verge one hundred yards from the property, came to a stop and killed the engine. According to the florist, Rebecca Ward was no longer there. The revelation that Ward was separated from his wife did come as a surprise, but he wasn't sure of its significance at this point in time. Overall things in Esher were going to plan and he felt he was finding some answers to the questions he had. His musings were suddenly interrupted by his ringtone.

It was James Malloy. "Listen!" said Malloy. "Good news! We've had the definite nod that there'll be no one following the van. Great, huh?"

"You sure?" queried Masson.

"Yeah. Sure. We got the info from the inside... You still up for it?"

"Of course. No probs..." said Masson. Problem or not, he had no choice but to get involved.

For whatever reason, it seemed the police had no idea of Divorty's criminal background, or if they did, they didn't have the resources to enlist a security back-up. It did not occur to them that a bunch of Divorty's mates were prepared to risk their own freedom to help him secure his. They seemed to view him as a low-risk burglar, out of his depth. Not his problem, thought Masson.

Malloy hung up and Masson returned to the matter in hand. From this near to the house he had an unrestricted view of the drive onto the property. He had no intention of staying for too long in case he was observed by one of the locals who would note his registration number, but he was keen to see Ward in the flesh.

One hour became two. The late afternoon was becoming dull and cool. The leaves on the trees were turning to copper as the sun drooped low across the horizon. In a couple of weeks, the leaves would begin to cover the ground in a carpet of amber and brown. A number of vehicles did come along the lane, but it was still quiet suburbia. The blue metallic Boxster parked onto the verge barely received a glance. Another ten minutes passed and he was considering an end to the surveillance, when the red Porsche appeared at the end of the drive and turned left onto the lane. Masson was almost too lulled into contemplation to react; nevertheless, he soon set off in pursuit. If Ward was driving the car then it would be interesting to see where he was heading.

Masson followed the Porsche out of the Esher area. Within minutes they were on the A3 and quickly travelling northbound into the tightly packed south London suburbs. Soon they'd reached the Richmond area. Despite the traffic between them, the flame-red body of the Porsche was conspicuous and Masson managed to keep up with him. Ward wouldn't expect anyone to be following him, so Masson felt okay on that score. It looked as if he was heading into central London.

They crossed over the Thames at Kew Bridge, then into Chiswick, winding east towards Hammersmith. Masson lost him for a few moments in traffic around the elevated section of the A4, but managed to accelerate past a couple of vehicles and spot him again as they came to stationary traffic. Masson was one car behind him. The time was getting on for five o'clock and the evening rush hour was starting to take hold. They edged their way into Kensington.

The Porsche turned right onto Earls Court Road and headed into the tight streets of south Kensington. The traffic was nose to tail at this point. Overhead it had become so dull that several drivers now had side lights on. There were a good number of pedestrians on the pavements in and around south Kensington and plenty of activity in the posh cafés and stores. Masson kept his eyes on the Porsche, but he got caught out at a set of traffic lights. The car went through them just as they were turning red. Masson had to pull up, only to see the Porsche's tail lights disappear into the distance. As soon as the lights changed to amber, he set off in pursuit. Too late. The Porsche was now out of sight. He banged the steering wheel column in frustration at the thought of losing him.

Though the Porsche was probably long gone, he drove around for a few minutes in the hope of spotting it. It was his lucky day. His frustration soon turned to joy. As he turned onto the Kings Road he passed a red Porsche 911 parked onto the kerb. He had to glance back in his rear-view to be certain it was the same car. The registration plate MAW 378 was a dead giveaway. He drove along the street, turned left and came by a car pulling out of a space close to the Brompton Hospital. Once parked, he quickly made his way back onto Kings Road and walked in a westerly direction to the spot where the Porsche was located.

There were a couple of well-heeled restaurants in the vicinity. He dropped the shades over his eyes, and blended right in with the other minor celebrities and wealthy residents. He walked past the Porsche and along the path to a restaurant, where diners were sitting in a garden under a glass canopy. He looked across the seating area and saw Rebecca Ward. She was sitting at a table for two, opposite a guy who he assumed was the driver of the Porsche, Marcus Ward. In her hand she held a slim flute full of champagne. Her long blonde hair was down this time, around her shoulders and she wore a silk scarf around her neck which matched the white jacket that seemed too thin for the autumn air. Masson couldn't stand and ogle so he walked on for twenty yards, stopped to look in the window of a chemist, then turned around and came back in the direction he had come.

From this side he had a better view of the guy she was with. He looked to be average height, average size, nondescript features. He was wearing a light jacket over a plain shirt, but no tie. Short, dark, cropped hair. Approximate age range of about forty to forty-five. A waiter had just approached them to take their order. Masson carried on walking. His view into the area was now obstructed by a line of high bushes that formed a boundary between the restaurant and the pavement, so he had no option but to head past the Porsche. At the next junction, to a side street, he paused and decided what to do. He quickly elected to hang about until they emerged. If they left in the Porsche he wouldn't be able to follow them, but he thought it unlikely they would leave in the car. Intuition told Masson there was a good chance they would go to a nearby flat or hotel as the meeting was far enough away from Esher to potentially be illicit.

Time passed and the night was drawing in at a rapid rate. The full beams of headlights on the Kings Road were on. Floodlights in the restaurant garden snapped into action. A further thirty minutes passed. He had zipped his jacket up to his neck against the cold nip in the air. A bus went by with its internal lights blazing. A breeze whipped along the street to send a discarded coffee cup tumbling down the road.

It was a further twenty minutes before they emerged and stepped onto the path. They walked side-by-side, comfortably, but not intimately, towards Sloane Square. Ward was about her height. He was slim and lithe and looked well maintained. He had a slightly tanned complexion. As they came towards Masson he turned away and headed down the side street at a pace, before pausing, and coming back. He watched them walk to the end of the street, seemingly unaware of his presence. They carried on walking past the Porsche and ambled along the pavement at a slow pace. Masson was right, they were heading somewhere local. He intended to stay a good thirty to forty paces behind them. They soon quickened their pace as if the cold, after the warmth of the restaurant, was now getting to them.

They were soon near Sloane Square. They crossed over the square, took a right onto Lower Sloane Street, then turned into a residential area of tall red bricked houses in Sloane Gardens. It was just a stone's throw from Sloane Square and the underground station.

Masson watched them eventually step off the pavement into the vestibule of one of the big, four storey Victorian houses that lined the streets. He doubted anyone would emerge any time soon, but he was proved to be wrong. Only five minutes elapsed before Ward came out of the house alone and walked away at a swift pace. He walked back up Lower Sloane Street and onto Kings Road. Masson followed him and watched him go to his car and get in. The car pulled away from the kerb, did a U turn in the middle of the road and headed back in the direction it had come. Masson watched the red tail lights fade into the distance. In that moment he reflected on what Tony Delmonte had told him at the funeral. Marcus Ward was having an affair with Suzanna Croft. If he had allegedly split from his wife, would this allow him to get Suzanna into bed?

After watching the lights on the Porsche go out of view he returned to the house on Lower Sloane Street. Once there he stepped towards the front door and looked at the names attached to the intercom unit. The names of the residents were:

Flat 1: N. Hasim
Flat 2: Miss J Erickson
Flat 3: J. Cortes-Smith
Flat 4: A. Asif
Flat 5: N. Chiles
Flat 6: Lequour
Flat 7: Unoccupied
Flat 8: Y. Pires-Mendoza

There was no reference to Rebecca Ward. Then again, why would she use her real name if she wanted to keep the location secret? If she even wanted it secret. There was definitely something underhand going on here. Maybe the Wards were in it together for a reason that as yet, was not obvious.

Content with his evening's work and what he had discovered, Masson decided not to chance his luck and attempt to contact her. He called it a night, walked back to his car and drove home.

Chapter 11

Thursday 1st October

The next morning, Masson awoke at seven. Over breakfast he contemplated his next move. There were some high stakes in this game: murder, double-crossing, and angry hard guys. The Wards were involved: certainly, Rebecca Ward had hired a hitman.

He knew from Delmonte that Ward was having an affair with Suzanna Croft, and that supposedly, the Wards' marriage was falling apart: perhaps motives to kill Croft. Whether Marcus Ward actually did the murder was another matter. He knew that Ward was still in contact with his supposedly estranged wife. He also knew that the Ward home was very close to the Croft home. In theory, Ward could even have murdered Croft for a reason that was not clear. Maybe Ward's aim was to get his hands on Croft's fortune by marrying the widow? He shook his head to himself. Conjecture would not do. He required stronger evidence. He decided his best strategy was to try and get the information out of the lovely Rebecca Ward.

Masson left home at nine and drove to the Sloane Square area. She could not stay in the flat all day. She had to leave at some point. It may be a long shot, but he had to take every opportunity.

He made it to the area of smart, period red brick houses that had long ago been converted to flats. There were plenty of people in and around this bustling area of the city. He managed to find a parking space not too far from the house, parked, then ambled to a spot on the corner by Lower Sloane Street and settled himself there.

He knew he couldn't stay in the area too long for obvious reasons. In these times of heightened security it wouldn't do to be caught hanging around. He didn't want to attract attention to himself. He would wait on this corner for twenty minutes or so, long enough to reasonably wait for someone, then stride away in feigned annoyance at the imagined latecomer, before coming back again later. The day was chilly in the shade, but reasonably warm in the weak, watery sunshine. The sound of the traffic on the street was a constant, as was the lingering perfume of the plants in the garden adjacent to Lower Sloane Street.

Over the course of the next twenty minutes, various people came and went from the row of houses. A postman in the familiar fluorescent jacket trundled by, bowling a trolley on wheels. The time was getting on for ten-thirty. For all he knew she could have left her flat hours before he arrived. After another ten minutes, he left huffily and walked down the street towards Chelsea Bridge.

At the junction with Pimlico Road he raised the collar of his jacket against a nip in the air. He stepped into a café, ordered a coffee, sat at a table and scanned through the pages of a morning red-top newspaper for half an hour. When the café began to fill and he had failed to purchase another beverage, the person behind the counter started to give him the evil eye, so he departed and walked back up the street to the house on Sloane Gardens. This time he approached the street from a different direction and propped himself up against a bollard. A droplet bounced off his lapel. Shit, he thought. If it began to rain heavily she would be reluctant to leave the flat.

He kept his eyes on the pavement in front of the row of houses. It was not long before someone emerged out of the house with a skip in her long stride. It was her: Rebecca Ward, no doubt about it. She turned away from him, walked along for a few yards, then turned onto the path adjacent to Lower Sloane Street and headed up to the square. She was wearing a short, shiny, tight-fitting burgundy jacket, grey sportswear pants, and white trainers on her feet. The same baseball cap she was wearing when he first met her covered her head. Her long pony tail was sticking out through the opening at the back.

He pushed off the bollard and followed her up the path. She was fifty yards ahead of him. She had a sports bag perched on her right shoulder. Her pace was languid, casual, but not exceedingly slow. He'd almost caught up to her when she stopped to cross over a road onto the middle of the square. He quickly reduced his pace and followed her across.

She made her way onto Eaton Place, where she had to wait for the traffic to ease before moving on to the pavement at Sloane Street and walking in a northerly direction towards Knightsbridge. He looked skyward. A rain cloud had broken and released a smattering of drops before the breeze rose and shifted it somewhere else. The traffic along Sloane Street wasn't busy. She walked on at a quicker pace. The strap of her gym bag slipped, and she had to pause for a moment to swing the bag onto her other shoulder, which suggested the bag was heavy. She crossed over Pont Street and sauntered by the boldly logoed designer shops.

He wondered what to do. He assumed that his face was red: he was angry. He wanted to catch up to her, push her into a doorway and demand that she tells him everything, but that wouldn't be a wise move for obvious reasons. There were people all over the place for one, and secondly, threatening violence just wasn't his style. He had to be far subtler.

As she approached a row of stores she suddenly veered off the path and stepped into a doorway, and out of view. He carried on for another ten yards, paused for a couple of seconds, then retraced his steps and came back. The business sign on the door read: 'The Sloane Health, Fitness and Solarium Centre'. He stepped back, looked up, and there posted on the windows of the next two floors were images of women in various fitness and aerobic poses.

He had an idea. He waited a minute to ensure she was not in the entrance, then went boldly inside. He found himself in an open space with a stairway going up to the first floor. A notice on the wall said: 'This way to health and fitness. Ladies only.' A pointed finger sign showed the way up the stairs. As he stepped onto the first stair, a woman coming down the stairs made eye contact. It wasn't Rebecca Ward. She looked as though she had recently completed a vigorous workout. He smiled at her. She responded in kind and carried on past him.

He quickly ascended to the first floor landing, went through a glass door and into a spacious reception area with a curved glass counter before an opaque glass divide. A rather attractive woman in a white beautician's uniform was sitting at the counter. Through the glass screen it was possible to see shapes of women working out on rows of multi-exercise machines. In the area beyond, the sound of techno pop was belting out a rhythm. To the right was another glass doorway that must have led into the changing rooms. As he came into the reception the pretty woman raised her head. She smiled.

"Can I help you, sir?" she asked.

"Hopefully," he replied. He rested his arms on the counter, looked into her eyes and smiled. "My partner and I are moving into the area in a few weeks. I'd like to be able to let her know that there's a decent fitness centre nearby. I'm wondering if you have any details about joining, she's really into her Pilates and such."

She reached over to a holder and took out a glossy leaflet. "Is your partner just looking for class activities or an individual trainer as well then?" she asked.

"Oh, definitely both," he replied.

"Our membership fees are very reasonable," she said. "We have a lot of respected clientele, everyone loves it here. There are even some big names, if you know what I mean. It's a great place to socialise and meet people," she confided.

Masson saw an opportunity appear before him. "Funny you should mention that. The lady who entered a couple of minutes ago – doesn't she have an early evening show – you know, that one on Sky? God, I can't for the life of me remember her name – what is it?"

The woman looked ill-at-ease by his blatant prying. She glanced at a log on the counter, then committed an error of judgement by telling him the client's name. "Do you mean Naomi Chiles?" she divulged.

"I'm not sure now. What's that again?"

"Naomi Chiles," she repeated.

He instantly recalled the name – N. Chiles – against the button for flat number five on the intercom unit at the door to the house. "The tall lady with the baseball cap on her head? Grey sports outfit?"

"Yes."

"Sorry. I must be mistaken. I'm sure that's not the name. She probably just looks like her."

She nodded her head. "Would you like a membership leaflet with our fees?"

"Yes, sure," he said. "Thank you. I'll take one and give it to her. I think she'll like it here very much," he added, with a smile.

He looked at the obscured dark figures behind the frosted glass barrier and wondered if one of them was the lady who called herself Naomi Chiles. The techno music continued to pulse out a rhythm as the figures moved in synchronisation to the beat.

"I'm sure she will," she said, as she handed him a glossy leaflet displaying the fees. He thanked her and left.

'Sara Croft', 'Rebecca Ward' and now 'Naomi Chiles'. He was intrigued even more. Any more aliases and she'd be a Russian sleeper agent. Something very odd was going on. He now had another lead to follow. He felt reinvigorated by his ability to find names and get answers. He flattered himself that it might be down to a certain amount of previously undiscovered detective talent, but then he pinched himself. If the truth be told, there was a large chunk of luck in it. On stepping out of the exit he headed back along the pavement to Sloane Street and walked to the house. He wanted to be there when 'Naomi Chiles' returned from the fitness centre.

He stationed himself at the end of the street on the Lower Sloane Street side, so he could observe the length of the road up to the square. One hour passed. It was now getting on for four o'clock. A nursery full of kids was just finishing for the day, with mothers collecting their offspring and nannies gathering the children in their care from outside the front door. He thought he might be attracting too much attention, so he back-peddled down the street towards Pimlico Road. He came back ten minutes later.

It was another fifteen minutes before she appeared on the path ahead of him. The tight jacket squeezed around her midriff. The grey jogging bottoms rippled in the breeze. She had her head down, peering at the phone in her left hand. The baseball cap was off. The bag was now on her left shoulder. She didn't look up as she approached the turn into the street where the house of flats was situated. As she came nearer, he stepped away and let her turn off the pavement and onto the path along the line of houses, then, deftly approaching her from behind he followed her at a distance of ten feet.

As she neared the step leading onto the porch he got right behind her, so close he could have grasped her ponytail if he'd wanted to. He was about to surprise the lovely Mrs

Ward, or was it Naomi Chiles? No one was near to them. As she paused to open her shoulder bag he stepped even closer. Just a matter of inches now. She could feel his presence on her shoulder and turned to look at him. At first there was no recognition on her face. Then she raised her eyebrows. She was about to say something, but could only utter a stuttering 'Uurgghh!'

"Hello. Long time, no see. How are you?" he said in a matter-of-fact way. She didn't respond. He grasped her elbow. "No histrionics now. There's a good girl."

He had no intention of threatening her with violence. That wasn't his style. But she didn't know that. She looked shocked by his sudden appearance, but didn't look as if she was about to scream. Those to-die-for features looked in control of her emotions. He extended his left arm around her midriff, felt the curve of her waist and held her close. He put his mouth to her ear. "Be cool and don't make a sound. You'll be okay. Open the door and let's go in. I could do with a drink," he whispered.

She didn't say a word. She put the key into the front door, opened it and they stepped into a marble-tiled corridor. There were doors leading into flats on either side of the entrance. The corridor then broadened out into an open area with a carpeted stairway going up to the first floor ahead.

"Where's your flat?" he asked.

"Second floor," she replied.

"How many flats are there?" he asked.

"Two on each floor."

"Let's go up."

They ascended the stairs. He was a step behind her. He stayed close and ready to grab her if she attempted to flee, but he didn't think she would be that stupid. No one was around and there was no sound except for the creak of the stair boards. She was calm and collected. She didn't appear

75

to be fearful, maybe just a little shocked that he had found her. As they reached the first floor landing he got by her side and they stepped onto the next step together. He could smell the delightful scent of her jasmine perfume: the same powerful aroma he had smelt at the first meeting.

"You weren't hard to find," he said.

She didn't reply. She stared down. She looked gorgeous. He didn't want to hurt her. He wouldn't. That was the last thing on his mind. On reaching the second floor landing she led him to the front door of her flat. The door had two glass panels in it. It was marked 'Flat Five'. She took the key, threaded it into the lock, turned it and opened the door.

They stepped straight into a reception with the lounge area set out behind a wooden frame, which was festooned with climbing plants and various ornaments and picture frames. Openings to the left and ahead led into other rooms. She stepped through into the lounge. He followed and let his eyes take it all in. The room was spacious and well decorated, the furniture and art-work arranged. It was orderly and full of colour. At the far end, a pair of floor to ceiling doors opened onto a narrow, railed balcony. Daylight was pouring in through the glass panels.

There was a green Chesterfield sofa against the right hand wall. A low walnut topped coffee table was set in front of it. On the other wall was a set of bookshelves that contained all manner of books and glossy publications. A single armchair that matched the sofa was placed in the corner. There was a wide screen television in the other corner; and a plain rug covered a parquet floor. On the walls were several photographs of close-up female faces in silver glass frames. She stepped a few paces towards the window, then paused and turned around to face him. Now that she was on home turf she must have felt her confidence increase. She opened the bidding:

"Okay. So what do you want?" she asked.

"Answers," he replied tersely. She took the cap from off her head, then slipped the bag off her shoulder and placed them both on the table, but remained standing. Then he asked, somewhat inconsequentially, "What's out there?"

"Where?"

"Down below."

"A garden."

"Nice place," he concluded.

"How did you find me?" she asked.

"I'm supposed to be the one asking the questions," he said.

"You won't hurt me, will you?"

"Not unless you want me to." He noticed the arrangement of several bottles and glasses in a cabinet. "How about a drink?"

"What of?"

"What've you got?"

"Brandy. Vodka. Wine."

"A glass of wine would be fine. Pour yourself one."

He watched her step towards the cabinet, take a bottle of white wine and pour a generous amount into two glass tumblers. She came forward and handed him a glass, then stepped over to the sofa, settled down on one end and tucked her long legs under her. She unclipped her ponytail and let her hair fall down her back. She was serenity personified. He began to think they might get along fine. On the other hand, she was one dangerous woman, alright. She coolly arranged murders. He needed to be careful. She looked at him.

"What now?" she asked.

"Depends."

"On what?"

"How you react."

"To what?"

"Questions."

She eyed him and put the rim of the glass to her mouth and took a sip of wine.

"That was quite a stunt you pulled off." She didn't respond. "Shame is you don't know who you're involved with." She remained mute. "A load of bad-arsed criminals who won't be as nice as me. Who killed Charles Croft?" he asked.

"I thought it was you."

He chuckled. "I know the criminal justice system in this country is messed-up, but that's going a bit too far. Was it Marcus Ward?" he asked.

"Marcus who?" she asked.

He smiled. "Come on. Let's not play games. Your other half."

She looked puzzled. "My other half. I don't have another half," she said in an indignant tone.

"He was here last night."

She let out a chuckle of her own, smiled and then shook her head. "Marcus Ward is not my other half. He's married to my sister, Rebecca. I'm Naomi."

Masson put the glass to his lips and took a long sip of the wine, using the time to think of a reply. "So, if you're not Rebecca Ward, where is she?"

"Last time I heard from her she was in Los Angeles with her film producer boyfriend. She's married to Marcus, but they're no longer together."

Masson glanced back to look at the criss-cross wooden frame behind him. There were a number of picture frames on it containing photographs. He couldn't help but notice the one in which two pretty girls were standing together, laughing. Two females who looked remarkably like twins. The penny dropped. "You're a twin?" he asked.

"No." Naomi looked towards the same photograph. "Rebecca is two years older than me." She ran her left hand through her hair to free it. He noticed that she wasn't wearing the diamond encrusted ring on her wedding finger.

"Where's the ring?" he asked. "The one with the big diamond."

"I don't have it. It isn't mine."

"So who gave it to you?" She didn't answer. "Ward gave you the ring, didn't he?"

She looked at her hand, then at him and tilted her head slightly to one side. "It's my sister's wedding ring. She gave it back to him when they went their separate ways."

He stepped towards the armchair and sat down opposite her. He looked at her and she at him. "You've opened a can of worms here. Divorty is in prison, but he may not be there much longer. Once he's out, all hell will break loose."

"Who's Divorty?" she asked.

He grinned, then threw his head back and looked at the ceiling. "Who's Divorty?" he asked in a rhetorical way. "He's the guy you hired to kill Charles Croft, but when he got to the house he was already dead. Someone got there before him and framed him for the murder."

"I know nothing about that," she said too quickly.

Masson smiled. "I don't know if I'm surprised by that or not. You do recall us meeting in Green Park, don't you? Or have you forgotten about that?" She didn't reply. "Who asked you to impersonate Mrs Croft?" he asked.

Naomi took a sip of the wine. He waited for an answer. "Marcus," she said.

"Marcus Ward?"

"Yes."

"I'm just the go-between in this. I passed the job onto Divorty, and he was going to do it. He's now mad as hell. If he gets out anytime soon, he'll be looking for answers."

"Why are you telling me this?" she asked.

"I thought that would be obvious. To protect you." She played with the fringe of her hair. "If Ward wants Croft dead there has to be a reason. What is it?"

"I don't know," she said. "He came here and asked me to do it."

"Do what?"

"Get in contact with this chap whose name he'd been given."

"Smetham?" he asked.

"Yes, I think that was the name."

"How much did he pay you?"

She thought about the answer for a moment. "Ten thousand pounds," she said. "I need the money. I'm a part-time actress and dancer. I occasionally work on cruise ships as a *hoofer*. I don't get paid a huge amount. When he came up with ten grand, what was I to say?"

"Who gave you all the details about the house?" he asked.

"He did."

"Ward?"

"Yes."

"Who gave them to him?"

"I don't know," she replied.

"Could it have been Suzanna Croft?"

"I don't know," she replied.

He thought she could have been telling the truth. "What's your relationship with Ward?" he asked.

"There is no *relationship*," she said unequivocally, stressing the word 'relationship'.

"He was here last night, wasn't he?"

"Yes."

"Does he screw you?"

"How dare you?!" she protested, raising her voice for the first time.

"So you don't know why he wanted Croft dead. Could it be that Croft knew or suspected he was having an affair with his wife and was threatening him to back off? Or had Ward lost a lot of money in a deal gone bad?"

"I told you. I don't know."

"I think Ward could have been planning to kill Croft for some time, so he set it up and then hit on the idea of framing a fall guy in order to get himself out of the frame. He's a clever man. Yes?"

"He's ambitious," she agreed.

Masson looked at her. He liked her style. Cool and calm. "Ambitious for Croft's fortune, I'd wager. Sees the long game. Divorce his wife, then marry the widow who will inherit the old man's fortune."

She nodded her head, and then finished the drink in her hand. He did likewise. He leaned forward to put the glass on a coaster on the coffee table. "Can I offer you some advice?" She didn't reply. "If you want to stay healthy and have a long life and I guess you do, stay away from Marcus Ward at all costs. His life could be in danger and yours with him."

She retained her unperturbed front, but maybe she was beginning to understand what he was saying. Masson continued to tell her the tale. "Divorty is on remand, but some of his associates are keen to spring him. I think they've got a good chance of succeeding. If he gets out, he'll be looking for answers. I'll tell him straight. First, he'll confront Marcus Ward, then he might come for you."

"Why are you telling me this?"

"Don't you listen? I told you. To warn you."

"I won't be around in a few days," she said. "I've got a dance troupe assignment on a boat for a month. That's why I go to the gym every day to loosen up."

"Good. Until you leave keep a low profile. Keep your eyes open. There could be some guys doing some investigating pretty soon. They won't be police and they won't be as nice as me. They're Liam Divorty's friends. If they don't get the right answers they'll torture you with a pair of battery rods. They'll attach them to your intimate places and enjoy it. They might even film it for prosperity." She shifted on the sofa, but retained an aloof exterior. Masson continued. "It didn't take *me* long to find you. It doesn't take a brain surgeon to know that Ward is having an affair with Suzanna Croft. Her husband was killed by someone who knows somebody else is coming to kill Croft. He gets there first, kills Croft, hides close by, sees the hired killer coming to do it, then contacts the police to tell them he's seen a burglar. If the police get there quickly enough, they'll nab him. They find the old guy dead. Therefore, any suspicion which may have potentially been placed on Ward is immediately reduced."

She listened to his words then sat forward. "Do you want another drink?" she asked.

"Sure." She reached towards the table and took his empty glass. He caught another whiff of her perfume. "How long have you been dancing?" he asked.

"Fifteen years. It keeps me fit and agile."

"I bet. You have a nice place here," he said, pointedly looking around. "How can you afford it?"

"I have a nice mother," she replied.

"I wish I had a mother who'd buy me a pad in Sloane Square," he said. "What's her name?"

She didn't reply. She went to the drinks cabinet, turned to look at him and smiled. "Are you trying to chat me up by any chance?" she asked.

"Do you think I am?" he replied. He got up from out of the chair and stepped towards the doors over the window. "Mind if I open the doors?" he asked.

"Be my guest," she replied.

He kicked his shoes off, stepped towards the window, took the doors and opened them inward. There was a metal rail across the opening and a grill at waist height to prevent anyone from falling over. He looked down to the garden below. Fifty feet below was a metal railing separating a communal patio area from the garden, then what looked like a shed of some description. She stepped towards him and handed him a full glass of wine. He looked at her and she at him. The growing sparks between them were starting to catch fire.

"You didn't answer my question," she said.

"Which one?"

"Are you trying to chat me up?"

"I think I did," he replied. He looked into her eyes, then at her lips. Then he raised his hand and stroked her cheek. She hadn't moved or taken her eyes off his so he wound his arm around her waist and pulled her lips to his. He had longed to kiss her from the moment he had set eyes on her. She smiled at him, and then she took his glass out of his hand.

She set his glass on a table and took his hand. "Come on, let's make some noise. I've got the place." With that she led him through the flat and into a bedroom. There was a curtain drawn over the window so the room was in shade. The bed looked inviting in the near darkness. She came close to him and placed her hands around the back of his neck, then kissed him again.

That evening Masson didn't pull up to his house until gone midnight. She'd taken him to her bed for hours. Her body was just as beautiful as he had imagined it to be. He hoped a lasting bond would develop. He had to protect her from Divorty and his friends no matter what. It was what any right-thinking guy would do.

Chapter 12

Friday 2nd October

When Masson stepped through the front door to his flat he found an envelope on the mat. He opened it. Inside was a hand-written note from James Malloy. This was significant on two accounts. First, it demonstrated that they really were going to try to spring Divorty, but it was also designed to show him that Malloy knew where he lived. The message was simple. It read:
'Two o'clock. Same venue. Be there.
JM'

The attempt to spring Divorty would now be moving from the preparation phase to the action phase. He felt philosophical about it. No doubt all the other members of the team would be at the meeting, crammed into the small room. He knew it was something he had to do. Turning them down would be like slapping Divorty and his friends in the face. That would result in them looking at him with increased suspicion. He had to be involved in the attempt to spring Divorty and be there to celebrate with them when he was free.

Holloway Road was busy at two o'clock on a Friday afternoon. O'Flynn's was not open for business until five. Masson arrived with a couple of minutes to spare. It was the guy he knew as Dave Toshack who opened the front door and let him in. The other members of the team were already in place, plus three other guys he had never met before.

Malloy introduced them. There were a couple of North Londoners called Ces Desmond and Devon Trent, plus a guy called Leroy Nelson. This made a team of seven to do the job. A right rag-and-bob-tail set of criminals; but still, a team. To get this kind of backing, Divorty must have ascended further up the crime ladder than Mason had realised. The philosophy of those assembled for the job was quite simple: Liam Divorty needed their help, and would do the same for them. You did what you had to for a mate.

When everyone was gathered they commandeered one of the tables and got down to work. The sunlight pouring in through the windows of the otherwise empty bar illuminated the scene with a bright hazy glow. Bottles of beer and packets of crisps were on the table, along with various other nibbles.

Malloy led the session. The plan was good. The route from the prison to the courthouse was known. The van carrying Divorty would be leaving Belmarsh at eleven on the dot, this coming Monday morning. Divorty was due to be in court at two in the afternoon. The attempt to free him would take place about twenty-five minutes into the journey. The actual journey time from prison to court was around thirty-five minutes give or take a few on either side. The attempt would come near the end of the journey just as the crew were starting to relax and beginning to look forward to their lunch break.

Malloy had assigned the job of quartermaster to Toshack. He had been able to get all the equipment required. This included the vehicles they would use, one of which was the ten-ton tripper truck that would smash into the front of the prison van. The rest of the team would then leap into action and wrestle the doors off the van. Toshack had his hands on a sawn-off shotgun. He was mad enough to use it. Other items were things like full-face crash helmets, gloves, crow bars, jemmies to prise the door off, and sticks for crowd control. Once Divorty was free, the team would make their escape in a people carrier driven by Devon Trent. The whole operation, from start to finish, shouldn't take longer than five minutes. It had all been carefully worked out and planned. Divorty would be taken to a safe-house, miles away, in north London. It all sounded too simple, but it might just come off.

To give Malloy some credit, he had thought of everything and every possibility. If something did go wrong, it wouldn't be down to a lack of planning. By the time the talking came to an end, one and a half hours had passed. As the meeting broke up, the team left the bar in groups of two.

Malloy asked Masson to stay back for a few minutes. Toshack was there too. Malloy wanted to know what, if anything, he had discovered in the time since they had last met. Masson told them. He had come to the conclusion that a man called Marcus Ward was directly involved in setting up Divorty. When Malloy asked him why, Masson explained that he had learned that Ward was having an affair with Charles Croft's widow. It was common knowledge in the town. The assumption was that he wanted to take up with the wife in order to get his hands on the fortune she would inherit. He pointed out that the two homes were in close proximity and this would have allowed Ward to go to the house undetected and kill Croft. He had broken in, murdered Croft, then made it look like a bungled burglary. Then he had lain in wait for Divorty to arrive. Once Divorty was on the scene he had called the police, anonymously, to report a person breaking into the Croft home. As the alarm went off, the police arrived and grabbed Divorty as he was trying to get out. Both Malloy and Toshack thought it was credible. Then Toshack asked him who had made the first contact to get the contract set up.

"Ward's wife," replied Masson.

"Why?"

"Search me. I haven't worked that one out yet," he replied.

Masson left O'Flynn's at four o'clock. He didn't know if Malloy and Toshack had bought any of it, though Malloy did praise him for his investigative work and the conclusion he had come to. Masson thought he was off the hook for the time-being.

That evening Masson called Naomi. He said he wanted to see her. She told him to come around to her flat. Though he shouldn't have, he did and, that evening, they made love. It wasn't just sex for him. He was a sucker for a pretty face and a sexy body, but there was also a connection. A spark.

As he was leaving, he told her he wouldn't be around for a couple of days at least. She told him that she had a flight to on Saturday to meet up with the cruise ship for the dancing job. She thought she wouldn't be back until the end of October. She asked him if he would do her a favour by visiting the flat whilst she was away to make sure everything was okay. He said he would be pleased to do that for her. On her return to London in a month they could meet up again and continue their relationship.

He considered going out to rendezvous with her somewhere at a tourist stop, then thought better of it. It wasn't a cruise for her, it was paid work. He dropped the idea. Before he left she gave him a set of keys.

Chapter 13

Monday 5th October

They were ready. The route, the timings and the duration of the journey were planned. Every inch of the route that the van carrying Divorty from HMP Belmarsh to the South-West magistrate's court in Lavender Hill, Battersea was known to the team. The men knew their roles and what was expected of them. The preparation had been first rate. Malloy and Toshack excelled in that department. They had driven the route from the prison to the court-house on several occasions and at different times of the day to assess the traffic conditions and find the best place to strike. They had timed it to the second. As Malloy had said at each meeting; precision and control would be the key elements to a successful outcome. Masson had no reason to disagree.

The police had no idea that one of the men in the van had friends who were determined to spring him. They didn't deem Divorty or anyone else in the wagon important enough to require back-up. A massive mistake. Masson felt somewhat confident they might just succeed. If Divorty did go down for the Croft murder then he might try to negotiate a kind of plea bargain and implicate Masson; therefore, it was better that he was inside the tent pissing out, rather than outside pissing in.

Monday soon came around. Malloy collected Masson from Holland Park Road at eight in the morning. He was driving an Audi saloon with false plates. Toshack was in the front passenger seat. They drove across London from west to east to a secluded car park in the Plumstead area. The drive to the prison would take less than fifteen minutes.

While waiting, they checked the final details and made sure they had everything. All the equipment was in the boot. At this time of morning, several people were walking dogs on the common land, but they were some distance away from the car. Malloy grabbed a holdall stuffed with overalls from the boot and silently handed one each to Masson and Toshack. The three men slipped into them and got back into the car. Masson was pensive, but didn't reveal it. He had not been involved in anything like this for some time. The last time was ten years ago when he helped a firm hijack a security wagon carrying a million pounds. It had been ages since he had felt the buzz of being at the business end of a job.

It was ten-thirty on the dot when Malloy pulled the Audi out of the car park and set out to a spot near to the prison. If the prison van kept to the schedule it would be leaving the prison at exactly eleven o'clock. Such was their intelligence they even had the registration number of the vehicle. Nothing was said in the car. Malloy concentrated on getting onto the A206, and after a couple of hundred yards the sandy-coloured walls of the prison came into view. There was a steady stream of traffic on both sides of the road, but nothing special for the end of the morning rush hour. Toshack used one of the burner phones he had in his possession and checked in with Matt Royce who was driving the tipper truck. He told him they were on the A206, then he swiftly terminated the call.

Malloy slipped off the road that led to and from the prison, onto the forecourt of a disused petrol station. There was a palpable air of tension as they waited in silence for what seemed like ages, but in actuality was only a matter of minutes. Just willing the van to appear at the top of the road, Masson felt his heart pounding in his chest. It would all kick off in the next twenty-five to thirty minutes, and then, there was no going back.

Suddenly, at two minutes past eleven, a white prison van drove up the slight incline to the end of the road and stopped at the traffic lights. It was right on schedule. This was it. Toshack got onto the phone. "It's on," he said. Then he used the second phone to put in a call to Devon Trent in the people carrier. As the traffic lights turned to green, the van went across the junction and turned right. In the same moment, Malloy started the car, edged out of the forecourt and slipped into the traffic. The back of the prison van was around fifty yards ahead.

One mile became two, two became three. In the back of the Audi, Masson felt ill, not with any nervousness, but with the motion of the car. Malloy swore as the car in front was slow to move away from a crossing.

"Plenty of time," Toshack said. "No need to panic."

"Who's panicking?" Malloy asked.

Toshack said nothing. He got back onto the mobile. "Just turning on New Cross Gate," he said.

Masson was not that familiar with this area of the city. He didn't recognise any of the streets or intersections, though he could see by the road signs that they were on Peckham High Road, then Camberwell New Road and heading in a north-west direction towards the Oval cricket ground in the distance. The traffic was heavy, but free moving. The sunlight was hazy and intermittent due to the slow, puffy clouds overhead. After a further fifteen minutes and four miles, they were at the junction with Kennington Park Road, turning left onto Clapham Road.

"Nice and easy does it," Toshack said.

Masson had his eyes pinned on the back of the prison van; there were several cars between them and the van. Toshack's mobile rang. "Yeah. Good," he said. "Just turned onto Clapham Road…Where are you, Matt?" he asked, then listened to the reply.

They continued on, moving in a gentle push towards the spot where they planned to attack the van. As the road split near to Clapham Junction north Underground station, the prison van carried on onto Clapham High Street. Malloy saw a gap appear behind the van. He put his foot on the gas, whipped around two cars in front, cutting nimbly back into traffic in front of them. Now there was only one car between the Audi and the prison van. In the next minute they came to the busy junction with Clapham Common. Meanwhile Matt and another two guys in the truck were heading east, along Nightingale Lane, to rendezvous with the prison van.

"Where are you, Matt?" Toshack asked, then listened to his response. "Good boy. We're on Clapham High Street. The van's one car in front of us… Some dickhead in a fucking clapped out Mini," he said, and gave a shrill laugh. They only had around three hundred yards before the van took a right turn onto Clapham Common Long Lane. Then all change. As they neared the junction, disaster struck. There was a barrier across the junction which read:

'Long Lane closed due to a burst water main.'

No one could have foreseen that. The prison van had no option but to stay left and go along Clapham Common on the south side. "Shit," said Malloy in a raised voice, then, "Where the fuck is he going?"

Toshack got onto one of the mobile phones. "Matt. Double back!" he shouted into the phone. "He's taken the other road. Long Lane is closed on our side."

They had planned to hit the wagon on Long Lane as it went down the side of the common. Matt Royce came over the phone on the open speaker. "What?" he asked.

"Turn it around," Toshack said quickly. "He's going to turn right onto The Avenue by the side of the common."

"Okay. I'll try to turn it around to head back down The Avenue and meet you at the next junction. The one just before Balham Hill."

"Okay."

At least they had their bearings, but if Matt couldn't do a three-point turn and get the truck in the other direction the opportunity might be lost. The traffic along Clapham Common south side came to a stop, which was no bad thing as it would allow Matt the time to do a U turn. As Long Lane was partially closed the traffic going into Battersea had no option but to take the diversion, which meant the road was now far more grid-locked than usual.

It seemed to be an age before the line of vehicles in front began to move. The prison van gradually edged its way to the junction with Balham Hill. Inside, Divorty must have been wondering if they would attempt to spring him. To the right was a low single metal rail that went along the edge of the park. Behind that were the lush green shrubs, the trees and the grassland lining the edge of the common. On the other side of the road was a low brick wall that separated the pavement from a row of big houses that overlooked the park.

Toshack got onto the phone. "Where are you, Matt?" he asked.

"I'm trying to turn the truck around," he said in an exasperated tone. "Is Devon behind you?" asked Tosh.

"Think so," he said.

"Shit," said Malloy, then added. "Fuck it."

"Let's do it," Toshack encouraged.

The prison van began to pick up speed as it approached the lights at the junction in the distance. One hundred yards quickly become fifty then…forty… thirty… twenty… ten. Then to the right the tipper truck appeared, racing towards the junction with The Avenue at a rapid speed. The prison van edged forward, onto the yellow hatching on the road that marked the junction, preparing to go straight on. The tipper truck picked up speed and came careering across the road in excess of sixty miles an hour. Everything went into slow motion. There was an almighty bang as the truck hit the prison van and smashed across its front. As the vehicles collided anyone in the near vicinity of the crash would have dived for cover. The collision of a ten-ton tipper, driven at a high speed, shunted the prison van off the road and half way up the path on its near side. The front wheels were on the path, whilst the back wheels were still on the road.

The guy in the Mini skidded across the road and narrowly missed an oncoming car on the other side before screeching to a halt. The gap allowed Malloy to pull up close to the back of the van. As the bang of the crash died, it was replaced by the blaring sound of the horn in the van going off. It was possible to see steam escaping from the front end. Glass and other debris were strung over the road. The glass splinters were glinting in the sunlight.

"Helmets!" shouted Malloy. In the excitement they had forgotten to put them on their heads. They each rammed a crash helmet on. Malloy got out of the car first, followed by Toshack. Masson was the last out. They met at the back of the Audi. It was Masson who opened the boot and they each grabbed a metal crow bar or a long metal jemmy. Speed was now imperative. Toshack took the sawn-off shotgun from underneath a blanket. Several people walking along the path had stopped to rubberneck the accident. The sight of a group of men in overalls and crash helmets rushing towards the battered prison van was frightening. But most of the onlookers, seemingly petrified, remained glued to the spot.

Malloy, Toshack and Masson quickly went to the back of the van where they were joined by Matt Royce and the other two guys from the tipper truck. All six men were tooled up and ready to break into the back of the van. Masson was aware of a cloud of dust and the acrid smell of burning rubber. "Out of the way," Toshack shouted. He raised the double barrel sawn-off shot gun to his waist, aimed it at the back door of the van and let off a round. The lead pellets tore into the metal panel, peppering it with holes and indentations. The team then gathered at the door and began to tear away at the door frame with the crow bars and jemmies in an effort to prise it off. Each had the end of a crow bar in the frame. They repeatedly heaved on them in an uncoordinated attack on the metal.

It seemed to go on forever, but was probably only a minute or two. The sturdy metal doors began to peel apart. Then suddenly, with a sound of grating and snapping, the welds popped and the door swung out. Malloy was helped up into the back. The guard manning the cells appeared at the doorway with blood oozing from a cut on the top of his head. Malloy simply took him by the shoulders and heaved him out of the way. He fell outside, onto the ground in a heap. His head cracked against the tarmac. After that he didn't make a sound, or move a muscle. Inside, beyond the van door was a chain-link cage door leading to the cubicles which held the prisoners, seated inside. Matt Royce joined Malloy and between them they managed to prise the cage door open. All the time the horn was still blaring.

Once inside the secure area, Malloy shouted, "Liam, where the fuck are you?"

"Here, quick!" came the reply.

They went to the cubicle where Divorty was held. Immediately, Matt and Malloy started working on the door. The rest of the team were standing at the back of the van waiting for Divorty to appear. About three and a half minutes had elapsed since they'd hit the truck. The traffic had stopped moving, the bystanders had all vanished, except for one elderly guy leaning on the wall and casually observing what was going on.

Between them, using the jemmies and crowbars, Malloy and Matt were able to prise the door open and pull Divorty out. Moments later, all three appeared at the back of the van and jumped down onto the road.

Now that Divorty was free, the gang looked to see if Devon Trent, the guy driving the getaway car, was in place. He wasn't anywhere to be seen. Malloy, crowbar in hand, looked up the road to see if he was coming. He wasn't. "Quick. In the Audi!" Malloy yelled.

In a moment of near total farce, the gang of seven headed for the Audi, just as the getaway vehicle, driven by Devon Trent, came hurtling along the pathway on the park side.

"Over here," yelled Toshack at the top of his voice, waving the shotgun. They instantly forgot the idea of getting into the Audi, and headed to the people carrier. They ran like crazy towards the vehicle, dropping the crowbars as they went. They pulled the sliding side door open and all seven men attempted to pile into the vehicle. Then came the sound of a siren from up ahead on Balham Hill. Like the getaway vehicle, driven by Trent, a police car was using the pavement to get around the grid-locked traffic. Malloy leaned out and shouted to Toshack who was still on the road:

"Give it to the bastards!" he encouraged.

Toshack didn't hesitate. He stood his ground, raised the gun and, as the police car came into range, gave it both barrels. Thankfully, he pulled it at the last second so the lead shot didn't hit the windscreen but instead took out the front lower panel. Steam hissed from the radiator. The sound of the shot scattered a couple of spectators who were standing on the corner, but also stopped the police car dead in its tracks. Now that the vehicle was not a threat, Toshack went to the people carrier and jumped inside. Trent put his foot on the gas, drove off the pavement, onto the road and sped away from the scene like a boy racer burning rubber on a local racetrack.

Masson had never felt so exhilarated in his life. He was shaking with adrenaline.

Trent hammered the vehicle up Clapham South side and made a left at the turn into Clapham Old Town before turning into a maze of residential streets. As the vehicle turned onto Wandsworth Road, Trent slowed down and became immersed in the heavy traffic. After a hundred yards or so, he slipped onto the kerb at a bus stop. The door opened and four of the team, including Masson, got out, minus the crash helmets and gloves, but not the overalls. Masson quickly disappeared down a side street and out of view, while the other three ran off in other directions. It hadn't gone without a hiccup, but at least they had done it. And they had Divorty. He was free from the police and free to wreak all the havoc he wanted.

Chapter 14

Masson planned to keep a low profile for the next few days. The first thing he did when he returned home was to turn on the television and listen to the rolling news at two-thirty. Sky TV were giving details about an incident in Clapham at around eleven-thirty this morning, when a van carrying six prisoners to the South-West magistrate's court in Battersea was attacked. At this time, it was unclear whether the driver of the van had been killed. The bandits had discharged a firearm and took a shot at a police car. It was thought that the officer had not been seriously hurt. Masson breathed out a huge sigh of relief. He hoped that the driver of the prison van and his mate had escaped any serious injury.

He turned the television off, went to his PC, logged on and looked at the news. BBC London was reporting the same incident. Early reports suggested that the driver of the van had been hurt, but his injuries were not thought to be life threatening. Again, Masson felt relieved. The last thing he wanted on his conscience was to learn that anyone had been badly hurt or worse. The report said the police were searching for a gang. The getaway vehicle, a stolen people-carrier, had been found abandoned close to Clapham Junction railway station. At this time the prison authorities, in conjunction with the Met police, were not releasing the name of the prisoner who had escaped from the van, just that he had been due to attend a hearing at two o'clock that afternoon. Another news agency was showing a video of the scene with the police in large numbers and rubberneckers milling about behind a cordon. The camera panned around to the front of the van with the tipper truck embedded in it to show the damage. The front end was completely destroyed. If the driver and his mate had survived death, it was nothing short of a miracle. The reporter then interviewed a passer-by who said he had seen the tipper truck plough into the van. The reporter said that the truck had been stolen from a building site in south London two days ago.

Masson then went back to the television. Sky News was airing an interview with another bystander who said he had seen six men in blue boiler-suits with white motorcycle helmets on their heads smash into the back of the van. He had seen a guy in a prison-style jacket jump out of the van, then they had all piled into a green Peugeot people carrier which sped off at high speed towards the junction ahead.

Masson felt physically and mentally drained. He felt numb, shot of all emotion and feeling. Over the next hour he took a long, hot shower, had something to eat, then collapsed onto the settee and fell quickly asleep. He was awoken at six o'clock by a telephone call. It was James Malloy. He kept it short and sweet: a 'friend' had called a meeting for Tuesday afternoon. He was safely tucked up back at home in north London and celebrating his return with a couple of beers. He was grateful to all who had helped him 'get home'. Though the meeting was not a party, it was a celebration of a kind. Masson was invited. Malloy would collect him from the 'usual place' at one o'clock tomorrow afternoon. Masson said he would be there. Malloy ended the call.

The invitation started Masson thinking. He had not expected to hear from Divorty so soon. He assumed he would have gone underground for at least a week, but it sounded as if he wanted to hold court as soon as possible. Whilst not unduly concerned, he did wonder why he wanted the meeting and how it would pan out. He had Naomi on his mind. She would be on the cruise ship by now. He considered trying to contact her, then thought better of it. He had to keep a low profile himself and stay out of circulation for the rest of the day. Or maybe the next few days.

For the rest of Monday he listened to the news at regular intervals. The BBC London News at ten confirmed that both the driver and the other guard in the cab had escaped serious injury. A police officer had been treated for minor cuts to his face. The guard in the back of the van had been treated in hospital, then released. Police were searching for as many as nine men. The prisoner who had escaped was named as forty-year-old Liam Divorty from Islington. He had been due to attend a hearing regarding the murder of former stockbroker Charles Croft, killed in Esher sixteen days ago. Anyone with information should contact Crime-Stoppers or their nearest police station. Masson asked himself how long it would be before one of the team was pulled in for questioning. He didn't know the answer.

He stayed close to home killing time, and generally trying to relax. He picked up a paperback novel that he'd purchased several weeks ago, but hadn't had the chance to open. He sat down and read the first paragraph, but had to put it down when he kept re-reading the same few words. He couldn't concentrate on it for more than five minutes. A maelstrom of conflicting thoughts was swirling through his head. He wondered what Naomi was doing. Lately, she was never far from his thoughts. He wanted her by his side, and he wanted her in his arms as soon as possible.

Chapter 15

Tuesday 6ᵗʰ October.

Malloy collected Masson from the pick-up spot on Holland Park Road. They didn't say a lot as they made their way through the early afternoon traffic. Masson had no idea where he was heading. What he did notice was the big slab of beer cans on the back seat of the car. Maybe they were going to have a party after all.

After driving in silence for a while, they chatted about banal stuff like the weekend television. Then talk turned to the excitement of yesterday. Malloy said he had nearly cried when he saw the turn-off to Clapham Long Lane was closed. It had only been by the grace of God that Matt Royce had been able to turn the truck around and get it in the other direction. Without Matt, Divorty wouldn't be the free man he was today. Malloy smiled and chuckled.

Masson asked him if he had seen the TV news this morning. A mug shot of Divorty had been shown. A senior cop said the police thought he was still in the London area, but they couldn't be certain. In reality, they had no idea where he was. They had no idea who had sprung him. The cop said they were confident of finding him in the next few days or so. Malloy said he hadn't seen the news. He said he wasn't concerned. He did reveal that Divorty was already talking about getting out of the country. What was certain was that he wouldn't be returning to his used-car business in Islington any time soon.

Malloy drove in a northerly direction to an area just inside the M25 circle. The day was cool and overcast. This morning, the very first frost of autumn had left a hint of mist, which had cleared when the sun broke through. It was now dull and grey, but the air held less of a chill. By one-forty they were in an area of Barnet around Cockfosters tube station at the northern end of the Piccadilly line. They had decided on a safe house on the edge of the city in the sprawling landscape of north London suburbia. Malloy turned onto a road of semi-detached nineteen-fifties style houses, some neat and tidy, others in need of some much needed tender loving care.

The safe house must have been rented from some local landlord with a lot of properties, the sort who was unlikely to ask questions. Malloy rolled to a stop directly opposite a semi with a bowed front and white walls. There were blinds over the windows on both floors. Cars of every description were parked on hard-standing in front of the houses. Before getting out, Malloy glanced behind and ahead. It was clear. They made their way across the path, through a gate and onto the property. Malloy had the slab of beers under his arm. A brown velvet curtain was covering the frosted glass front. Malloy tapped on the door once, and a face appeared behind the curtain. It was Matt Royce. When he saw Malloy and Masson he opened the door and let them inside. They stepped into a hallway and through, into a long lounge that ran from back to front.

Liam Divorty was sitting at a dining table in the back section of the room. The interior was bare, with nothing much in the way of colour, imagination, or furniture. Masson was aware of a musty smell, as if the house had not been in use for some time. Divorty observed them enter, then he saw the slab of beer cans under Malloy's arm and his face lit up. Behind Divorty was a sliding patio door that led out onto a ragged, overgrown back garden that looked as if it had been neglected for some time.

As Masson came into the room, Divorty greeted him with a nod of the head, although his eyes looked tired, and his face was stern and unsmiling. Prison food had not been to his liking, because he had lost a bit of bulk. Or maybe he'd decided to diet or had taken advantage of the gym facilities. Whatever.

"What a fucking shithole this place is," Divorty grumbled. "Miles from anywhere."

"It's best to stay out of the city until the heat dies down," replied Malloy, defensively. Faced with a reputation like the one Divorty had, there was good reason to be cautious.

"Yeah, yeah… I suppose," he admitted grudgingly, but he didn't sound wholly convinced. Malloy stepped forward and placed the pack of twenty-four beer cans on the table.

"Got any smokes?" Divorty asked. Malloy gave him a pack of twenty from his pocket.

"Thanks."

"You're being a right moody cunt," Malloy said.

Divorty snarled. "You'd be a moody cunt too if you were jammed up in this shithole," he said. He looked to Masson. "Molly tells me that you've being making enquires and got to who set me up."

"If you mean, do I have a good idea who did it, then, yes, I've got a good idea."

"Care to share it?"

"From what I can tell it was a guy called Marcus Ward."

"Marcus Ward! He sounds like a porn star. What's the score?"

"He lives a stone's throw from the Croft guy. He's being having it away with his wife. I guess that's why he wanted rid of the old man."

"He still sounds like a porn star. And?"

"She's due to inherit a fortune on his death, but couldn't wait, so I guess the pair of them hit on the idea of killing her hubby. To take the suspicion off them they arrange for someone to come into the house and make it look like a botched burglary. At least, that's how it looks to me."

Divorty considered the scenario for a few moments. "That figures. Whoever killed the guy had ransacked the bedroom to make it look like a burglary gone wrong." He paused. "But look," he said. "Why didn't they just let me go ahead and do it? If they just wanted rid of the bastard, why go to all that trouble and risk it going wrong and end up taking the rap?"

Masson was taken aback. That was a good question, one which he had not considered. He thought for a moment.

"Well," he said, "I guess they could have assumed that if it was all too clinical, a professional job, the suspicion would fall on them." Then another thought occurred to him: "They would save themselves the second payment."

"Now, that figures," said Divorty. He pulled at the pack of beers, tore the plastic rings off and wrestled a can out of the pack. He pulled the ring-top open, put it to his lips and took a swig of the contents. "Where's this guy at?"

"Who? Ward?"

"Yeah, him."

"Esher. Literally lives in the next lane to the Croft house. He could have garden hopped to get there, killed the old guy, and then observed you entering. He calls the cops. The local force receives an anonymous tip off and they race round there. The alarm goes off. They get there just as you're leaving."

Divorty didn't say anything for ten seconds. It looked as if he was thinking it through. "Why don't we all go around there and ask him where our forty thousand is? He owes us and I want to ask him what the fuck he's up to."

"Who?" Malloy asked.

"This Ward," Divorty replied. "Who'd you think?"

"Let's wait a while," Malloy said. "Lie low for a few days then see how the land lies. Then if you want to have words with this geezer we'll do it then."

Wiser counsel seemed to have won the day as Divorty nodded his head. "Okay, okay," he said. He took another mouthful of the beer. He was restless and eager to get back into the game, but realised it was best for him to keep his head down. After all, the Met would be desperate to find him – having been made to look like a complete set of tools. They had a score to settle with him. And with the other members of the crew for that matter. The problem with Divorty was keeping him happy. He wouldn't want to sit here for a week watching daytime television, doing nothing. He wasn't that kind of bloke. It just wasn't his style.

Malloy stepped out of the room and into the adjoining kitchen. He emerged moments later with a bottle of water in his hand. He ripped the seal open, pulled the cap off and downed half of the contents in one.

Divorty opened the packet of cigarettes, took one out and lit it. He was continuing to mutter under his breath.

"Fuck sake. What's up with you?" Malloy snapped.

"Who the fuck does this guy think he is?"

"Who?"

"This Ward guy. I want to go 'round there now and sort him out."

"Okay," said Malloy. He had given up trying to persuade him to drop it. "Let's go and see him then. Matt, you drive."

"No, Matt. You stay here. Molly, you drive." Divorty was giving the orders.

"Okay, okay," said Malloy.

"Tom," said Divorty. "Tell me about Croft's wife. She's the one who gave you the dough, isn't she? Where is she?"

"She was at the funeral, a week ago. I saw her there."

"Was she the one who gave you the £40K?"

"Yes," he lied, imagining Naomi's face.

"Is she at the Croft house?"

"Mmm. I don't know. Could be. She's got a place in Paris too. Maybe elsewhere. Croft was loaded."

"I want to see her."

Malloy stepped forward. "Look, I wouldn't. Too dangerous. The cops might be at the house."

"Liam, he's right," Masson interjected. "You've just got out – the first place the cops would make a big show of protecting is the Widow Croft. Stay away."

Divorty thought about it for a few moments, and again, *seemed* to take the good advice on board. "Yeah. Maybe you're right. Let's not go to see her, but this Ward bloke is different. I want to get even with him."

Divorty was a loose cannon. He was calling the shots, but not thinking them through in a rational manner. Neither Malloy nor Matt Royce had the balls to try and talk him out of it, and Masson didn't dare draw attention to Naomi, or the real Suzanna Croft. They chatted for another ten minutes whilst Divorty finished off two cans of beer.

It was close to three-thirty when they finally agreed to take the trip to Esher. It was a very dangerous move in many respects. Going back to the scene of the crime was risky. But it didn't seem to register with Divorty. He was on the edge of a meltdown. He got up from the table, took his jacket off the back of the chair and swung it around his shoulders. He took a baseball cap and fitted it onto his head and pulled the peak low down over his face.

Once out onto the street, Malloy, Masson and Divorty got into the car. Malloy drove out of the area. Rather than go through the heart of the city, he elected to drive around the M25 in an anticlockwise direction. It took them an hour to get to the M3 junction, then another thirty minutes to reach the outskirts of Esher.

"So what are you going to do when we get there?" Masson asked Divorty.

"See if he admits setting up me. What'd you think?"

"What then?"

"Ask him for forty thousand. The guy he wanted dead is dead. So he's got what he wanted. I'd say that, in a sense, we've fulfilled our part of the bargain. Ain't we?" he said.

"Sure. You've got a point," Malloy said.

Masson had to agree with him. He gave Malloy the directions to Esher Lane. They were soon on the leafy lane with its neat grass verge and array of sycamore and willow trees. There were slightly more leaves on the ground than there had been six days ago, when he had lain in wait in the hope of seeing Ward. Was it really just six days ago that he'd followed him into Kensington and Chelsea? It seemed so long ago now, but the calendar didn't lie.

The area was quiet. Some of the homes looked unoccupied, even abandoned, probably because the residents had departed for a long winter holiday in some southern hemisphere paradise. The light of the day was beginning to peter out at five-forty.

Masson pointed out The Vicarage as they were about to come level with the first of the two closed metal gates. Malloy slowed the car and approached at a gentle pace. They could see onto the empty pebble courtyard. That didn't mean to say Ward wasn't at home. The car could have been in a garage, or on loan to a friend perhaps. Unlikely, but possible.

"Nice place," Malloy said.

"Yeah, real nice," Divorty said. "Just like the Croft place."

The two houses were completely different, but Masson chose not to question Divorty's opinion. Malloy picked up speed and continued up the lane. "What are we going to do?" he asked.

"Drive into the town. Find a pub. Have a beer then come back later when he might be around," Divorty said.

Masson wondered what he planned to do if they found him at home. Kill him? Possibly.

Malloy said, "Okay. Let's do that." He drove out of Esher in a westerly direction and into the area around Weybridge. They eventually found a pub off the beaten track. Once inside, Divorty had a couple of pints of lager. Malloy stayed on water. Masson had red wine.

It was getting on for seven-thirty when they got back into Esher. The night had drawn in rapidly. It was cool and chilly in the dark of the evening which had descended over the town. Lights burned in the neighbouring houses. As they reached the house on Esher Lane, they could see the red Porsche 911 parked on the forecourt in front of the house.

"He's home," Masson said. "That's his car."

Malloy drove by the first gate, swung across the road, through the open second gate and onto the property. The sound of the car wheels crunching on the pebbles would have alerted anyone inside that a vehicle had just pulled up outside of the house. Malloy stopped close to the doorway under the porch. A light was on in a downstairs room. Masson didn't have a clue about what was going to kick off. Divorty seemed hell bent on harming Ward. Divorty didn't care. Someone he didn't know had railroaded him and that hadn't gone down well with him.

Divorty suggested that Malloy wait here, just in case they needed to bolt quickly. Malloy said okay, he would stay in the car. Divorty was soon out, followed by Masson, and they stepped towards the big red front door under the colonnade porch. Divorty first rapped his fist on the entrance, then saw the doorbell button and pressed it. Within twenty seconds a light appeared in a pane of glass to the side, then they heard a lock mechanism turning and the door opening. A face appeared in the narrow gap, then the door opened wide. It was as if the guy inside assumed it was a door-to-door salesman of some description, or maybe the police. Masson recognised him immediately. It was the same man he had seen with Naomi Chiles in the restaurant garden. Ward looked put out by these sudden unexpected and unwanted visitors.

"Er…Yes…Can I help you?" he asked. His accent was plummy and educated. He had a touch of arrogant, upper-class snobbishness about him.

Divorty smirked at him. "Yes, Marcus. I think you may be able to," he said.

The guy stepped back, raised an eyebrow, and looked down his nose at Divorty. Wrong move!

"You don't know me," Divorty said. "But here's a little sign of friendship." He swung a fist and buried it into Ward's stomach in a spot just above his groin. On being punched, Ward staggered back several paces. Divorty stepped inside without being invited in. Masson followed him in and closed the door behind him.

In front of them, Ward was doubled up in pain. The blow had knocked the wind out of his sails.

"Can you help me? Well, I certainly hope so, Mr Ward," Divorty said in a theatrical manner. "You owe me £40,000. That's how much you can help me."

Masson glanced around the interior. They were in a reception room with doors leading off to the left. To the right was a stairway leading up to a landing with big windows looking out onto a patio at the back of the house. The area was decorated in a quaint style with various prints on the walls, and a number of expensive-looking oriental vases placed here and there on tall, spindly tables.

Ward was doubled up with a combination of shock, and pain from the punch still shuddering through his body. He was wearing a grey wool sweater, dark trousers and slippers on his feet. His handsome dark complexion now looked sweaty and pale. Divorty glanced around. "Let's go this way," he said, grabbing Ward by the back of the neck and tugging him through an open door.

Masson followed them, stepping into a large sitting room, dominated by a luxurious white leather L-shaped settee. The unit was illuminated by tall vase lamps on matching tables at each end. The decoration was elegant, though a little cluttered by the many ornaments and bric-a-brac lining the various shelving units, and the mantel above the fireplace. A replica gas fire with imitation flames, and comforting yellow lighting from the lamps, warmed the space. A pair of French doors led onto the patio and the garden at the back of the house. Stringed orchestral music was playing from a pair of high speakers aside a huge music centre.

Divorty forced Ward to sit on the settee. Though he looked stunned he had recovered from the blow to a degree. He looked scared and fearful of the strangers in his lounge. Divorty sat down in the other section of the settee. He stared at Ward.

"Do you know who I am?" he asked.

Ward raised his head, then opened and closed his mouth, finally managing "No," in a semi-whisper.

"Liam Divorty at your service. Here to collect the money you owe me. £40,000 on completion of a job. Where is it?"

"I haven't got it," he said.

"You know you owe me. Right? Don't you?" Ward nodded. "At least we're on the same wavelength." Ward didn't reply. "Let's start from the top. You hired my services to kill a man called Croft and you, or the person you sent to set up the deal, paid half the fee, and agreed to pay another £40,000 more for a successful completion. You still with me?" Ward nodded again. "Well, there was a successful completion, wasn't there? That said, I've come to present my bill. You owe me £40,000. Where is it?"

Ward looked at him. His expression was one of pain and dread. "I don't have it," he said.

"Wrong answer. You set me up, didn't you? Don't deny it. You're shagging his missus, aren't you? Suzanna, is it? You aren't going to get one over on me, mate."

Divorty eyed a drinks cabinet shaped like a big bronze globe and located near the French doors. "Any chance of a drink? Tom, fix us all a drink, will you?"

Masson stepped towards the globe, pulling out his handkerchief as he walked. He flipped up the lid, and looked in at a number of bottles containing a wide range of liquors. Glasses and tumblers were stacked on a shelf below. There was a bowl containing ice cubes.

"What'll you have, sir?" he asked.

"Surprise me," Divorty smirked. "Mr Ward, a drink?"

"No," came the muted reply.

Ward had a stack of tiny white napkins in the cabinet. Masson grabbed a few and used them to grab a bottle of vodka, and pour some into a glass. He added a ready-cut slice of lime and a single ice cube from the bowl. With the glass held in a napkin he handed it to Divorty.

"You not having one?" queried Divorty.

"None for me," Masson replied. "I just work here."

"Suit yourself." Divorty turned to look at Ward.

"You'd better start talking," he said. "Did you kill the old man?" Ward didn't reply. "How are you going to get me the money you owe me?"

"I…I do have it here," he admitted with defeat.

"Now we're getting somewhere." Divorty took a sip of the vodka. He raised the glass to Masson. "Lovely. My compliments to the barman," he said. "So where is it then?" he asked, glaring at Ward.

"In a safe in my study."

"How much is in there?"

"I don't know."

"Well, let's go and see, shall we?"

Divorty put the glass down onto the side table, stood up, went to Ward and pulled him onto his feet. "You lead the way," he said, spinning Ward around and giving him a shove. Ward staggered a bit then led them out of the lounge, across the foyer, by the front door and into another smaller room, under the stairs, which looked to be his office. There were several short filing cabinets on one side, and a computer desk on the other side. A pile of assorted newspapers were neatly stacked on top on the cabinets; above them was a shelf containing hardback books and stacks of glossy travel journals.

On the floor in a corner was a medium-sized metal office safe, around two feet wide by three feet high. Ward clambered down on his knees to open it. He took the spindle, turned it this way then that a number of times, grabbed the handle, forced it down and pulled open the thick metal door. With that, Divorty took hold of his shoulder and shoved him to the side. Ward was sent sprawling across the floor.

"I can't be too sure you're not going to surprise me. Can I?" Divorty snarled. Sinking down on his knees, he reached inside and withdrew a number of documents and a silk bag. Crumbling the documents into the hand holding the bag, he opened it with the other hand and pulled out several wads of banknotes which were secured by paper bands. He waved them in the air. "How much?"

"About one hundred thousand," Ward whispered.

Divorty whistled, then he concentrated on counting out £40,000. It took him a few minutes. Once he had counted out the money he shoved the wads of cash into his jacket pocket. The rest of the notes and the bag and documents he tossed to the floor. "Okay, let's finish our drinks. I think my business here is finished."

With that done, Divorty took Ward back into the lounge and forced him down into a seat, then sat opposite him. Masson remained standing at the back of the settee observing the proceedings. Divorty took his glass of vodka and put it to his lips. He took a long sip, then put the glass down onto the side table, sat back and crossed his legs. He looked at Ward.

"You wanted him dead. Didn't you? So you could get your hands on his money by getting into bed with the wife. You fucking low-life slime-ball. You came up with the plan to kill him. The only problem is that you needed someone else to do it so no one would suspect you. So you break in or go to see him knowing his wife won't be there. You kill him and make it look like a burglary gone wrong. You wait for me to arrive, then call the police and, I don't know how you did this, but you make sure the alarm will come on. Didn't you?" Ward didn't reply. "Didn't you?"

Ward waited for a few moments, then his shoulders sagged and he seemed to give up any pretence. He nodded his head and mouthed the word "Yes," admitting all. Masson wanted to smile, but refrained from doing so.

Within a second of Ward saying 'yes', Divorty vaulted forward, jumped on him, forced his weight down onto the man and straddled his torso. Then he wrapped his hands around his throat and attempted to throttle the living daylights out of him. There was no other way to describe it. He wanted to kill him with his bare hands. Ward didn't have the strength to fight back. He tried to kick his legs, but Divorty was far more powerful than him. Before he could finish him off Masson acted. He jumped onto Divorty's back.

"Leave it!" he shouted at the top of his voice. He took hold of Divorty's shoulders, and attempted to pull him off.

"Leave it. Leave it, for Christ's sake! You've got the money now. He's not worth it!" he shouted. Using all the strength he could muster he managed to pry Divorty off Ward. Divorty seemed to just give up. He relented and took a step back. As he did so, Ward put his hands to his own throat and took in several deep gasps of air. He looked terrified. Meanwhile, Divorty stepped back, slumped onto the seat he'd been in before, and calmly finished his drink. Ward had had it coming to him, but Masson was pretty sure he had just saved his life. If he had left it any longer Divorty would have throttled him to death. Less than a minute later they walked out of the room, across the foyer, out of the front door and into the car. Nothing was said.

As they drove away, Masson wasn't worried. He knew Ward wasn't calling the police. The last thing he'd want would be scrutiny. If the police started to ask him difficult questions on why anyone would want to hurt him, he could implicate himself in the recent events. Ward was stupid, but not that stupid.

One hour and fifty minutes later they were back at the house in Barnet. They dropped Divorty at the safe house and left him with Matt Royce. No doubt they would start on the rest of the cans of beer as soon as he stepped through the door.

Malloy said little as he drove Masson back to west London. He dropped him off at the pick-up point on Holland

Park Road. They both knew that Divorty was out of control, but they didn't want to admit it to each other. It was difficult to predict what he would try to do next. Maybe now that he had the £40,000 and frightened Marcus Ward almost to death, he would be satisfied. But there was no way of telling how it would work out. Masson feared that Divorty could take them all down, but he didn't share his thoughts with Malloy. Maybe Malloy was thinking along the same lines, but didn't want to say it out loud to Masson.

Chapter 16

Masson didn't venture outside his flat for the next couple of days. By the time the weekend came it had been four days since the visit to see Ward. Masson had not heard from Malloy or anyone else. He hoped he would not hear from anyone for at least another week. He was beginning to feel a bit more relaxed, but all that changed late on Sunday afternoon when his phone rang. It was Malloy. He sounded pissed off by Divorty's latest witless behaviour, and told Masson that Divorty was becoming increasingly restless and paranoid. He complained incessantly about being trapped in that house with not much to do except drink increasing amounts of alcohol and watch daytime television.

Malloy said Divorty was on the point of cracking. He was becoming a bloody nightmare. No one knew who he was going to lash out at next and threaten. Matt Royce was on edge and on the verge of pissing off.

Masson wanted to advise Malloy to consider getting someone to lure Divorty to a dead end and kill him, because, if the truth be told, Divorty was becoming a liability to them all. Giving him that advice would be like signing his own death sentence. Besides, he should leave it up to those more qualified to make the hard decisions. That was what he thought, but he never said it. Maybe Malloy was thinking along the same lines to, but kept it to himself.

"What about a different safe house?" Malloy finally suggested. "It needs to be somewhere different. Central maybe. Where he could get out more and blend into the crowds."

Masson thought it sounded like a reasonable idea. Malloy said that some of the neighbours in the road may have been aware that the same men were coming in and out of the house, but one of them didn't emerge at all. The whole thing was becoming increasingly unstable.

"Okay," said Masson. "I'll look around for a new safe house."

He rang off. Masson went back to the television. There was an advert for Christmas cruises. Christmas cruises in October for crying out loud. Then it came to him: Naomi Chiles's flat near Sloane Square was unoccupied. Divorty would be able to stay there for a couple of weeks whilst Naomi was out of town. It was empty and he had the keys. That way they wouldn't have to find a new place and go through the myriad of questions a landlord might ask, and they wouldn't have to lay out a penny. It wasn't ideal, but it was a solution. He called Malloy back within the hour and told him he had a place for Divorty to stay in the beating heart of the city. He could use it for two weeks, tops. He told Malloy the flat belonged to a friend who had gone to Europe for a short vacation. The flat was close to Sloane Square. In this area Divorty would be anonymous. He would be just like one of many transients passing through.

"I like it. Yeah, I really like it," said Malloy. "Leave it with me. I'll get back to you."

It didn't take Malloy long to ring Tom back. Divorty was keen to get out of the house and into central London. A flat near Sloane Square sounded perfect. Malloy revealed that the plan was for Divorty to stay one week, then he was getting out of London all together. He was heading to Spain to link up with some mates who were in the Malaga area, running a sports bar for expat Brits.

Divorty asked for Masson to collect him from the house in Barnet as soon as possible. He was also going to give him £8,000 from the money he took from Ward. As long as he was out of the flat by the time the owner came back it wouldn't be a problem. He agreed to collect him within the hour. The news that Divorty was heading to Spain came as a bonus. He would be out of his hair in a week. If Divorty played it right he could be out of London for many years to come. For the first time in days, Masson thought things were falling into place and that it would all work out fine in the end. As soon as he had finished chatting to Malloy he drove to the house in Barnet to collect Divorty.

By the time Masson arrived at the house, Divorty was packed and waiting to go. He had crammed his belongings into a canvas holdall. He was on his own in the house. Royce had gone. As soon as Masson pulled up outside, Divorty came out of the house with the holdall in his hand, wearing jeans and a jacket. He had a beany hat pulled low over his head. He slid into the Boxster next to Masson, exchanged a few pleasantries, then they were away. Divorty didn't say a lot, though he seemed pleased to be going to a place in town. He could become lost in the general hubbub and just another face in the crowd. Masson asked him when he was planning to go to Spain. He wasn't given a definite answer to the question.

They were in the Sloane Square area within the hour. It was a Sunday night and there were not a huge number of people milling about at seven in the evening. Masson took him down the street where the house was located and parked outside. They stepped across the path, through the front door and up the stairs to the second-floor flat. Once inside the flat, Masson showed him around, then handed over the set of keys. Divorty was pleased. He said it was great, just what he wanted. When he asked Masson who owned the flat, Masson told him it belonged to a bird he had met. She was out of the country on a dancing assignment on a cruise ship, which was true. Divorty said he would be hoping to be out in a week to ten days, as soon as his mates in Spain gave him the green light to travel there.

The Old Bill in Spain had been sniffing around their sports bar, poking into bets and payoffs. The cops would soon get bored. As soon as the way was clear they would contact Divorty and ask him to join them on the Costa.

Divorty was familiar with this area of town and would blend in in no time at all. Masson asked him to contact him as soon as he was about to go, in order that he could collect the keys. Divorty said okay. Before Masson departed, Divorty gave him the £8,000 he'd promised. It was his second ten percent cut. Masson smiled and took it, but in truth he didn't want it. He was done with being the go-to man for a killer for hire. He felt that his relationship with Divorty was winding down. He wasn't saddened by that. On the contrary, he was rather pleased their sordid relationship was coming to an end.

Monday 12th October
Not twenty-four hours elapsed before Divorty contacted Masson and asked him to meet him in the flat.

"Have you got a problem?" Masson asked, dreading the question.

"Nah. I just need a favour."

"Shoot."

"I've been in touch with the guys in Spain. I need to do a few things first. I'm too hot to get out and do them. Can you help?"

Masson wanted to hang up the phone, but this was a way to get rid of Divorty. He said of course he would help him all he could, and would come round the flat that evening. He ended the conversation by asking Divorty if he wanted anything bringing. Any clothes or food, or anything else he could think of. Divorty said 'good idea'. He asked Tom to pick up the necessary items to make an omelette. Masson said he would, and be around shortly.

Just under an hour had elapsed from the end of the telephone conversation to the moment Masson stepped up to the front door of the house in Sloane Gardens. He pressed the button on the intercom unit. Divorty answered it within seconds and buzzed him in. Masson had a plastic shopping bag in his hand containing the items Divorty had requested.

On knocking at the door to flat five, Divorty opened it and invited him inside. He looked well. He was wearing a pair of knee length shorts and a plain, white shirt. The flat was as warm as toast. Masson went to the chair in the corner, just beyond the criss-cross wooden frame and sat down. Divorty was sitting on the Chesterfield. The flat looked okay. Thankfully Divorty had treated it with respect. He had even put a can of beer on a coaster on the table top.

The curtains over the high doors at the window were open to allow the insipid light of the day to rain in. In the shorts, Divorty's legs revealed a display of large veined muscles and a tattoo of the Arsenal club crest on the back of his calf. At over six feet tall, lithe and broad shouldered he had the physique of a rugby player. He had regained some of his bulk, from hanging around safe houses with little else to do except eat. Little wonder that Ward hadn't been able to force him off. He relaxed into the sofa, stretched out his long legs and eyed Masson.

"How long have you known this bird?" he asked.

"A couple of months," he replied. "Why do you ask?"

"Is that her?" He turned his head to look at the photograph of the female face in the frame on the wall above him.

Masson looked at the picture hanging there. "No. She's there." He pointed to a picture frame on one of the shelves. "That's her on the right. The other one is her sister."

"Nice looker," said Divorty. "Where'd you meet her?" Surely he had not got him here to talk about Naomi, but maybe he had. "What's she do?"

"Naomi. She's a professional dancer. That's where she is now: on a cruise ship dancing for the paying customers. She's away for a month. That's why the flat's empty."

"Sounds nice," said Divorty. He pulled his legs up. "Funny thing is, that picture is also on the wall of the house in Esher."

"Which picture?"

Divorty turned to look at the picture on the wall again. "That one," he said.

"Which house?"

"The Croft house."

Masson looked at the picture in the silver frame. It was a photograph taken by a professional photographer. The subject was a female in close-up holding what looked like a sunflower close to her mouth. Then he saw it for the first time. It was a photograph of a woman who looked remarkably like Suzanna Croft, taken about five years ago more or less. There was no doubt about it.

"Is it the same? Are you sure?"

"Yes," Divorty assured him.

"Coincidence then. Must be a popular copy like the one of the girl in the tennis gear scratching her arse."

"I can't say that I've seen it before. Bit odd that I see it in two different locations in a short space of time."

He had a point, thought Masson. Then a second thought went through his mind. Divorty's line of questioning could be leading somewhere unpleasant.

"Yeah, okay," replied Masson. "Suppose you're right. What's your point? What are you getting at?"

"Nothing much. Just wondering," Divorty said in a defensive tone. "Maybe it *is* a common photograph."

"Anyway, what did you want to see me about? Something about getting something for you?" Masson was calm and collected, but in the back of his mind he did wonder why Naomi Chiles would have a photograph of Suzanna Croft in her flat. Meanwhile, Divorty seemed to take the explanation at face value. He turned the conversation back to the reason why he wanted to see Masson.

"Can you do me a favour?"

"What is it?"

"Go see Devon Trent?"

"Yeah, sure. Why?"

"Take him these." He got up off the sofa, stepped across to Masson and handed him two passport size photographs. "He'll get a passport for me. Arsenal are in Spain next week playing Valencia. Tell him I'm on the trip. He'll be able to organise the rest. A ticket and the travel. There's a grand for his trouble." He reached into his back pocket, pulled out a wad of notes and counted them to the value of £1,000.

Today was Monday. The game in Spain was next Tuesday evening. This meant that Divorty would be out of the country by this time next week.

"Sure I can. Just one question."

"What is it?"

"Where can I find Devon Trent?"

"He hangs out in a bar called 'Gunners Retreat' in Highbury. On the corner of Highbury Park Road. If he's not in there, someone will know where he's at."

Now that that had been sorted, Divorty wanted to change the subject. "Tell me about the woman who approached you about the job."

Masson pursed his lips. "About thirty. Nice looking. Fit. Elegant. All that kind of thing."

"Good looker yeah."

"Yeah. I'd say so. Especially if you like bottle blondes, with too much make-up and big hair."

"I always thought that was your ideal woman."

"No. Not anymore. I much prefer the petite type."

"So what's with this one? Isn't she a blonde?" Was Divorty suspicious and trying to catch him out?

"I said prefer. Doesn't mean I get," Masson said.

Divorty smiled then chuckled an exaggerated laugh. "Anyway, if you can contact Trent and tell him I need a new passport and tell him I'm on the trip for the Arsenal game."

"Sure," Masson replied. "Not a problem."

Masson decided to hang about for a few minutes. He didn't want to give Divorty the impression that he was keen to get out. He decided to chat to him about anything that came into his head, but he felt sure that Divorty was suspicious of him. Perhaps suspecting that he wasn't telling him the truth. He was right.

Masson gave him the plastic bag containing eggs, butter and bread and some oil to make an omelette, then departed from the flat at three o'clock. As he got into his car he did wonder why Naomi had a print of Suzanna Croft on the wall of her flat. Was there more to this than met the eye?

The 'Gunners Retreat' bar was indeed on the corner of Highbury Park Road and a dead-end street. At three-thirty on a Monday afternoon he would be surprised if he found the place open. The windows looked dark and dirty. They were covered with an assortment of posters: an Arsenal fixture list, pictures of players and a reference to some forthcoming gigs in Finsbury Park.

Masson tried the door. Surprisingly it was open. He stepped inside, paused, and looked around. With the posters on the windows the bar was in semi-darkness and felt eerie. On an Arsenal match day, it would be packed to the rafters with fans. Today there were two local guys sitting at a bar on raised stools, each nursing a bottle of beer. As Masson came in, they observed him with suspicion etched onto their faces, maybe assuming he was a copper. The floor area wasn't large, hardly twenty feet square. No tables. Just standing room behind a rail that curved around the floor. A guy behind the counter looked up at Masson.

"Yeah?" he asked stiffly.

"Looking for Devon Trent," he said.

"Who wants him?" he asked in a brusque manner.

"A friend of James Malloy and Dave Toshack," he replied.

The guy instantly chilled. "Wait here, man," he said, then he stepped around the counter, poked his head through an opening and called, "Devon!" in a raised voice.

Devon Trent emerged a few moments later and looked into the bar. He saw Masson near to the entrance and gestured to him with a wave of his fingers to join him at that end of the bar, far away as possible from the two guys who were sitting there. Masson stepped towards the end of the bar and followed him into a room. Inside the room around half a dozen guys were sitting on chairs watching a hard-core S&M bondage movie on a wide screen TV.

Masson didn't waste any time. He handed him the two passport photographs, then gave him the message from Liam. Trent told him to come back on Friday. He would have a passport for him, along with an air ticket to Valencia and a ticket for the football game. It would be £800 in total. Masson gave him the thousand in cash and told him to keep the change. He would be back at one o'clock on Friday to collect the items. As soon as the business had been done he left the bar and went home.

Chapter 17

Wednesday 14th October

On Wednesday night there was a development in the case. In a press conference, the Chief Constable of Surrey police announced that they were looking for forty-year-old Liam Divorty to help in their enquiries not only into the murder of Charles Croft, but also the prison van escape. This was nothing new. The main development was that police colleagues in north London had found the house in Barnet where he had been holed up. They had missed him by five or six hours. He was now believed to be in the central London area. His mug shot was once again plastered across the television screen. A BBC reporter standing outside of the Croft house gave the public a summary of the case. He said Mrs Croft was believed to have returned to the family home in France.

    If Divorty was watching the same broadcast, he may have concluded that the police were closing in on him. The switch to the flat in Sloane Square had come at a good time, but the net was tightening around him. Masson was fearful. He half expected the police to nab Divorty or one of the other members of the crew. There was the possibility that if the cops picked up any one of them, it could result in his own arrest. He was going to see Divorty on Friday to take him the items he required to follow Arsenal to Valencia and in doing so get out of the country. Friday could not come soon enough.

Thursday 15th October

    The Thursday morning tabloids were full of the two linked cases. One ran a story on the inside pages that dubbed Divorty as the 'Stockbroker Strangler' and described him as Britain's most wanted man.

Friday 16th October
    Friday arrived. Masson had not heard from any of the other players. It was as if everyone in the loop had gone into lockdown mode. It had just turned one o'clock when he left his home to travel the three miles to Highbury to meet with Devon Trent in 'Gunners Retreat'.
    As he entered the bar, a number of customers, pints in hand, turned to eye him suspiciously. Rock music was thumping out of a juke-box. There was the aroma of weed in the air. The barman, the same guy he'd seen on Monday, was behind the counter pouring beer into a glass. Voices had become lowered, but as soon as the barman acknowledged Masson they returned to the previous level. The barman greeted him.
    "What can I get you?" he asked.
    "Devon Trent," he replied.
    "Back room."
    "Thanks."
    He stepped along the counter and into the room where the guys had been watching the bondage movie. The room was now vacant except for Devon Trent sitting at a small table with his legs outstretched and resting on a chair. He had a joint smouldering in his fingers. He was wearing a heavy bomber jacket with a fur lined collar.
    "Hi," he said. Masson replied in kind.
    Trent slipped a hand inside the jacket and withdrew a brown envelope. "Take a load off," he said and took his feet off the chair. Masson pulled the chair back and sat down. The chairs the guys had been sitting on to watch the smut movie were now stacked on the side wall along with boxes of crisps and various other snacks. Trent opened the envelope and extracted several items. One was a passport, hot off the press, an airline booking in the form of an e-ticket printout, and a

ticket to the game: Valencia FC versus Arsenal in the first group stage match of the UEFA Champions League. He handed the passport to Masson.

Masson opened the folder, and there under the cellophane cover was the photograph of a glum looking Liam Divorty. He was now Mister Kenneth Wilson of Oxford. Masson was not a forger, and therefore had no idea if it was a quality counterfeit, but it looked not dissimilar from his own passport. It was in all likelihood stolen, picked by someone with nimble fingers, who had then sold it on to someone else who'd threaded the photograph of Divorty inside, and had carefully sewn it back together. Looking at the airline booking, Divorty was Mr Kenneth Wilson there too. All seemed in order.

Divorty used to travel to Europe to watch Arsenal as often as he could, before the Croft disaster. He knew from experience that a plane load of noisy, rowdy, football fans were waved through immigration, at both ends, with just a cursory examination of their travel documents. There was no reason to believe the trip to Valencia would be any different. The flight was leaving Gatwick at mid-day on Tuesday. The game kicked off at eight o'clock and would finish by ten. The return flight would be in the early hours of Wednesday morning. It was a return journey Divorty had no intention of taking.

It was a couple of minutes before Masson left the bar, after first politely declining the opportunity to have a beer with Trent.

"Nothing personal," he said, "I've got to get back to Divorty to ensure he doesn't fall too far off the wagon."

Trent smiled. He seemed to know that Masson was referring to Divorty's drink problem, which in his case was a lack of supply. In truth, Masson wanted to give him the packet as quickly as possible and encourage him to be on his way. Divorty would no doubt ask him to take him to the airport on Tuesday. He would be pleased to oblige him, and then he would be out of the country, hopefully for many years to come, or forever.

It had just turned one-forty five on a day that had become warm and pleasant for mid-October. It was hard to believe that it was nearly one month since the death of Charles Croft. Masson parked his Boxster on the street just one hundred yards from the house off Lower Sloane Street. The area was lined with cars, but there were few people around. As he stepped off the street and approached the door he glanced behind him to make sure no one was following. He pressed the button on the intercom unit and waited for a reply. It required a second attempt before he received a response.

"Yeah. Who is it?" came the groggy reply. Divorty sounded half-cut. Masson assumed he had been on the sauce.

"It's your benefactor, mother-fucker," he said, mimicking some famous film dialogue.

"Come up."

The front door buzzed open. Masson entered and took the stairs to the second floor. He knocked on the door to flat five and entered. He had the packet containing the passport and the other items in his hand. As he entered the flat he could see that Divorty was sitting on the Chesterfield settee with his legs outstretched and resting on the coffee table. He had both windows wide open so a wave of fresh air was wafting into the interior. The dark metal of the grille was silhouetted against the light. The coffee table was littered with empty beer cans. A slab of twelve unopened cans rested next to him on the settee. Divorty cocked his head at Masson, looking at him as if to say, 'what the fuck'. Divorty's eyes were glazed, and when he took his eyes off Masson, he looked past him into the corner of the room. Masson did likewise, and got the shock of his life.

Naomi Chiles was sitting in the armchair in the corner. A gag had been placed over her mouth. Her hands were tied behind her back and her feet were bound at the ankle. She was wearing a white plaid jumper and pastel slacks. Her long blonde hair was down around her shoulders. She raised her head to look at Masson and tried to say something, but her words were distorted by the gag. He could see that her eyes were red and puffy as if she had been crying. Masson looked at Divorty. "What the fuck have you done?" he demanded.

"Who's this cutey?" Divorty retorted. His words were slurred. He was obviously drunk or teetering somewhere on the scale between merry to pissed.

"She's my bird!" shouted Masson.

"You're punching way above your weight," Divorty said, then he hiccupped before laughing out loud.

Masson quickly stepped towards her. The gag was a cord from a dressing gown and he had forced something into her mouth, possibly a sock.

"Leave her," Divorty instructed.

"Fuck you, you moron," he replied. This would either subdue him or make him more aggressive.

"Fucking well leave her," Divorty warned.

Masson ignored him. The gag could easily suffocate her. Did Divorty care? Probably not. Masson picked at the cord which was tied at the back of her head, loosening the knot. He attempted to pull it off, but as he turned his head he was aware that Divorty was getting up off the sofa and coming towards him. He had his hands raised in an aggressive manner and his movements were increasing in momentum. In response Masson stepped towards the centre of the room and raised his fists in order to defend himself if Divorty came at him.

"You backstabbing cunt," Divorty said, stepping towards the shorter man. In the next step he threw a wide punch. Masson was able to raise his right arm in time to block it to stop him from clubbing him around the head. In response he swung a left fist that caught Divorty on the left side of his head.

Divorty creased his face into a snarl. He seemed intent on harming Masson all he could. Masson was able to see a second incoming punch and managed to duck out of the way.

Meanwhile, Naomi was desperately trying to get the gag out of her mouth.

"You cunt," Divorty snarled. Although he was under the influence and unsteady on his feet, he still posed a massive physical threat. He lifted his arms, brought them together and made an attempt to clamp them around Masson's head. Masson was able to dodge out of the way and turn to him. He threw a second punch to Divorty's head that hit him in the same spot as the first. He backed away into the middle of the room and set himself into a defensive stance, only for Divorty to come barrelling towards him. Divorty managed to get his big thick arms around Masson and clamp them around his midriff in a vice-like hold. They were virtually face-to-face, so close Masson could smell the stench of beer on his breath. Divorty was a powerful man. If he got Masson into a bear-hug he could literally squeeze the air out of his lungs. Masson could feel the clump of his hands digging into the small of his back. Moving his head back he was able to bring his forehead back, then propel it forward to headbutt him. Divorty's nose shattered, his head snapped back and he lessened his hold, then let go. Masson was able to get hold of Divorty's left arm and turn him one hundred and eighty degrees. Blood was oozing out of Divorty's nose. His eyes were glassy. He instinctively put his hand to his face and looked incredulously at the blood streaming out of his nostrils onto his fingers.

As he dropped his defence Masson hit him again with a peach of a punch that caught him flush on the jaw. Divorty staggered back a pace. Masson followed up with a kick to the groin which caused him to double up in pain. He made a long 'urrggh' and groaned out loud, but he still came back. He swung a punch that connected with Masson's right shoulder, causing his arm to go into instant spasm.

As Masson was left-handed he was able to swing a punch that connected. Divorty stepped back a couple of paces and dropped his arms to leave his chest exposed. Masson put his head down and charged at him with all his might, hitting him plumb centre in his chest. The force caused him to step back again and leave himself undefended. Masson followed up with a kick jabbed at his upper torso. Divorty took another step backwards. Then he seemed to recover his senses and looked to go back on the attack.

Masson charged at him again and hit him in the chest. Such was the force that Divorty was now at the window with his back resting against the railing. His hands were down by his side. He turned his head slightly to glance down. As he did so Masson charged him for a third time. The forward momentum caused Divorty to lean back over the ledge of the rail. Then gravity took over. He lost his balance and his grip on the rail, and slowly, like a falling tree gradually picking up momentum as it falls, his legs tipped up. In a series of almost slow-motion robotic movements his heavy frame took over and he went over the rail and out of window. Moments passed before the next sound Masson heard was a thump from below, as Divorty hit the ground.

He rushed to the window and looked down. Divorty had landed on the set of railings forty feet below the window. One of the spikes had gone through him from back to front and was protruding out of his lower stomach. He was impaled. His arms were flayed out on either side. His head was jolted back. His legs were bent at an unnatural angle. He was dead or very close to it.

"Shit," said Masson under his breath.

Naomi let out a muffled scream. She had managed to work the tie down and was trying to shove the gag out. He went to her, and pulled the rest of the wadding out. Then, despite a dead feeling in his right arm he pulled her out of the seat and managed to untie the strapping from around her wrists.

"Who is he?" she gasped.

"Was," he corrected, turning his attention to her ankles. "Liam Divorty. The man you hired to kill Croft."

"Is he…" She stopped in mid-sentence.

"Yeah. He's dead."

"Oh my God!" Naomi stepped across the room as if she wanted to look out of the window.

"No! Don't look down," he urged. He grabbed her arm to stop her from peering out. She halted mid-step, then sagged against Masson. He wrapped his arms around her, then stroked her hair with his good arm. He kissed her on the cheek. They stayed still for the next ten seconds in each other's arms.

Masson breathed a deep sigh. He was trying to think out loud and come up with some constructive thought. He had just had to fight for his life. He was both mentally and physically fatigued. He was trembling as the adrenalin left his bloodstream. He looked around the flat at the cans of beer on the coffee table.

His right arm began to tingle, then ache. He shook it out. He tried to shake reason into his head. "Let's figure out how we're going to explain this." He paused briefly then asked, "Who's upstairs?"

Naomi looked at him quizzically. "What?" she asked.

"Who's in the upstairs flat?"

"It's empty," she said.

"Quick. Get me a kitchen knife." She looked increasingly puzzled. "Please. Naomi. Just do as I say."

Naomi stepped out of the lounge and went into the kitchen. She returned moments later holding a large bread knife. Masson knew it was a long shot, but it might work. He took the knife from her.

"Get his stuff together and put it in his holdall." He nodded his chin toward the pile of cans, the strewn clothes.

She paused, looking around at all the stuff Divorty had scattered around. She rubbed her wrists.

"Please. Just do it," he repeated. "Now, babe. Now." He stepped towards the front door, opened it and looked out onto the landing. Hopefully, none of the other residents had heard the commotion in the flat, seen him fall or heard the thud as he hit the railings.

Masson stepped out of the flat and took the stairs to the third floor. Once at the door to the flat above Naomi's, he fixed the knife blade into the door frame, put his shoulder against the frame as best as he could and tried to force the door open. It took some effort, but he managed to trip the simple lock. When the door was open he stepped inside the flat. The lounge was a big bare space without any furniture whatsoever. Nothing, but for the thick pile carpet on the floor. He stepped towards the high doors at the window and forced them open. Seventy feet below Divorty's body had not moved. Even from this height, Masson could make out the pool of blood spreading on the stone floor.

He left the room; then as quietly as possible he closed the door and went back down the stairs to the second floor and entered Naomi's flat. She was frantically trying to cram all of Divorty's items into the holdall.

"That's good enough," he said. "Don't have to be too neat. Give me the bag." He glanced around. "Just a minute! Collect those cans off the table, and those last few off the floor." Naomi blinked, then did as he instructed and dropped them clanking into a plastic bag which was lying near to the front door.

"Hurry," he encouraged. She didn't say anything. "Shit, where are the keys?"

"What?"

"The keys to the flat. He had them to get in here."

He frantically strode around the room, eyes wild. Much to his relief he found them on the table by the sofa. He took the unopened pack of twelve cans from the table and wedged them under his arm. "The bag," he requested. "And close the doors at the window. It might work," he said.

"What might work?" she asked. "You really think we can hide all traces of that bastard? Surely somebody saw *something*! Heard…. something." She lapsed into silence.

He didn't reply. She gave him the bag containing the empty beer cans and the holdall crammed full of Divorty's clothing. Armed with the bag containing the empty cans, the holdall and the unopened pack of cans, he stepped out of the flat and went up the stairs to the third floor. Once inside the flat he went into the lounge and emptied the contents all over the floor. Next, he opened the holdall and threw the items around. He placed the unopened pack of beer on the floor. He felt inside his pocket, took the packet containing the passport and the other bits and pieces, and put them into the holdall. He wiped at the holdall's plastic handle with the carrier bag, then shoved it into his pocket.

Before stepping out he checked the scene. It was as good as he could hope for in the circumstances. He stepped out of the flat and closed the door on the way out. Quickly, but carefully, he went down the stairs and back into Naomi's flat. He didn't say a word. His mind was racing. She had closed the tall doors over the window. He looked at her and they shared a concerned face.

"You okay?" he asked.

Naomi nodded her head. He waited for a minute then took his mobile phone and called 9-9-9.

Chapter 18

Before the police descended on the house, Masson cleaned the flat as best as he could to erase all evidence of Divorty's presence. He used the plastic bag from the cans to line a trash can; he told Naomi to clean the bread knife thoroughly and place it back into the cutlery drawer. It was a massive long shot and he knew it, but it might work. Hopefully, as it had turned out to be a nice day, few residents would be at home, stuck inside. Since it was a weekday, anyone not out in the sun would be at their place of employment. Hopefully nobody had seen Divorty fall from the second-floor window.

It was fifteen minutes before the police arrived. Two cars full of uniformed police officers arrived on the scene. Masson met them at the ground floor. He showed them into the house then through to the back. They asked him what he had seen and heard. He said he and his girlfriend were sitting in the lounge room, chatting, when they observed a dark shape go by the window. It was followed by a thud. He got up, opened the window doors and looked down to the ground to see the body splayed over the railings. He had called 9-9-9 immediately.

The police asked him if he knew the victim. He said that he didn't. As far as he was aware the flat upstairs was unoccupied. He assumed that the victim had either come down off the roof or had fallen out of the window in the flat above. The officer asked him if he had heard anyone in the flat. He said he hadn't. The officer asked if he could speak to Naomi. Masson asked if he would delay speaking to her, as she was upset by the whole episode and had gone for a lie down. The officer said that was understandable and they would speak to her later.

The second team of cops then went up to the third floor and looked into the flat. It appeared that the victim could have been a squatter who had managed to gain entry to the house and found the empty flat. After all, the list on the intercom said: 'Flat 7 Unoccupied'. It didn't take a genius to work it out. He had drunk himself into a stupor, opened the doors over the high window, lost his balance, toppled out over the rail and fallen to his death.

The police searched his bag. They found a passport in the name of Kenneth Smith, an airline booking and the ticket for a football game in Spain. At first the police assumed he had stolen them. They also found £8,000 in cash.

Within twenty minutes of arriving, the police had cordoned off the house to prevent anyone from getting in or near. A 'scene of crime' team were dispatched within half an hour. Divorty's body was covered with a white sheet. The explanation appeared to be simple. The victim had gained entry to the house, had found the empty flat and broken in. The marks on the door suggested he had used a blunt instrument to prise the door open. He had a large amount of alcohol with him, which he had drunk throughout the day. He had opened the doors over the window, somehow lost his balance, and had fallen out.

No one would question his broken nose or bruised knuckles. The impact of the fall would have caused them.

After the initial questioning the police left Masson alone. He returned to the flat. Naomi was beside herself with fear. Masson asked her what she was doing back home. What had happened to the cruise? She told him the boat had developed a technical problem that meant it couldn't sail. The vessel had docked in Livorno, Italy. All non-essential staff and passengers were then taken to Pisa for a flight back home to Gatwick Airport. She had arrived in London at ten o'clock this morning, then she had taken the train to Victoria and from there took a taxi home, only to find a stranger in her flat. Divorty had grabbed her as soon as she had walked through the front door, gagged her then tied her up. At one stage he had threatened to rape her if she tried to escape.

Masson told her he was Liam Divorty – the killer for hire – and that he had been sprung from a prison van eleven days ago. He informed her that Marcus Ward, her brother-in-law, had been attacked by Divorty. If it wasn't for him pulling Divorty off Ward, there was a good chance that he would have been murdered. She didn't react to any of this. The trauma of the last few hours had left her feeling numb and unable to grasp a lot of what he was saying.

It was eight o'clock in the evening when the police eventually removed Divorty's body and took it away for further examination. The cordon was lifted at nine. The residents who had not been able to gain entry to their flats were allowed into the house.

It was nearly midnight. Masson and Naomi were in the flat together. The light was low, the TV was off and they were just sitting in silence. The last of the police officers had gone two hours ago. In that time, they had hardly spoken two words. They were still traumatised to a degree by what had happened. It was hard to grasp that Divorty was dead.

Naomi was curled up in the armchair in the corner of the room; she had her arms wrapped around her torso as if she was holding herself close for self-reassurance. She was holding a glass, full of white wine in her hand. Masson was sitting opposite her on the sofa. Both of them were tired, but by the look on Masson's face it was obvious to see that he was in a thoughtful state of mind. It was almost possible to see the cogs turning in his head as he contemplated what could have happened, and what the truth might be.

At the end of the day, he wasn't one hundred percent certain that Ward had killed Croft in an effort to smooth a path to his wife. In the back of his mind he wondered if

Divorty had killed him, then denied it, or if someone other than Ward or Divorty had done it. He considered the scenario that Naomi Chiles had been in the house with Croft and she had killed him. After all, why did she have a photograph of Suzanna Croft in her flat? Divorty had seen it.

    Masson considered a scenario in which Naomi Chiles and Suzanna Croft were having a love affair and that Charles Croft knew this. Or Naomi was having an affair with him or both of them in some kind of a love triangle. She had killed him in order to get to her. Or Charles wouldn't leave Suzanna Croft so they could be together. After all, Naomi could have stayed with Ward the night of the murder, left the house at eleven o'clock and entered the Croft home to see Charles. Maybe to have sex with him for money, then killed him. She reset the alarm and observed Divorty enter, then called the police before returning to the Ward house. It was possible. Of course, he could ask Ward, but decided against such a plan. The only person he could ask was sitting right in front of him. He reckoned she held many of the answers.

    He looked at her, and took a deep breath. She eyed him then she took a sip from the drink in her hand. "There's still a lot about this that I don't understand," he blurted out.

    She narrowed her eyes. "What do you mean?" she asked.

    "I don't think Marcus Ward could have killed Charles Croft."

    "Why not?" Her body language seemed to stiffen as she spoke, then she stretched in the seat and yawned in a way that was not natural. A game of intellectual chess was about to begin.

    "He doesn't seem like the type of man who could commit cold bloodied murder. He doesn't have it in him. It needs a special kind of person to kill another human being and he just doesn't have it."

Naomi shrugged her shoulders in a manufactured way. "All right. If he didn't do it, who did?" she asked.

"I think you know the answer to that question. I think you know a whole lot of answers."

She took another sip of the wine, this time taking more of the liquid into her mouth. She was thinking about a reply. Clearly, Masson had hit a nerve. He was on to something and suspected she knew far more than she was letting on.

"Why do you think it wasn't Marcus?" she asked.

"He's not the type. Too nice. Too rich. Too comfortable to commit murder. He'd be crazy to jeopardise all that."

"You think?" She was continuing to play the game, but she knew he was getting closer. She might even know the name of the real killer and the reason Croft had been murdered. She smiled at him and kept her turquoise eyes on his. He retained a face that was studied in reflection. He wasn't going to say another word until she told him the truth. Her mouth tightened.

"If I tell you, it stays within these four walls. Agreed?"

She was calling the shots. "Absolutely," he replied. "Why would I want to broadcast it around?"

She unravelled her legs, sat back in the seat and crossed her legs. "A man called…" she paused for a second… "Peter Smetham killed Charles Croft."

Masson knew the name: Peter Smetham. He was a south London man with links to some gangster types who ran criminal enterprises. Smetham had been his contact to reach the supposed wife of Croft all those weeks ago.

"Peter Smetham?" he clarified.

She nodded her head. Now it was Masson's turn to look puzzled. "Why?"

"Long story."

"Care to share?"

"He lost a lot of money in one of Charles Croft's get-rich-quick schemes."

"How much?"

"Enough. As much as £200,000."

"And how do you know that?" he asked.

She took a sip from the glass. "Because Peter Smetham is my father."

Masson was stunned by this revelation. "Your dad!" he exclaimed.

"Yes. My dad."

"But I don't understand. Your name is Chiles. Not Smetham."

She shook her head so vigorously that the ends of her hair danced. "No. Chiles is my stage name. It's my mum's name. My real name is Naomi Anthea Smetham-Chiles. I guess Chiles stuck. So I continued to use it."

Masson listened, but the fatigue in his head seemed to be playing tricks with his mind. He was finding it difficult to see the full picture and grasp the connections.

"Honestly, I'm struggling. Perhaps you ought to tell me from the top."

She pursed her lips, then she adjusted her legs, pulling them under her again. "Charles Croft persuaded my dad to give him a lot of money and said he would invest it for him with a big guaranteed return. But it was nothing but a pyramid scheme and, when some investors wanted their money back, there was nothing left in the pot to pay everyone. Those who came in late lost out. My dad asked for his money, but Croft said it had all gone. My dad's not the kind of person to walk away. He threatened Croft, but Croft ignored him. Said he was broke and couldn't or wouldn't pay him back a penny..."

"Don't tell me. Marcus Ward was one of the other investors," said Masson.

Naomi smiled at him, with a beam that could have melted even the coldest of hearts. "How did you guess?" she asked.

"Let's just call it intuition."

"Marcus didn't lose as much as my dad, but he still lost enough."

"If Croft sold them a bum deal, why didn't they go to the police?"

"You're joking! Right? It was a dodgy scheme," she said. "The police wouldn't have done a thing."

"So where did Marcus Ward get involved in this?"

"My dad and Marcus Ward know each other. They're Freemasons. My dad even introduced Rebecca to Marcus."

"Now you're kidding?!"

"No. Why should I be?"

"Geez."

"They agreed to do something about Croft. They weren't going to let him get away with it. It took them six months to come up with a plan to get him: hire a contract killer to take him out." No wonder she'd gone along with it. She was a criminal's daughter.

Masson sat up a bit. "Whose idea was it to use a contract killer?"

"I don't know." She moved a strand of loose hair from her face and took a sip of wine.

"Did Ward agree to pay the fees for hiring a killer?"

"Yes."

"I wondered why he didn't ask questions when Divorty accused him of killing Croft and asked him for the second payment of £40,000." He slouched back down.

"He was protecting my father. After all my dad is his father-in-law."

"True….true…." he mused, closing his eyes.

"They're all family," she agreed.

Eyes still closed, he added, "Some of this I had suspected. Killing Croft would give Ward a free run at Suzanna Croft, and of course, access to the Croft fortune."

"Yes. They were already having an affair. If Marcus marries Suzanna, he'll make sure that my dad gets all his money back."

"I'm really starting to like Marcus Ward. He seems *all heart*," Masson said, a bit sarcastically.

"Not really. He's a schemer, but he's out of his depth."

"So. What happened that night? The nineteenth? He looked at her, eyes half opened.

"The night Croft was killed?"

"Yes."

"My dad paid him a visit. Suzanna said the coast would be clear."

"Your dad killed Croft and made it look like a burglary gone wrong, then he waited for the killer - Divorty - to turn up?" he asked, sitting up, stunned by the cheek of it. A guy he had recommended – and which could have been him – such a casual set-up was cold. Really cold.

"That's about the size of it." Sip.

Masson shook his head, then he ran a hand over his heavy eyelids. He waited for a moment to see if she had anything else to say. She didn't. He glanced over his shoulder to look at the picture frame containing the photograph of the pretty lady holding the sunflower to her mouth. "What's your connection to Suzanna?" he asked. He jerked his chin toward the image. "That *is* her, isn't it?"

Naomi cut her eyes toward the photo. "Yeah, that's Suzanna. How do you know that?"

"Divorty saw it in two different places. Here, and in the Croft house. He got suspicious. So what's the connection between you two?"

"We danced together in a troupe, about five years ago. There was me, Suzanna and my sister Rebecca, plus three guys. We were on a cruise ship for a year. Sailing out of Miami and taking rich Americans around the Caribbean."

"Small world..." he muttered.

He managed to stand, and stepped towards her. He leaned over her, took her face, held it and clamped his lips onto hers. She wrapped her arms around his neck and kissed him.

That night they went to bed, but only to sleep. They didn't move 'til ten o'clock the next morning.

The next day.

It was not until midday that the police were able to identify the body as that of Liam Divorty, using the tattoos on his arms and legs. The man half of the Met police were searching for had been found.

Within an hour of discovering that the victim was Liam Divorty, the street was swarming with cops seeking answers. Initial reports suggested that the injuries sustained by the victim were consistent to those caused by a fall from a height. The toxicology report said that he was nearly twice over the legal drink-drive limit. An alcohol-induced accident fit the scene. No reports mentioned the broken nose, the bloody face. The fall had caused those injuries, plus a tough guy like that must have been violent. No point in expensive, time-consuming DNA studies either. The cops had their killer.

House to house enquiries took place. No one in any of the surrounding flats with a view of the back of the house had seen the victim fall out of the window.

However, the police were not thorough with their investigation. Masson thought it would be only a matter of time before the police realised that Naomi Smetham-Chiles was the sister of Rebecca Ward, the estranged wife of Marcus Ward, and who had been having an affair with Suzanna Croft. The chance of it being a coincidence was huge. But the police being the police, under-resourced and not able to devote detectives and hours to carry out a full investigation, maybe would never be able to join the dots. Perhaps the be-all-and-end-all was that Liam Divorty was dead.

The Malloy gang wouldn't care that much. Divorty had become a liability, better off dead than causing trouble for them in the long term. Masson might get some initial grief, but it would blow over and they'd all be the best of friends.

Masson didn't think Naomi had told him the truth, or at least, all of it. Maybe he didn't care. For now, he now had Naomi in his life, and Divorty was out of it. Why spoil a good thing and worry about who killed a swindler like Charles Croft?

The End

The Lady Below

London, England…
Friday 19th May 2000

Chapter One

Ms Grabowski had lived beneath my wife and I for the best part of the past two and a half years. Actually, if the truth be told, that wasn't correct. We had lived above her. According to the letting agent for the property management company, Mr Amis, she had resided here for thirty years. Since 1970. Just five or so years after the block was built in the mid-1960s. I'm ashamed to admit I didn't know Ms Grabowski's first name.

She was perhaps the longest of the twelve sitting tenants who resided here and called 'Park View House' their home. It was in a quiet part of Golders Green, north-west London. About six miles from the centre of the city. Just a mile or two from the start of the M1 motorway and slap bang next to the North-Circular. It was a Jewish area, though my wife and I were not Jewish. We had no religion. Therefore, we could be loosely termed as agnostic or atheist, or whatever they call people who had little interest in religion. Not that my wife or I begrudged anyone who regularly attended a church, a mosque or a synagogue. Whatever floated their boat. We resided on the first floor of a three-floor block, with four flats on each floor and a car parking space at the rear.

My wife and I knew Ms Grabowski, if only to nod to on the occasional time we saw her in the communal entrance or out on the street. She looked to be well into her early 80s.

Despite her age she was an attractive lady who always took pride in her appearance. We had noticed that, over time, she was finding it increasingly difficult to get around. She had in the past six months taken to using a walking stick. She was, in some ways, a reserved, private person so we never really enquired about her personal circumstances. The chap from the property management company told us she had always lived alone and appeared to have no family to talk of. She was a good-natured lady, who when we saw her always said hello, and had a smile on her face, despite the pain caused by the arthritis. She seemed to have no visitors, though I had noticed that, during the past eighteen or so months, she had been visited every twelve to sixteen weeks by a man who looked to be in his late 70s. A tall, portly chap, who usually wore a light baggy suit, smoked a cheroot and looked as if he liked good food and drink for he was a rotund shape. When we arrived home, one day, I had seen them coming out of the door to her flat and I had heard them talking in a language that sounded, to me, like German. My wife, Leah, a trained teacher by profession, had been with me at the time. She thought it could have been either Czech or Hungarian. Ms Grabowski did speak English but with an accent that sounded eastern European or east German. I wasn't sure and never asked. I thought the male visitor, the large chap, visited her periodically, but we didn't keep a record.

We had not seen or heard Ms Grabowski for a few days. We occasionally did hear her, in the flat below, closing a door or playing music that sounded like a Viennese waltz. Or an orchestral piece from some Austrian composer. Three days past and still no sound and we had not seen her leaving her flat. I was beginning to get a little concerned. In the early evening of the fourth day, Friday 19th of May, I contacted Mr Amis. The long and short of it is that Mr Amis called the police and arranged for them to meet him outside the entrance to the block. Mr Amis, using his pass key, entered the flat. He and the police officer found Ms Grabowski. She was sitting in an armchair, with her head slumped to one side and dead to the world. Imagine our shock when Mr Amis knocked on our door at six-forty-five that evening, to tell us that she had passed away, just twenty feet below our feet.

 We later learned that there was no evidence of foul play. Natural causes and old age was what went on the death certificate. Though she was 83 years of age that was hardly old these days, and in terms of the sharpness of her mind. Three hours after the discovery of her body she was taken away, inside a body bag lying on a stretcher, and placed into the back of one of those black vans, without any windows. Both Leah and I were stunned by the sudden turn of events. Whilst we were not close to her, she was a private person, we were no less devastated to lose such a fine lady. To think that she had been sitting there, dead, in the seat for at least four days. That would put her date of death to Tuesday 16th or Wednesday 17th. I chastised myself for not going down there sooner to check on her. In reality there was very little we could have done to prevent her passing.

 Mr Amis asked me if I wouldn't mind keeping an eye out should anyone come to visit her. Of course, I said I wouldn't mind. He gave me a card with his contact details on it. He then produced a key to the flat, which he asked me to take, just in case. I took it from him. He asked if I would go into the flat should I hear a noise. I wasn't so sure about that, but what could I say? I had already agreed to keep an eye on the place. Despite it being a sudden death, because of her age, it was very unlikely that the local coroner would ask for a post-mortem.

 Mr Amis confirmed that Ms Grabowski had moved into the flat in 1970. She had resided here as a tenant, not as a full or part owner of the property. She must have been financially stable because the rent was £1,000 a month. Not a piddling sum in the year 2000. According to him, she had never been married and had no children. He thought she was Jewish and had come to England from Holland two years after the end of the second world war. June 1947 to be precise. She would have been thirty years of age at that time. I asked him how he knew this. He informed me it was what she had told the property letting agency in 1970. It was still on the records. Leah and I had little reason to doubt his words. Where she had lived in the twenty-three years from 1947 to 1970 was anyone's guess.

Chapter Two

Several days elapsed in which we had not heard a word from Mr Amis or the police. Obviously the flat couldn't remain empty for months or even weeks. The property letting agency had a profit to make. There was a shortage of accommodation like this and no doubt the flat would be occupied in a short space of time. But first someone would have to arrange a time to come to empty the flat of her possessions, and find a place to store them until it was decided what to do with them.

I had only been in Ms Grabowski's flat on two occasions. Both times, I hardly made it past the front door. From what I had seen it did look full of old furniture, knick-knacks and bric-a-brac, though she wasn't a hoarder. The entrance hallway, which split the flat in half, did feel a little cramped. That and the rest of her furniture, assuming she had a lot, would require some shifting. It wouldn't be done in a day. As she had no family, we wondered who would inherit the possessions she had left? I guessed that once Steven Amis got around to it, he would have to make arrangements on the best way of disposing of them. Perhaps a local charity would benefit? Of course, that was all assuming Ms Grabowski hadn't made any wishes on what was to happen to her possessions after her death.

Thursday 25th May

It was now exactly six days after. Thursday. I had come home at around six-thirty. I worked in a Canary Wharf office tower for a firm of insurance providers called 'Heathcote & Hamilton'. I was an actuary. A job I'd done for the previous six and a bit years since leaving university. Leah worked for Brent Council. In the education department as a teacher in a local school. She specialised in dyslexia tuition for pupils suffering from the inability to read. My wife and I had no children. Just a two-year-old Labradoodle crossbreed dog, called Chipper. He was a bundle of fun and a mass of red hair.

We had been home for about one hour. I was sitting in the lounge with one eye on the tv, though the sound was low, my other eye was on a report I had brought home to read. Leah was in the bathroom. I heard what I thought was the sound of the doorbell to Ms Grabowski's flat. It had a distinctive loud single chime. I quickly got up from my seat, headed out of the lounge, onto the corridor and on towards the front door. Light was blazing in through the high window at the other end of the corridor. I opened the front door, stepped out onto the communal landing leading to the stairs, down them and onwards to the ground floor. As I reached the bottom of the carpet covered staircase, I looked to my left to the doorway of Ms Grabowski's flat and put my eyes on the top of a hairless head. It was the large portly chap I had seen previously at the flat about four months ago in January. I recall it was January because it had been a snowy, cold day. On this occasion he was wearing a dark heavy wool jacket. He turned his head to see me take the last two stairs. He reminded me of a former wrestler I had seen on tv when I was a kid. Some foreign sounding name. Professor Ivan Mastic, or suchlike. The chap stood about six feet two tall. When compared to my five feet nine, he dwarfed me. A pair of lifeless slate grey eyes were set on me. His jowls were loose, and his cheeks had deep lines running through them in a sea of rosy pink flesh.

We looked at each other for the few brief moments. Each willing the other to say the first words. The blank look on his face seemed to suggest he knew something was untoward. Ms Grabowski had not answered the doorbell.

"Shalom," he said, possibly thinking I was Jewish and could speak Hebrew, or whatever.

"Hi," I replied, then hesitated, as I wondered on how best to break the news that Ms Grabowski had passed away. Assuming he didn't already know. I noticed his large circular belly perched on the edge of his belted trousers. His jacket was a zip front, cheap looking, black sports jacket, though I suspected it had been a while since he had played any kind of sport. I estimated his age to be seventy-eight, give or take, a couple of years either side. His eyes were on me, but he had only turned his body say ninety degrees to me, so his bulk was still facing the door.

"It's Ms Grabowski," I said. I had reached the bottom of the stairs and had my left arm resting on the top of the banister to support my weight. His mouth was open slightly to reveal the cutting edge along the bottom set of his teeth. His head went back a touch. He had an enquiring look on his face. "She passed away," I said in an appropriately soft, sad tone.

His reaction clearly illustrated that he had no idea she had died. I wondered for the first time if he spoke English, but then I realised he had understood my words.

He remained mute but had turned his large frame another ninety degrees to face me. His bulk just about filled the width of the corridor. His large paw like hands came up and he wrapped them over the top of his head and held them tight. He gave a despairing tut sound, closed his eyes, then clenched his teeth. He had clearly understood my utterance.

"She is dead?" he muttered with a question mark at the end. He had an accent that was hard to distinguish. It wasn't British. More Germanic. Whether that was Germany, the Czech Republic, Austria, Slovenia, or Hungary, or wherever was hard to say. I spoke a few words of German.

"Es tut mir Leid," I said. Which means 'I'm sorry'. I couldn't recall the words for 'she died last week' so I uttered them in English. I guessed by his reaction that he understood German as well as any native speaker. His reaction was one of shock. She couldn't have been ill the last time he had visited so her death must have been totally unexpected. He mumbled a few words that were totally lost on me.

"I'm so sorry," I said. The chap looked glum and even stunned. I wondered if he was her brother, half-brother, cousin or some other relative or just someone she knew from the synagogue or wherever. Then something odd occurred. He actually turned back to the door, reached out, took hold of the door handle and tried to open it. But the door was locked and didn't open for him. He put his eyes on me.

"Who has key?" he enquired in his thick accent. There was no way I was going to admit to him that I had a key. Why should I? Did he want to get inside the flat? If yes. Why? He had no authority, whatsoever, to gain entry.

I shook my head. "I don't have a key. If you want to get inside you should be talking to the management company who lease the flats."

"Who?" he asked.

"Well, there's Mr Amis, he should be able to help you. He'll have a key. You'll need to speak to him."

His round face broke into a frown. He didn't look best pleased that I didn't have a key and he would have to ask the letting agent. He kind of grunted and snarled at a low growl at the same time. But not at me. There was a sudden sound behind me, as the double glass topped door leading into the vestibule came open. I looked to see one of the other tenants. A resident on the top floor enter the building. He looked at me and we exchanged a wan smile, then he glanced at the German chap before continuing on his way up the staircase to his flat. I knew him as Mister Anstead. He made his way up to the first-floor landing. He was just one of the other ten tenants. I watched him take the last step and turn onto the landing and go out of my view. Using it as a delaying tactic, while I wondered what to say to the German chap. I didn't have to worry. In the next second and without a word passing from either of our lips, or any other prompting, he brushed past my right arm, stepped away from me and the door to the flat. I observed him go to the double door, step through them and onto the marble floor vestibule. I heard the front doors coming open. I don't mind telling you that I was relieved that he had gone of his own volition. I blew out a sigh, dropped my hand into a trouser pocket and wrapped the fingers around the key lying there.

Chapter Three

Monday 29th May

A further seventy-two hours passed. Despite both the policeman from the local station, and Mr Amis having my contact details, I didn't receive any update from either of them. Therefore, we had no idea on how things were going forward or how they would conclude. I had told my wife of the visit from the large German looking and sounding chap. The very same chap we had witnessed with the late Ms Grabowski on a couple of occasions.

My wife and I hoped that whoever took the tenancy, of the now vacant flat, was a person who didn't make a lot of noise, and followed the rules and regulations laid down by the property management people. Just like Ms Grabowski. We were a little snobby, like that. The tenants in the other ten flats were a mixed bunch of young professionals, singletons, a few elderly and DINKYs like Leah and I. Meaning **d**ouble **i**ncome, **n**o **k**ids **y**et. Leah and I had been married six years. Children was something we'd consider in the next couple of years. I was twenty-eight. Leah twenty-seven. Plenty of time for children. Of course, we did have Chipper to keep us amused and busy.

It was now Monday evening. It was nearly the end of May. It would be June on Thursday. We were looking forward to the weekend and a visit to the furniture superstore, on a retail park in Essex, to get a couple of things. That evening, before I turned in at eleven pm, I was going to take Chipper for a walk in the park. It had been a gloomy day, weather wise, well down on the average for the back end of the month. A warm high was lingering somewhere else. More to the west of the greater London area, though next week was supposed to be going to be okay. I took Chipper the half a mile into

Golders Green park, not the field of grass at the back of the house. I let him roam and do his business. I had remembered to bring some of those scoop-the-poop bags with me. The traffic in the area was sporadic.

As I sauntered across the open land, I recalled the visit of the German chap and wondered what to make of it. Not a lot as it happened. I had no idea what he was seeing her for or why he wanted to get into the flat. A car came by blasting out the driver's choice of music, I didn't know if it was garage, acid, grunge, Britpop, R&B, or rap or what. They all sounded the same to me. Geez, I was losing it. I would be twenty-nine in three months. Where the hell had my youth pissed off to? Where had the time gone? Wherever, I wished it would come back. I was from an age when Depeche Mode were the big thing. Culture Club. The Jam. The Pet-Shop Boys with West End Girls. My tastes varied. I liked anything if it had a good beat and a pulse.

On that night I got home for ten past eleven. The light had dipped one hour before. As I walked along the street, on which the house I lived in was located, I noticed a car parked, facing the façade of Park View House. As it was a dead-end cul-de-sac it couldn't go forward. I noticed any unfamiliar vehicles in the immediate neighbourhood. This was one of them. It didn't belong to any of the people who resided in the block or on the street. Maybe it was a visitor. We, residents, all parked our cars in the car park at the side of the house, for which we each had an allotted parking space. I owned a Mini Cooper, though I hardly drove it nowadays. Leah used it when she had to go off on her work to a different school from the one she was based at. This stranger vehicle was a Mercedes SL something model. It was a car with a long chrome bumper and plenty of bling. Like something you'd see in a Merc drivers' convention or in a classic car parade. It was a left-hand drive model, but with a GB sticker and UK number plate. I glanced in on my way by to see a dark-haired chap sitting in the driver's seat. There was another chap in the passenger seat, but I never got a good look at him. I didn't think a right lot about it and carried on to the end of the street, up the step, through the first set of doors into the marble floor vestibule, then through the second set of doors. I was in my flat in a minute and in bed by half past the hour.

It may have been about two a.m. when I was aware of a sound from below. I think I had woken up a few moments before by one of Chipper's barks. Then I was aware of a sound from outside. It sounded like a crashing cymbal hitting a patch of concrete. The resulting crescendo reverberated like an echo in a hollow chamber. I was now more than half awake. Once again Chipper let out a bark. This time more solid.

I rolled the edge of the duvet back and peered towards the window that looked out onto the street. At this time of the year, it never really got dark as the dawn was only a couple of hours away. My wife, at my side, let out a long snore. I stressed my hearing to snapping point and thought I could hear a crack of glass. Perhaps a vandal, or an opportunist thief, had climbed over the metal rail fence and was trying to force open a window. But that wouldn't account for the sound of the crashing cymbal. Maybe I had imagined it. Chipper, who was in his basket in the hallway between the two halves of the flat, became restless and I could hear him scratching at the bedroom door. "Okay, Chipper," I called out to him. He was like a living surveillance device. He could hear things we couldn't. He knew something wasn't right. I pushed the duvet all the way back, swung my legs around and planted my feet on the carpeted floor. Just then there was a third sound that sounded like the window frame in the flat below being forced open. All twelve flats had the old style of push up sash window frames. A preservation order prevented the building's owners from upgrading the window to modern UPVC frames, therefore they were the old-fashioned release catch and push up type.

Leah turned around and forced the top half of her torso upright. "What is it?" she asked.

"Shhh. I've heard a sound from below," I replied.

"Such has?"

"God knows. Maybe a break-in."

"Where?"

"Below."

"What Ms Grabowski's?"

"Yes. I think so."

I stretched my arm out and reached for my robe on the chair by my side of the bed. I took it, got up, slipped it on over my pyjama bottoms, took the belt and tied it tight around my waist. The light at the window suggested it was later than I thought. Perhaps three-ish? Who the hell would be in the neighbourhood at three in the morning? I glanced through the gap in the curtain and saw the branch of a tree move.

We had a view out of the bedroom onto the front and the cul-de-sac street that led onto the nearby Finchley Road. Those at the rear had a nice view of a small local-authority maintained park about half the size of a football field.

Perhaps the noise had been caused by the strong breeze, which would account for the sounds. In the still and quiet of the morning sounds travel far further than during the day. My eyes went to the bed-side carriage clock. The glowing numbers blinked at me and said: 03:25. What I must have heard wasn't a break-in, but the wind rattling the window frame. But then I could hear a clatter as if someone below had walked into an item of furniture and knocked over a metal ornament.

Leah, who was wearing the top half of my pyjamas, was getting out of bed. I ventured to the bedroom door, took the handle, opened it and stepped onto the corridor, that split the two bedrooms from the other three rooms. I headed towards the front door. The key was in the lock. I took it, opened the door and stepped out onto the communal landing. The stairs going down were only a few feet away. The sleep in my head had all but gone and I felt cognizant and ready to face down what I could be about to meet. I stepped the few steps to the staircase and began the descent to the ground floor. There was a splash of streetlight on the floor, coming in through the glass in the doors that led into the vestibule. The last person to enter had to make sure the front door was closed and locked. That was the house rule.

I didn't rush. I gingerly made my way down the staircase and ran my hand over the smooth handrail. The creaking of the wooden boards might have told someone listening that there was a presence on the stairs. I made it to the last step and took a firm grip of the top of the banister. By the time I had made it to the bottom my heart was beating profusely, and the beat was banging against my chest. Once my feet were on the flat surface of the ground floor landing, I turned one hundred and eighty degrees, to face the stout wood panelled door to flat number 1. Then I realised I didn't have the key with me. On coming level to the door, I couldn't do anything but take the handle, push it down and try to open the door. The door was still locked tight. I didn't know what I would have done if I had found it open. Nothing, other than run back upstairs, grab my phone and call the police. Anyway, I rolled my fist tight, raised my hand and banged it against the door. Now that I had made my presence known, I didn't need to be silent. I would, if I had to, wake the entire house. "Who's in there?" I shouted out loud, then instinctively pressed my ear against the wood surface. It was a stout door, so I wouldn't have heard much of anyone inside. Not even someone bashing a big bass drum, never mind a tiptoeing burglar. I rapped my tight fist for a second time against the panel and repeated the question in the same bellicose manner.

"What's happening?" enquired a voice from the other end of the ground floor landing. It was one of my near neighbours. A Miss DePaul. She was standing there with a male partner. I didn't know him. They had both dressed in bath robes, in haste.

She was a lovely girl. Very blonde and attractive. She had an amazing figure, which I had noticed on several occasions.

"I don't know," I replied, then knew that sounded stupid, so I quickly followed up by saying: "I think there's someone breaking into what used to be Ms Grabowski's flat."

I wondered if she knew she had passed away? Or had ever met her?

I saw my wife, now wearing her opal blue bathrobe, appear above me at the top of the stairs. She looked down at me. It was then that I thought the best course of action was to contact the police, so I rapidly went back up the staircase, two steps at a time. "I need to call the cops," I said. By the time I had got to the landing, two of the three other residents on the first floor had opened their doors to see what the hell was going on.

"I think there's a break-in below," I explained in the way of an explanation. "I'm going to call the police," I added.

Once inside my flat I headed straight into the lounge, found my mobile phone and pressed 9-9-9 into the face. Then from below I heard another sound. With my mobile phone in my hand, I quickly went to the window and looked down to the ground. Incredibly, I was just in time to catch the backside of a dark-complexioned figure, climbing out of the window directly below me. He, or she, made off between the side of the block and a black railed fence that formed the boundary between the block and someone's back garden fence. The sight of the dark-haired figure made my heartbeat increase. I had to catch my breath and take in a huge drew of air into my lungs to prevent myself from becoming giddy. After a gap of about thirty seconds a voice came out of the phone, it caught me off guard for a brief moment as my thoughts had diverted elsewhere. It was the civilian controller asking me which service I required.

"Police, please," I replied quickly.

After a further delay lasting closer to forty seconds, I was finally connected to someone in a control unit.

"Police. What is the nature of your call?" A lady asked me in a blunt question.

"I think someone is breaking into a flat below mine."

"What is your address?"

I gave it to her, then I supplied her with all the information she required. She asked me for my age and my occupation. Which I thought were odd questions to ask in an emergency. She asked me how I knew there was a burglary taking place? I told her about the sounds I had heard, then seeing the man with the dark head climbing out of the window that would have opened into the lounge below mine. It was at this juncture that I informed her that the previous tenant, Ms Grabowski had, ten days ago, been found deceased. I referred to the community police officer who had attended, but couldn't for the life of me recall his name. I also told her I had a key for the flat. She strongly advised me not to try to enter the flat, but to wait until there was a police officer in attendance. I told her I had no intention of going into the flat. She had already put out a request for a passing patrol car to divert here to attend the scene. The last thing she told me was to wait in my home, with the door locked, until I observed the police arriving. I said okay.

Chapter Four

Things like this in police matters can run slow but, give the police some credit, they arrived about twenty minutes after the call had been made. Two uniformed police officers turned up. I saw their marked Met Police car pull up outside, then I went downstairs to open the front door. I meet them outside on the steps. I had put on a pair of jeans over my pyjama bottoms, and donned a jumper over a sports vest.

As was the trend in the new age of coppering at the start of the new millennium, it was a male-female combination. He was a young, light skinned Asian heritage chap. She a rather nice-looking young lady with her long golden hair done up tightly and secured by a scrunchy. He introduced himself as PC Ravinder Chatto. She was WPC Tina Sprake.

"What's occurred?" he asked, then put his eyes on me and gave me a 'tell me all' face.

"About three-twenty. I heard a noise from below, so I went down to investigate. I banged on the door, then I came back up here to make a call to you guys, that's when I saw someone climbing out of the window."

"When was this?" she asked.

"About twenty minutes ago. Twenty-five at the most."

She went to the door to Ms Grabowski's flat and tried the door, finding it locked.

"I've got a key, upstairs," I volunteered.

"Can you get it?" he asked.

"Sure."

"Did you know her well?" he asked.

"Ms Grabowski?" He didn't reply. "We knew her, but we didn't know her well if you know what I mean." The police officer gave me a 'what the hell' face. "What I mean is that I know a lot of people, but I don't know them well enough to say I know them, really well."

He nodded his head. "If you can get the key, please."

"Of course."

I vaulted up the staircase, to find Leah standing on the landing with the key in her hand. I gave her a whimsical look, took the key from her and made my way back downstairs. I handed it to PC Chatto. He threaded it into the door, opened it and stepped inside, followed by WPC Sprake, but she paused at the entrance as if to ensure that he entered first to check that the place wasn't full of burglars.

It was about two minutes before PC Chatto returned. He informed his colleague that there was evidence of a break-in. The burglar had looked through drawers in a cabinet, a couple of sideboards and even a desk. The person or persons responsible had long since vacated the scene. She followed him back into the flat, then got onto her communication device to report their findings and request that a SOCO team (scene of crime) be summoned to attend to dust down for fingerprints, any shoe tread marks and such like.

PC Chatto returned after about a minute. "What did you see?" he asked me.

"When?"

"When you saw this individual climbing out through the window."

"Just the back of this chap coming out."

"Can you describe him?"

"No. Not really. I only saw his back."

"What was he wearing?"

"A thick black jacket, dark trousers. He had gloves on his hands."

"Sounds like a pro," she said, then added: "Not an opportunist." I didn't know if she was talking to me or her colleague, so I didn't reply.

"Was it just one person?" he asked.

"Just him," I confirmed.

They asked me a couple of questions about the sounds I had heard. It was then that I disclosed that the previous tenant had passed away last week, last Tuesday or Wednesday to be precise. Though her body was not discovered until Friday evening. Therefore, the flat was now vacant.

"Do you know anyone who may have been responsible?" he asked.

I told them about the chap who had been to the flat on Thursday evening at six-thirty. Then I recalled the unfamiliar car I had seen with the two people inside. He asked me if I had gotten the number plate. Sadly, I hadn't.

The SOCO team arrived at seven-thirty, then a second pair of uniformed police officers arrived, plus the local community bobby who had been here when Mr Amis entered the flat to find Ms Grabowski. His name was PC Ronan Harrison. Shortly after him a pair of plain clothed officers arrived. Both male. There was a DI Hamish and a DI Doyle. They both entered the flat, stayed for fifteen minutes, then left, without saying a great deal.

All the police had gone by eight-fifteen. PC Chatto had locked the door to the flat, but left the key in the keyhole. I was informed that the property letting agent, Mr Amis, had been contacted and he would arrange for the window to be sealed and boarded up to stop a second invasion, should anyone attempt to get in again. Once all the cops had gone, I returned to my flat. The first thing I did was to call my place of work, to tell my boss, I would be about one hour late this morning, because I was 'helping police with their enquiries.'

Tuesday 30th May

On that Tuesday evening, I stayed on at work until six-thirty in order to make up for the time I had lost that morning. Though I was in a middle management role, and fairly high up the food-chain, the senior bosses wanted their pound of flesh, so I hung about until later than normal. Things like this were noted and regarded as normal. I did ensure my boss knew I was still there until late. We didn't, as it turned out, do a great deal of business after five-thirty. My expertise was in the trading of currencies which was why we had an office in Canary Wharf, close to the big banks and some of the currency brokers who had made the wharf their place of business. Yes, you really could purchase insurance to guard against sudden, unexpected fluctuations in the currency markets and thereby lessen any loss.

I arrived home at eight-thirty and settled down to relax and watch some tv, before Leah and I sat down for something to eat. On this evening, it was a pizza fresh out of the box. It was nine-fifteen when I received a telephone call from one of the plain clothed police officers I had briefly chatted to this morning. His name was DI Doyle. DI Cillian Doyle, to be precise. With a name like that he was bound to be of Irish origin. He spoke with a London accent. He asked me if I wouldn't mind if he popped around for a quick chat about the break-in. He would be here at say ten o'clock, assuming I hadn't anything planned. I told him, I hadn't. I'd be free to meet with him. He said he would be with a lady DI called Patricia Arnold. I think he said Arnold, though it may have been Harold or Howard. He ended the call at that point by saying he was looking forward to meeting me later.

Sure enough, at precisely ten o'clock, I received a buzz at the front door intercom. I answered the call on the telephone.

DI Doyle introduced himself. I told him I'd come down. I went downstairs to the front door, opened it on the latch to be greeted by two DIs from the Metropolitan police standing there.

DI Cillian Doyle was, perhaps in his mid to late forties. His carefully arranged thatch of brown hair was just starting to reveal a grey speckle at the fringe and around his ears. He had dark soulful eyes and a wispy smile. His dress sense was stylish without being over brash. His appearance suggested he looked after himself because his stomach was relatively flat, and he had a round, solid chest. DI Arnold was tall and svelte. In a double-breasted jacket and matching trousers, she looked like a tv journalist. She had red hair, more auburn than ginger. Her white cotton blouse was crisp, and her cologne was tangy. She had a trim figure for someone who appeared to be mid-thirties, forty at a stretch.

I invited them in and led them up the stairs onto the first-floor landing and into the flat. I showed them into the lounge and asked them to sit on the sofa. The pair of them let their eyes wander, as you do, in an unfamiliar setting. They took in the modern items of furniture and the array of glass ornaments Leah collected. I think they were suitably impressed with the surroundings. DI Doyle took out a notebook from a jacket pocket, opened it and consulted something written there. He appeared to be an astute chap. The natural light coming in through the long window, overlooking the side of the block, was strong enough for him to see his notes. Our flat wasn't open plan, but it could have been because of the number of glass doors that allowed light to shine through. It had a decent size lounge, with a kitchen-diner on one side, and the bathroom on the other, so the three rooms were in a kind of T shape. The two bedrooms were across at the other side of the central corridor.

Doyle raised his head and put his eyes on me. He was perhaps wondering where my wife was. Leah had taken the opportunity to get out to take Chipper for a walk in the park at the back of the house.

Doyle smiled at me. "We'd just like to go over a couple of things. I understand that a person of interest visited the flat belonging to Ms Grab-ow..Grabow…Grabowski." It took him a trio of efforts to get it out. After all, it wasn't a typical British surname.

"If you're referring to the large chap with the brusque features and the German accent then yes, that's true," I replied.

"Can you describe him to us?" DI Arnold asked. She had a gentle London accent with a twist of a Berkshire, Home Counties, edge.

"He was about six feet, two. Large frame. Maybe eighteen stone, probably more. A large bald head. Bulbous eyes and a pug nose. I'd say you could call it pug."

"How old?" he asked.

"About seventy-eight at a guess."

DI Arnold pursed her lips. "What was he wearing?" she asked.

"Err. A light jacket and matching trousers."

"You told colleagues he had an accent."

"Yeah, difficult to be precise. But I'd say German. I said something to him in German, just a couple of words and he seemed to understand what I was saying."

DI Doyle ran a thumb over his chin. "So, you'd say German?"

"If pushed. Yes. Somewhere from that neck of the woods."

"How about Austrian?" she suggested.

"Yeah, Austria. They speak German there. Don't they?"

"It definitely wasn't the same man you observed climbing out of the window?" he said. I didn't know if that was a question or a statement of fact.

I shook my head. "Definitely not. He was much younger. Slimmer. Far more agile. He had close cut dark hair. It looked like it was thinning at the front to form a wedge. A peak. The other fella had no hair. Before I got a look at his face he was going out of my view."

"Would you recognise him, if you saw him, again?" she asked.

"Who? Which one?"

"The chap coming out of the window."

"If I saw him from behind and from the top, then yes."

DI Doyle let out a light cough, then adjusted his posture. The cushions were soft and spongy so it was easy to get lost in them. DI Arnold was still sitting on the edge of the seat with her legs turned away from me and tightly clamped together. She once again reminded me of someone on television.

DI Doyle rubbed a hand across his forehead. "The Austrian-German connection is an interesting one."

"Why is that?" I enquired.

"We understand that Miss Greta Grab-ow-ski was Austrian."

"I never knew that. I didn't even know her first name. I thought she may have been Czech or Hungarian, but I suppose Austria is near enough. How do you know?" I enquired.

"That's what it said on her application for British citizenship made in the 50s."

I nodded my head in an absent way. "Okay. Fair enough." I narrowed my eyes. "The 50s. I thought she had come to England in 1947."

"She may have done, but she didn't apply for citizenship until 1951."

"Oh, right," I said. As if I cared little about the connections.

"We know that she was in Bergen-Belsen concentration camp when it was liberated in 1945."

This revelation hit me like an unexpected curve ball. I responded to the news by blowing out a tuneless whistle. "Phew, I knew she was Jewish, but I had no idea she was in a concentration camp. She never mentioned it to us."

"It's not something many people like to talk about," DI Arnold commented, as an aside.

"You can understand that," Doyle said.

"Yeah, that's true," I said, nodding my head to back him up. We were silent for a few long moments. I was intrigued, by the revelation. "How do you know she survived Belsen?" I peevishly enquired.

"It's detailed in her application. She even had the tattoo on her arm. The one they gave to Jewish prisoners," she revealed.

"I never knew. She never told us anything about herself. Not that we ever had a long conversation with her or anything. She seemed to keep herself to herself."

Just then there was a sound of the front door coming open, followed a second later by the sight and the sound of Chipper scampering and panting. He came tearing into the room and ran around, sniffing and wagging his tail. He didn't appear to notice the visitors, then ran out into the hallway to climb into his basket. Leah came into the lounge and clapped her eyes on the visitors. I instantly introduced her to the two detectives.

"You won't believe what I've just learned," I told her.

"What?"

"Ms Grabowski was in a concentration camp."

"Oh, my word. That's terrible," she said.

"How did she survive?" I asked the police officers, but didn't expect an answer.

"This is the amazing thing," DI Arnold said. We didn't reply, as we waited for her to tell us what was so amazing. "Ms Grabowski could play the piano and the violin. She had to entertain the camp guards. It is widely assumed this is what saved her from the gas chambers in Dachau."

"Oh, my God. Yes, that's amazing," I said, but not in an overwhelming way. Still my wife tutted at me as if she was expressing her disquiet at the way I had reacted. "No. It really is amazing," I repeated. I chose to gloss over any continuing controversy by feigning a brief coughing fit.

"But why would anyone want to break into her home?" my wife asked the officers. It was a dam good question, I thought.

"We simply don't know," admitted DI Doyle. "Until we locate those responsible, then we'll never know."

The cops were clearly looking for something from us, but what? "I mean I don't think there's anything of great value in there. Is there?" I asked.

Neither of them replied, though I thought I saw DI Arnold's eyelids narrow and her lips tighten.

"Clearly he was looking for something, and who knows maybe he found it," said Leah. She was being very perspective. I was impressed with her performance.

"They?" DI Doyle said.

"I only saw one," I confirmed.

"We seem to think there could have been two of them," he remarked.

"Why?" I asked.

"Because of the number of drawers that were opened in a short space of time," replied DI Arnold.

"You may have only seen the second one leaving."

173

"It's possible, I suppose," I said.

"Was he carrying anything?" DI Arnold asked me.

"I didn't see him carrying anything. Though I only saw him for less than a few seconds. I suppose he could have thrown something out onto the grass."

The conversation carried on like this for the next couple of minutes. The time was beginning to drag as were the questions. I asked them if they knew if there were any plans for the flat. They didn't know what plans the property management company, who were also the letting agents, had for the flat. It was nothing to do with the police, or me, if the truth be told.

It was getting on for ten, forty-five when the two detectives left Leah and I to get on with what remained of our evening. Tomorrow was Wednesday 31st. It would be two days shy of two weeks since the discovery of Ms Grabowski's body.

Chapter Five

Wednesday 31st May.

As soon as Leah and I had finished our evening meal at eight pm, I turned on my pc. I managed to find a 'Jewish Chronicle' web-site that provided some historical context of the 'final solution' or in other words, the Holocaust. I ran the name of Greta Grabowski through a search facility. I got a single hit relating to someone of that name. Yes, for sure, a person of that name had been born in Vienna, Austria in 1917 into a Jewish family. In May 1938, the Nazis had invaded Austria, annexed it and taken it into the wider German volk or Reich. It was more than likely that the Grabowski family were taken to Dachau concentration camp in the summer of 1938, or thereabouts. I surmised that her parents and any siblings may have died there in the gas chambers. In 1944, as the Russians pushed south and west into Germany, the Nazis had to transfer thousands of prisoners from Dachau to other camps to try to hide their crimes from the Red Army. Specifically, to the Bergen-Belsen camp in Lower Saxony in north-west Germany. At the time the camp was a prisoner of war camp for the estimated 20,000 Russians who had been captured. With the influx of numbers, the camp grew larger and the prisoner population rose to approximately 60,000 to 70,000 by the middle of 1944.

Had Greta Grabowski survived because she could play the piano and the violin? That would appear to be the case. She was forced to entertain the camp commandant and his underlings, whilst they ate and gorged themselves on good food and wine, whilst the camp inmates had to survive on rations that were hardly enough for an animal to live on. Greta probably lived on the food left by her tormentors.

Over the course of the following ten minutes, I read an account of her life. How she had survived the gas chambers of Dachau, that had taken hundreds of thousands of innocent lives. Just reading about the death camps brought a tear to my eye. Man's inhumanity to man filled me with a sense of hopelessness and a maudlin sadness drifted over me. I relayed the accounts to Leah, but didn't go into a lot of detail. It was hard for us to think that Greta had lived in the flat below us for two and a half years, thirty in total, but we had no idea of the things she had been through.

I hit the image prompt at the top of the page. A dozen or so pictures appeared on the screen. Pictures of the Jewish prisoners wearing the familiar light and dark vertical striped uniforms given to them by the Nazis. There were a couple of photos of someone who may have been Greta Grabowski. Both of them were in the age of twenty to twenty-five years of age. To think she was twenty-seven years of age when the British, along with the Canadians and a small number of Americans, liberated Bergen-Belsen on 15th of March 1945. It was impossible to say the images were definitely the lady who lived below, because we had only met her when she was in her eighties. After all, twenty-seven years of age to eighty-one was a huge fifty-four-year span. She had shoulder length blonde hair, a sparkle in her eyes and a svelteness of frame. The advantage of youth over advancing years. She had the look of a member of the Aryan race rather than Jewish, but that didn't mean much to the Nazis.

Both Leah and I were intrigued by the story and that we had lived above her for the time we had. She had been through a great deal in her life, losing her parents and siblings. Witnessing what she had seen in such desperately terrible places such as Dachau, then Bergen-Belsen. It must have been traumatic. But she had survived, unlike many of her brethren. She was freed in 1945, moved to Holland, then made her way to a new life here in England and made Golders Green her home for the past thirty years. This area was still by and large a majority Jewish area, but perhaps not as large as it was in the 1950s, 1960s, and 1970s. The area was changing slowly. Not that it mattered to us. We had few qualms about a changing ethnic landscape.

We did wonder if Greta had been a frequent visitor to the local synagogue. There was one close by to us. The Western Reform branch on Temple Fortune. Many practising Jews in the area would meet there for social events and the like. Perhaps they were unaware that Ms Grabowski had passed away, assuming they knew of her existence in the first place. I decided to give the local synagogue a telephone call, rather than pay a visit, to ask, but I put off the idea for the time being.

Chapter Six

Saturday 3rd June

The weekend soon came. We tended to relax on weekends. Free from the stress of our jobs. I would spend the time lazing around the flat. It was noon on Saturday. Maybe I'd call the synagogue tomorrow or the day after.

At one o'clock on Saturday, in the afternoon we took Chipper for a walk and to visit a local supermarket to stock-up on a few essentials, like milk, butter and breakfast cereals. We set off for the furniture store in Essex at two.

We returned home for five-thirty. We hadn't purchased anything from the furniture depot. Chipper was so tired he fell asleep in his basket. At six we heard a knock at the front door. It was Steven Amis, the chap, from the property management company who owned the block. His role was primarily to organise any repairs to the building and to ensure there were no tenants breaking the rules and making it difficult for their neighbours. He informed us that he had contracted a building maintenance company they used to do the repairs. They would be here on Monday. They were going to fix the window frame the burglars had broken through. He had little to say in the way of news about when the flat was going to be emptied so it could be re-let. I speculated there was a thick book full of regulations and guidelines that had to be adhered to before the flat could be emptied, though I had no idea of the ins and outs and the requirements. He asked me if I still had the key to the flat, thinking possibly that the police had taken it. I informed him that I had given it to the first copper to arrive, but he had left it in the keyhole, so yes, I still had the key. I was surprised when he didn't ask for its return. He asked me if I wouldn't mind keeping it a while longer and if I'd keep an eye on the flat for him. I reluctantly said 'okay'.

Sunday 4th June

The following day – Sunday – I turned on my pc after an early breakfast at 9.00am to find the telephone number for a local synagogue. At 10 o'clock, I rang the landline number, but terminated the call after three minutes when I didn't get a response. I thought about leaving a voice mail with a request to call me back, but I stalled at the last second, and decided not to do that. Mainly because I didn't know what to say. I considered sending an email, but didn't know what to write so I went off that idea as well.

After a light lunch of ham and salad sandwiches I elected to take Chipper out for a walk in the park. I had one of those contraptions that ejected a hard sponge ball out of a holder. He would scamper off across the grass to retrieve it and bring it back for me to project it back to where he had just been. Even he got cheesed off by this after the sixth time, when he steadfastly refused to go and get it, I had to retrieve the ball myself. He just lay down on the grass and pretended to doze. It was getting on for two-thirty when we got back to the flat. The afternoon had turned breezy, though the wind was warm, and it was pleasant out of the shade.

The pair of us, Chipper and I, were arriving back at the house containing our flat. As I headed towards the steps going to the front door, I dropped my hand into my trouser pocket and found the key for Ms Grabowski's flat.

I took a couple of moments to have a look round in a semi-furtive manner. Many of the other ten tenants were never here on weekends. I had never seen Miss DePaul on a weekend in the time I had lived here. I reckon she went to stay with her parents or a boyfriend on a weekend, though I didn't know for sure. There were many singletons, like Mr Anstead, professional types who went home for the weekend and only used this place for weekdays. I knew, Mr. Anstead, was a consultant at one the big hospitals over in north-east London.

I went up the two steps to the front door, through it, and into the vestibule. I was soon in the area by the staircase, with the door to Ms Grabowski's flat at my side. I paused for a moment to listen for any evidence of a nearby presence. There was no sound of anyone close by. The door that led into the back garden and the car park was closed. The entrance to flat 2, Miss DePaul's home, was further along the landing. Flats 3 and 4 where on the other side. Sunlight was streaming through a large, tall arch shape window that looked out on the back garden. It was sprayed over the orange-cream patterned carpet on the floor. All was still and quiet. I felt a little clandestine in what I was about to do. Thinking that I was bound to be discovered by someone, maybe Mr Amis or the police. But that was unlikely. I came up with an explanation just in case I was discovered inside the flat. I'd say I had heard a noise and opened the door and went in to investigate. After a brief delay, while I thought about the consequences of being caught, I approached the door, took the key from my pocket, threaded it into the keyhole and turned it. The bolt sprang open. The gold coated numeral 1 screwed into the panel surface looked chipped and scaly and as if it had lost some of its gold patina.

I had Chipper's lead wrapped around my clenched right-hand fist. The door came open with a slight whine of the hinges. The first thing that struck me was the soft, blast of warm air racing out to meet me, then the shade. The blackout blind over the window at the bottom of the corridor was all the way down to the bottom so it was in shade. I had been inside the flat on two previous occasions, but never beyond the doorway. Once, I had helped her take some shopping into the flat. The other was when some of her mail was inadvertently put into our box, I had returned it to her, therefore I had never had the need to go further than the front door.

The floor was covered in a thick, but old carpet. A plain mauve colour. I recalled the ornately engraved picture frames that had hung on the walls on both sides of the corridor. I could just make them out in the gloom. One was of a tutu wearing ballerina on her tiptoes. Arms aloft as she performed a kind of pirouette.

I had to tug on Chipper's lead to persuade him to follow me inside. Maybe he was distracted by the fusty air. He seemed reluctant to enter. It was his first time in here, so perhaps he was a little fearful. Up ahead there was an old-style sideboard. A solid piece of craftsmanship when things tended to last a lot longer than they did today. A light shade on the end of a long flex hung from the ceiling. Once we were inside, I closed the front door behind me.

I tentatively headed down the corridor towards the second door on the left, the one that led into the lounge. It had the feel of an elderly person's home. The sideboard was adorned with a few stout ornaments. It was the exact same layout as our flat. A carbon-copy. Three doors on the left, two on the right that led into the bedrooms. Glass doors to compensate for the lack of internal light.

I stepped past the door leading into the kitchen. I paused for one brief moment to listen for any sound. I heard nothing, other than a revving motorcycle engine, somewhere on a surrounding street. That quickly faded. I could hear the tick-tock of a clock on the sideboard. The stale fusty air I had just breathed in made his nostrils pucker. It was now eleven days since she had died. More than a week since her body was discovered.

Chipper, at my feet, let out a bark. 'Shush', I scolded him, before I followed that with a more lenient 'good boy'. He didn't know what he had done was wrong. 'Okay, quiet,'

I whispered. My imagination was beginning to wander. Wonder what I might find. Probably nothing. I soon made it to the door going into the biggest room, the living area. Leah and I referred to it as the lounge. I took the handle, forced it down then pushed it open and peered inside. The wide window, the one on the outer wall, to the right, the one the burglar or burglars had climbed through was covered with a piece of laminate hardboard. There was a pencil width of light along the four edges. The fixtures and fittings looked like the originals put in when the house was constructed in the mid-1960s. I could make out a settee in the centre of the room, in much the same place as ours. A couple of big sideboards and chests were set along the edge of the four walls. A sit-up and beg type of armchair with a high backrest was on one side. Large, fancy carved picture frames contained paintings from a bygone age, though in the gloom the pictures on them were hard to distinguish. Maybe one was a portrait and the other one was of a galleon on the high sea. I reached for a light switch where I thought it would be. A large single lampstand with a frilly lamp shade came on to douse the room in electric light. I couldn't ever recall hearing a tv and as I looked around, I couldn't see one now. On the sideboard, on one side, was a large glass encased display unit containing what might have been a stuffed bird. The spindle device of a carriage clock, inside a glass doom, was rotating. The room, overall, had quite an eerie feeling to it. The floor was carpeted. Then I saw the picture frame on a side table next to the sofa. It contained a single photograph, very similar to the image I had seen on the internet when I looked for information on Greta Grabowski. Was it her? I had no way of knowing for sure.

    To be honest there wasn't a great deal to see or take in during a swift inspection. Chipper pulled on his lead to such an extent he nearly had me over. I reached down to the harness hugging his torso, unplugged the lead and let him free. He went off to sniff around the flat and headed down the corridor towards the exit point. A thought came to me that I had no right to be snooping about like this. Perhaps I should go before someone came in and asked me to explain what the hell I was doing. With that in mind I stepped down the corridor to the exit. However, before I stepped out, I couldn't resist the urge to take a quick peek into the kitchen. I opened the door gently and peered inside. There was a single combined gas hob and oven. It was a stand-alone. It wasn't part of a fitted unit. There was nothing in the way of modern conveniences like a microwave or a toaster. She did have an eclectic kettle. On a work top there were a pair of coffee and tea caddies, a tea-pot and one of those half circular bread bins. A tea towel was draped over the top of the grill, high above the gas rings. The main feature was an old-fashioned Belfast sink, which were coming back into fashion, through this one looked like the original from when the block was constructed in the mid-1960s. It had two big old-style silver taps. Light was visible through a glass partitioned side wall. There was no outside window as the kitchen ran down the length of the internal landing, just like our flat. I stepped out of the room, took hold of Chipper by his harness, opened the front door and took a few paces onto the ground floor foyer. I closed the door behind me, locked it and took the key out of the keyhole. From here I went up the stairs to my own flat, opened the door and went inside.

  I thought that a return visit to the flat was very much a possibility, but probably later in the evening when the chances of being disturbed by a fellow resident, or whoever, was highly unlikely. Perhaps later this evening.

  On the first Sunday in each month - March to October - Leah met with a group of her teaching chums. It was a book reading club. Each member took it in turn to host. Tonight, wasn't our flat. We didn't have that joy for another three months. This evening, she would be out from about half past seven to a quarter past ten or thereabouts, depending on how interesting or not the book they were discussing was. This month's book selection was 'The Dice-Man' by Luke Reinhardt.

On returning to the flat, I found her in the bedroom getting ready for the evening. I didn't tell her I had just been in the flat below, having a nosey around. Nor that I planned to go back for a longer look later.

On this Sunday evening – Leah left the house at seven-fifteen to attend the soiree with her literary friends. She was using our shared Mini to drive to her friend's home. I waited for a further fifteen minutes to ensure she didn't come back. Then I went into the corridor to rouse Chipper from his basket. I toyed with the idea of leaving him to have a sleep, but he might come in useful as an early warning device. I hooked the lead onto his harness and said 'walkies'. He really was a barrel of fun. I don't know what we would have done if we didn't have him. I took his lead and led him to the front door, and out. He must have thought he was going for a walk in the garden or the park. We were going to neither. We went down the stairs at a careful pace. At the bottom I tugged on his lead to take him away from the doors leading into the vestibule. Instead, I took him to the door with the gold painted number 1 attached to the surface. I fed the key into the keyhole, turned it, heard the bolt spring open, took the handle, pushed it forward and stepped into the flat. I remembered to take the key out, close the door, and lock it from the inside.

Chapter Seven

With the time heading towards the mid-evening the light inside was in shade, but it was still bright outside. We were still a few weeks away from the 21st of the month, the longest day of the year. I let Chipper off his lead and dropped it to the floor, so he was free to roam about. He elected to sit on his two front legs and just take it in. I headed along the corridor, opened the door into the sitting room and entered. The pencil beam of light around the edges of the makeshift barrier appeared to be sharper than before. It was so dark I had no alternative but to turn on the lampstand light. I glanced round the room. I was quite taken by the oldy world charm of the paintings and the old furniture. I swiftly turned to the cabinet - come sideboard - adjacent to the wall running down the length of the outer landing, approached it and once there I opened the top drawer. I felt a sensation of suspense go down the length of my spine. I did feel a tad nervy. I put my hand into the drawer, grabbed a number of papers, pulled them out and rested them on the top surface. They were, mostly personal papers: a few bank statements, letters from an insurance company to remind her to renew a policy. That kind of thing. Some paid bills. A letter from a bank to inform her of a change in interest rates. The second drawer contained a pile of linen, bed sheets, and a tablecloth. Despite the lamplight it still wasn't bright. Perhaps I should have brought a torch with me. The third and final drawer contained an assortment of knitting patterns, knitting needles, some balls of wool. Pins and darning needles. Nothing to get too excited about.

    I moved from there and went around the room in a clockwise direction. The second item I looked in was a Georgian or Elizabethan chest reproduction. It had four curved drawers. I found an assortment of papers. A few more bank statements. She had over £6,000 in one bank. In a second, she had £5,600. Then I found a batch of blue envelopes containing writing on blue paper. Letters. Geez, they looked old. The paper felt as if it would crumble in my hands. They were creased and the ink on the sheets was just about visible. I looked at the envelope to see the name of the recipient had been blacked out as if by a censor in a prison. There was about two dozen envelope's all containing letters, written on the same blue writing paper.

    I took one of the envelopes. The name of the person to whom it was intended had been blacked out. The address was in a foreign language. There was no stamp. It must have been removed or there wasn't one in the first place. Maybe the latter. All looked as if they had been here for some years. The paper was aged, crinkly and very fragile. They were person to person letters. Perhaps they were love letters. I couldn't detect the words. They were in a language I didn't recognise. The words looked almost Cyrillic. Maybe Russian, Bulgarian, or Ukrainian. One of the letters, had the date '1943' written across the top in blue fountain pen ink. But no idea of day and month because it had also been blanked out by a censor. I heard a sound from outside. Possibly a car drawing into the car park at the side and rear of the house. I suddenly felt the chill of a draught. I observed Chipper saunter into the room with his lead trailing behind him. I put all the blue envelopes onto the top of the chest. I opened another drawer. It was full of trinkets and bauble like costume jewellery. Along with some coins. I had little idea if they had any value. Probably not. Perhaps they were pieces she had collected together from the time she came to London in the aftermath of the second world war.

    I carefully searched through the rest of the furniture in a diligent fashion. Alas, I didn't find anything else of great significance. I was contemplating leaving. Chipper was becoming restless. He had gone towards the boarded window and was pining. Maybe he thought he would never see the light of day ever again. I took his lead and led him away from the window. A quick glance at my watch told me I had been in here for getting on for twenty-five minutes. I exited the room, turning off the light on my way out. I didn't think I would find anything of interest in the bathroom, so elected to give it a miss. I entered the largest of the two bedrooms. It was the room immediate below the one we used as our main bedroom. Because of the layout of the block, the second bedroom didn't get much in the way of natural light so in many respects it was nothing more than a spare storage room.

Ms Grabowski also used this room as the main bedroom. There was a mattress that wasn't a single, but neither was it a double, more three-quarter size. The bedclothes and pillow were still in place. The floor was carpeted with the same carpet as the lounge and the corridor. The wallpaper was dark and old, and peeling off in several places. There was a sideboard or dresser on one side and an upright wardrobe on the other. The curtains were closed over the window that looked out over a narrow segment of lawn, then the black rail fence to the street beyond, at the front of the house. I thought about turning on a bed-side lamp, but thought better of it in case someone saw the light through the window.

I searched in the dresser. Chipper was pulling on the lead, so I let go and let him scamper. He immediately trotted off, went through the open door and out of the room. I pulled open a sliding drawer in the dresser, but found nothing other than a few pillow cases. All I had found of interest were the old, ancient letters, some dating back to 1943, several bank statements which suggested she had about £11,000 in the bank, several old bills and the like. I noticed the lack of picture frames and photographs of loved ones. Nothing to tell me who she was. But I knew who she was. She was Greta Grabowski.

I opened the wardrobe door to find a couple of items hanging there, like a robe, a couple of winter coats, a few flowery dresses, skirts and blouses on coat hangers. There was an old-fashioned canvas suitcase at the bottom. Maybe it contained an incredibly valuable Stradivarius violin. The one she had played in Dachau, and Bergen-Belsen for the amusement of the camp commandant. Not that I would steal it or anything like that.

I took hold of the case handle, lifted it out and took it to the bed, where I laid it on the mattress. I opened the two catches and lifted the lid. It contained nothing other than a few silk scarves, a fur stall, and a couple of pairs of shoes. I closed the lid, made sure the catches were locked, then took the case back to the wardrobe and put it back where I had found it. Chipper had drifted back into the room and was now trying to squeeze underneath the bed. Something he did in our flat. His head was down, and his backside was arched up as he tried to burrow underneath.

"What are you doing? You idiot," I said. I could hear him snorting, almost as if he had located a mouse or a cat, or perhaps he had smelt something rancid. "Come on," I encouraged. I dropped to my knees, took hold of him by the torso and tried to coax him away. He came out from underneath and his head sprung up, as if it was on a coil. "Let's go," I said. "Back home."

As I was still on my knees, I stretched forward to have a look under the bed. Much to my surprise there was something solid there. A black shape. I had zero idea what it could be, other than it was a box of some description. Maybe not so much a box, more like a chest. I stretched my arms out, reached forward as far as possible, put my hands on either side of the box and pulled it out across the carpet. It was a chest. Made of slatted wood. About a foot square. Dark wood. Like a small, pirate's treasure chest. There was a metal plate attached to it with some words engraved into the metal in a Cyrillic language. I had no idea what they said.

I took the lid, gave it a tug and it came open. The chest was full of white sheets of paper with what looked like handwritten lists scribed onto them. I quickly thumbed through the sheets. I could see and smell they were old. The writing, all hand written in blue fountain pen ink was hardly legible. What I did see was the Nazi insignia at the top of each page. There must have been fifty sheets, maybe more. I took all the sheets, carefully so as not to rip them along the crease, took them out and placed them on the floor. What I found underneath them amazed me. A set of old, dog-eared and partially cracked black and white photographs, probably dating back sixty years ago, possibly more. Mostly close-up, single mug shots of women staring ahead at the camera. All of them were wearing a similar dark jacket, with the insignia on the left arm. Like a crescent shape crest or emblem and what could have been wings and a swastika.

I put my eyes back on the first sheet of what I assumed were lists of names, but I had no way of knowing for certain. It looked like a list of names from top to bottom, maybe forty per sheet, then six columns from left to right. The fusty smell of the paper and the dust went up my nostrils and made me sneeze. I examined the lists. The first column was a name, or so I thought, followed by two digits in the second column. This may have been an age. The third column might have been the name of a town or a city, or a district or whatever. The fourth had a single word in it. I didn't know what it was. Then a fifth column which may have contained the name of a place. The sixth and final column had in the vast majority of them a X written there in either red or blue pen. It appeared to me as if different writers had written the X's as they were different shapes and colours of ink. Six columns of information, going across the sheet from left to right.

Each sheet must have had forty rows on them, from top to bottom. There must have been fifty sheets. At the top of each sheet was a date, written in hand, in a language that may have been German.

I didn't have a clue what they were or what they represented. I was intrigued by the Nazi insignia. The swastika inside a circle on the top of each page, plump centre. I turned my attention back to the black and white photographs. There were about two dozen of them. All the same size. All the faces looked at the camera with blank, stiff and stern stares on them. Then I turned the photographs over and saw the same swastika image embossed onto them. A cold waft of draught came over me. Were these the faces of concentration camp guards? They didn't look like anyone who had been forced to wear a uniform. A victim of Nazi repression. I swiftly collected the photographs and carefully arranged them together. I looked at them, one at a time. Of the twenty-four photos, only two appeared to be male. The sitters were all in an age range of say twenty-two to thirty-five years of age. Though, of course, it was impossible to be accurate. If I had to guess I would say that the mean age was twenty-nine. The mode was probably the same. Could it really be that I was looking at the faces of some prison camp guards?

Chipper came to sit by my side. He puckered his nose at the fusty smell of the sheets of paper. Despite the age the quality of paper was quite good, so they were not too flimsy. I had no idea what I was looking at. No idea if I had found something of interest. I turned my eyes back to the photos and examined the faces once again. Almost as if the answer would jump out at me. It didn't. I could only guess on how

Greta had acquired this treasure trove of material. The women in the photos tended to be similar. Similar faces, hairstyles. Same blunt, humourless expressions. Perhaps they had been forced to have their photo taken, against their will. They were mostly blonde. Aryan race. Not one of them looked like a young Greta, but why would they? She was a victim. Not a perpetrator of crimes of man's inhumanity to man. A thought occurred to me. Had Greta taken the lists and the photos when the Bergen-Belsen camp was liberated? Maybe she had been able to sneak into the commandant's office and take them to present as evidence to those who would investigate Nazi crimes. But she had never handed them to the British liberators.

Chipper had gone out of the room. I heard him sneeze, then bark. "Chipper, Shush," I chastised, forcing the words out through gritted teeth. He may have been warning me about a returning tenant or someone outside the door. I took hold of him and held him tight. I stayed motionless. I didn't hear a sound. A glance at my wrist told me the time was eight-fifteen.

After a pause of about ten seconds, or so, I collected the white, fragile sheets together, then the photos and placed them all back into the box. I wondered if this is what the burglars were looking for, but then again, perhaps they were nobody but opportunists who had somehow learned that the tenant had passed away. Knowing her to be Jewish they assumed she had left loads of value merchandise for them to steal. It probably had nothing to do with the items in the box, or the blue envelopes containing the letters, but maybe it had. They were more historical value than anything else. I still had no idea what the lists were. No idea at all. I wondered why Ms Grabowski would leave them lying in the box? Gathering dust for eternity. I closed the lid, took the box and placed it on the mattress, then I got to my feet. My thighs ached for twenty seconds. Geez, I had to get back into the gym and use the leg-press machine, sometime soon. Once I was steady on my feet, I took the box, held it tight under my arm and carried it to the door, out onto the corridor and up to the front door, whispering at Chipper to come with me. The box wasn't heavy, far from it. We got to the door, I opened it and tentatively peered out to see if anyone was on the corridor. There was no one. Then I realised I had forgotten to collect the twenty or so blue envelopes, so I went back into the living room to collect them from where I had left them on top of the sideboard. I placed all of the envelopes into the box, then I stepped out, back along the corridor to the front door, then out and locked the door behind me. Chipper followed me, and we headed up the staircase to the first floor. We were back in my flat in less than twenty seconds with the box in my possession. I consulted my watch. It was twenty past eight. Leah wouldn't be home until about ten-fifteen.

Actually, on this night, she didn't arrived home until ten-thirty. Her face was red and flushed. The book club was little more than an excuse for a group of ladies to get together to meet and enjoy a good selection of libations, usually in the form of prosecco.

"How did it go?" I asked her.

"That was one of the most boring books I had ever had to discuss," she said with a slurp.

I widened my eyes and pursed my lips. "Okay. What's next on the reading list?" I enquired.

"Flaming *Gone with the Wind*," she retorted.

"Oh dear. Who chose that?"

She sighed. "Megan 'bloody' Coverdale."

I knew Megan to nod to. "Sounds about right," I said grinning like a Cheshire cat.

Chapter Eight

Thursday 8th June

Four days went by in the blink of an eye. It was Thursday evening. I got home from work at 7pm. It was now nearly three weeks since Ms Grabowski's body had been discovered. Four days after I had found the box under the bed. I had hidden it in a cupboard, used for storage, in the spare bedroom. If I showed Leah the contents, she would badger me into giving it to the authorities, but that would reveal I had taken it out of the flat, without anyone's permission. The consequences could be serious. The key to the flat was another issue, I no longer wanted it and was half thinking about contacting Mr. Amis to request he collect it from me at the first available opportunity. We had still not heard from him about when the men were coming to fix the window frame, because it still hadn't been done. I have to admit that I did think about going back into the flat and returning the box to the place I found it. But, in truth, I was too intrigued by what it contained and what I had discovered. What were the list of names? Assuming they were names. Were they a list of some of the people who had perished in the gas chambers in Dachau? I knew from my research that there were no gas chambers at Bergen-Belsen, just a lot of detainees crammed into a small place. Who were the black and white photos of? The Nazi insignia perhaps suggested they were camp guards. Then there were the letters. Perhaps they might explain what the lists were and whose faces are on the photos.

    The letters looked to be written in a language that wasn't German. Maybe Greta spoke another language: Hungarian, Ukrainian, Czech, Slovakian or whatever. In truth, I didn't know if there was a language called Slovakian.

In order to learn more about the Bergen-Belsen camp I went on-line for an hour to look up all the links I could find. They were, by and large, ghastly and horrific. The camp was constructed as a POW facility, but in 1944 it was expanded to take in a host of different groups of people. This was because of the advance of the Red Army across huge sways of Nazi captured land in Poland, and today, modern-day Ukraine. Prisoners in other camps had to be transferred west. In Bergen-Belsen disease and starvation spread like wildfire. The camp became a Concentration camp for Jews, gypsies, political undesirables, and anyone the Nazis had a problem with. There was a separate women's camp, containing mostly Jewish inmates. Many of the five hundred or so SS guards committed heinous crimes, along with many of the capos. Capos were mainly non-Germans who assisted the Nazi's to run the camps. It was estimated that as many as 70,000 to 100,000 people may have perished in Bergen-Belsen.

When the camp was liberated on 15th of March 1945, the scenes that greeted the liberators were like something from a living hell. There were up to 16,000 corpses of men, woman, and babies littering the site that was believed to be approximately forty-five acres in size. Some of the senior SS guards and the camp commander were detained to answer for their crimes. Some of them were executed following trials. However, it is believed that a good number of the female guards were never arrested and managed to escape in the mayhem and chaos that ensued. Most by simply melting in with the inmates and fleeing. There were still some small-scale skirmishes between the allies and Germans taking place in and around the camp even though the commander had agreed to the allies' demand that he surrender the camp.

The head of the SS, Heidrich Himmler, had issued orders that as much of the evidence of Nazi atrocities be hidden from view, but this proved to be a virtually impossible task, mainly because of the speed of the allies' advance. When the British, Canadians and Americans entered the camp the crimes were all there to be seen. It led the former, BBC presenter Richard Dimbleby, one of the first reporters to arrive at the camp, to describe the scenes that greeted the liberators as some of the most unimaginable to humankind.

Wow, I thought when I read the accounts. How had Greta Grabowski, an Austrian Jew, transferred from Dachau to Bergen-Belsen in 1944, survived? It was because she was young and could play both the violin and piano to the camp guards. The infamous Josef Kramer was the camp commandant. He was tried for his crimes, found guilty and executed in December 1945. Some, if not all, of the female guards who had moved west with the prisoners were just as bad as their male counterparts. Of course, I knew something about the 'final solution' of the Jewish problem, but not the extent to which the Nazis had gone. I felt sickened to the stomach. After reading the accounts I was determined to learn more about the lady we had lived above.

The company I worked for 'Heathcote & Hamilton' occasionally employed an organisation, based in Bloomsbury for translation services. If I took a couple of the letters to them, they would, for a fee, translate them into English for me. That way I could read what they said. It might cost me anything between £200 to £400, but it would be worth it.

The following day, Friday 9th, I put in a call to Translation Services, from my own mobile phone whilst I sat at my desk, during my lunch-time break. I didn't want my company to accuse me of a conflict of interest, so I did it in my own time and on my own phone. I called them using my name, not that of 'Heathcote & Hamilton'.

The upshot was that if I posted the letters to them, or better still if I came into their office, they'd do the translating and let me have them back in a few days. I replied by saying the letter paper was a bit old and flimsy so the best thing for me to do was to drop in there in person. I agreed to go to the office after the weekend, on Monday, during my lunch break to give them five of the letters. I had a couple of days to think about it. With plenty of time to change my mind if I wanted to back out. I didn't. I was determined to go through with it.

Monday 12th June
  Before I left home for work on Monday morning, I randomly selected five of the twenty-four letters. Leah had already left for her school job, so she didn't see me selecting them. I chose five of the letters ranging in dates from what I thought was April 1942 to March 1945. I had no idea what they would reveal. Knowing my luck, I'd probably chosen five letters that wouldn't tell me much. I knew from my conversation with 'Translation Services', that they would charge me £50 per letter. £250 in total. I had that money in cash in my pocket. I did wonder if I was throwing money down the drain. It was one reason why I didn't tell Leah. She would have gone spare if she knew how much I was spending. However, I was still very much intrigued by the content and dying to know what they said. I knew from my limited knowledge of German, that they weren't written in that language. The more I thought about it, the more I was convinced the language was Czech, Hungarian, or even Serbo-Croat. I didn't think they were either Russian or Ukrainian. What I did know is that they weren't one of the widely spoken European languages, such as Spanish or French, or one of the less common languages like Italian or Dutch. After so many years some of the ink had faded but I didn't think this would hinder the person doing the

translating as logic would determine the next word. The quality of paper was quite good. All in all, I assumed the person doing the translating wouldn't have a massive problem trying to decipher them.

I could imagine the chaos in Europe at the end of the war in 1945, with millions of displaced people wandering around the continent. Some wanting to return to their homeland or others wanting to head west to avoid falling under Soviet influence. Many of the low countries, Holland and Belgium and parts of France would have been chaotic. After all this was in the day well before computers and IT systems to keep track of people. Europe after the war must have been a complete basket case. There would be no surprise that displaced people like Greta Grabowski with no family remaining in Austria would have been eager to get into the relevant calm of England in 1947. But hey, I was no expert on such matters. Neither was I an expert on the holocaust. But I could just about imagine the turmoil and chaos at the time.

When I got to work on Monday, I informed my colleagues that I was going to take a slightly longer lunch break than normal, as I had a personal task to do in Bloomsbury. I would stay until five-thirty to make up for the time. I didn't mind working for Heathcote & Hamilton'. It wasn't a bad firm to work for. My job was to calculate risk where movements in currency were concerned. We used formulas and logarithms to calculate insurance premiums for companies involved in large purchases of currencies to offset a loss should the value of a currency suddenly dip due to a revaluation, and major shocks caused by war, political turmoil and even natural disasters. I had worked here for six years. I was in the middle management bracket. I enjoyed a competitive salary and perks and bonuses. The senior management team often used the threat of redundancy to get their pound of flesh. It never came to anything. If one of the senior team left or retired, I thought there was a good chance I would get a leg up the greasy pole. Though, several of my colleagues would have said the same.

It was one pm when I left the office in Canary Wharf. I took a taxi into the centre of the city. I was arriving outside of the office of 'Translation Services' at one-thirty. It was on a side street running off Judd Street in the heart of Bloomsbury. I had five of the blue envelopes in my document holder. Actually, there were two sheets in each envelope, with scrawling back-to-back writing on each sheet, making four sides in total. The writing wasn't the biggest, but neither was it small.

The office of 'Translation Services' wasn't much to write home about. Just a narrow store front, between a ladies' hairdressing salon on one side and a sandwich shop on the other. The front was a door, a plate glass window, then beyond that a counter, so in effect it was like a food takeaway shop. Behind the counter was a frosted glass window in front of an office. A light was burning behind the glass. I opened the front door and stepped inside. The setting was bland. A plain tile floor. There was a calendar and some notice about upcoming events at a local music venue. Some information about what the firm provided on plain blanch walls. As I entered the premises a single chime sounded. I stepped up to the counter. My black leather document holder was tight under my arm. There was no one at the counter, but that changed in an instant when a glass door swung open and a grey-haired lady emerged from the office. She was wearing a tweed jacket and skirt combination. Thick rimmed bifocals over her eyes. The lenses had those little semi-circular inserts for close up reading. She looked in my direction and smiled. "How can I help you?" she enquired.

"I called the other day. I have five letters I want translating."

She didn't ask me for my name or how I had acquired the letters. It was nothing to do with her.

I opened the zip of my document holder, dipped my hand inside and extracted the envelopes. Taking my time to handle them carefully to emphasis they were a tad flimsy.

"They're old. A bit fragile," I emphasised. I carefully and deliberately placed them down, one at a time on the counter top. "I'm not sure what language they are," I said. She sniffed, perhaps smelling the aroma of old paper. She could see that the paper was indeed old, but not like something from a medieval manuscript. I explained that I had selected five letters from a haul of twenty-four. Telling her that I had found them in a biscuit tin I had discovered in the attic in my home. I don't know if she believed me. She probably didn't care that much. I told her that each envelope contained two sheets, with back-to-back writing on each sheet, no doubt to save paper at the time. She didn't say a word. She never asked me where I had got them. She must have believed what I told her. Just then the door, leading onto the street, opened and a chap appeared. Ironically, perhaps, he was carrying a document holder not too dissimilar to my own.

The lady took the first envelope, and carefully extracted the first of the two sheets. She lifted it close to her eyes to examine the writing and poured them over the text. I could see her eyes moving and the reflection of the blue paper in the lens of her spectacles.

"It looks like Hungarian to me," she said, without looking at me. I chanced a glance behind me to see who the chap was, but he didn't look like anyone I knew or recognised.

"Okay," I replied. "I did wonder," I added. Now I knew for sure it wasn't a secret code.

"No, it's definitely Hungarian." She placed the sheet on the counter, then ran her eyes over the other four envelopes, but didn't pick any of them up.

The door behind her came open and a chap in his fifties came to attend to the new customer. He handed the fellow a file from his holder then left immediately. Just saying he'd be back in three days.

"When do you want them back?" she asked me.

"As soon as you're able to provide me with a transcript," I replied. "What about the payment?" I asked.

"One hundred and eighty pounds," she said. "Come back on Wednesday at this time. We should have them ready for you by then."

"Thanks. I'll do. What about payment?

"Pay us when you return," she said.

"Fair enough," I replied. "Will cash do?"

"Cash is fine."

"Good. I'll see you on Wednesday," I said smiling at her. I assisted her to pick up the five envelopes. It was a few moments before I left the shop, vowing to return in two days to collect the transcripts. I wedged the now empty document holder under my arm as I stepped out onto the pavement.

Chapter Nine

That Monday evening, I arrived home at seven pm. Another day at work had been wiped off the calendar. I calculated that I only had another six thousand, five hundred days of work before I retired. Not that I wanted to wish my life away, or anything. If the truth be told, I didn't mind my job or having to go to work for a living. Loads of people did it.

It was close to seven-thirty when I settled down with Leah for a simple pasta meal with shreds of chicken in a rich tomato sauce. We consumed half a bottle of red wine between us. We were both feeling a little light headed by nine. I had just sat down to watch the tv, some documentary on BBC2, when the telephone rang.

It turned out to be a chap who introduced himself as Simon Greenberg. I didn't know anyone of that name and asked him who he was. He said he was calling from the local Golders Green synagogue. He was returning the call I had made to him. What was it? Getting on for nine days ago. I wasn't sure when it was. Still, he was calling me back. Which was good of him.

I had little reason to doubt he was who he said he was. I wondered how he had got my landline telephone number? I asked him. He had called my mobile, got no reply, then heard the recorded message on which I read out the landline number. It was as simple as that.

"What can I do for you?" he enquired, after he had reminded me that I had called the synagogue first.

"I thought I'd better inform you about the passing of Greta Grabowski," I said. "She was a Jewish lady who lived in the same house as us. In fact, it's not a house, it's a block of flats. She passed away about three weeks ago." I'd lost the precise date. The time seemed to have gone so quickly.

"Who?" he asked.

"Greta Grabowski. She was, I gather, eighty-three years of age." It was then that I wondered if she had ever visited the synagogue. There was no reason to assume that was the case. Maybe she had, but had stopped attending some years before Leah and I arrived here.

"Where did she reside?" Greenberg asked. Talking to him on the phone, I couldn't hazard a guess at his age, though he did sound more middle aged then a young or older man.

"In the block of flats just off Park View, close to the park. Just off Cleardown Gardens. In the Temple Fortune part of the green."

To be honest everywhere in Golders Green was close to Temple Fortune. It was a central thoroughfare running through the neighbourhood.

"It's not a name I'm aware of," he replied.

I was confused. "What Park View House or Ms Grabowski?" I asked.

"The name of the deceased lady."

"Oh. Okay. No harm done." There was a pregnant pause. "What's your role at the synagogue? If you don't mind me asking?" I asked as a kind of filler question.

"I'm a deputy," he said. I had no idea what that meant. He seemed to grasp my confusion. "I assist the chief rabbi to run the synagogue," he clarified.

"Okay," I uttered in reply.

He asked for my name, which I was happy to give him. Then I confirmed my address. Telling him it was about a quarter of a mile from the main Golders Green synagogue, the Jewish cemetery and the crematorium.

He said he knew the building.

"Will you check if Ms Grabowski was ever a member of the synagogue?" I asked. To be honest I didn't know if the synagogue had members like a social club. The terminology was alien to me.

Simon Greenberg said he would check and get back to me in a few days' time. I thanked him for calling me back, then referred to a funeral. I went on to explain that she had no known family that I or Mr Amis, from the property management company, knew about. If she wasn't a practising member of the Jewish community, how did we go about organising a funeral for her? He admitted that he didn't know. Nothing, according to him, similar to this episode had occurred before. He said he would have to consult with the rabbi.

I thanked him again for his call and for promising to speak to the rabbi and get back to me. We chatted about when I could expect his follow-up call, then we said goodbye and parted company. To be honest, I had no idea why I was concerned about a funeral. Perhaps, it was a sense of guilt that I hadn't gone down to the flat sooner to ask if she was okay. It was nothing to do with me. I simply wanted to ensure she had a funeral arranged by the synagogue.

I had only just put the telephone down on Simon Greenberg when, ten minutes, later it rang again. The time was nine-thirty. It was Steven Amis. He apologised for calling this late in the evening. I told him it wasn't a problem. He told me that tomorrow, Tuesday, Ms Grabowski's flat was going to be emptied. He had made contact with a storage company, based over in Wembley. They would be here, first thing at 7am, to begin the task. They envisaged it would take about six hours to empty the place. Everything: furniture and fittings, personal possessions, clothing, carpets, curtains. The entire kit and caboodle. It was all going into a storage unit until it was decided what to do with it. Apparently, investigations were underway in Austria to determine if she had any relatives there. They might be entitled to the contents; plus, anything she had left in the bank. I didn't tell him she had at least £11,000 in two accounts. Enquiries were underway with solicitors to discover if she had left a will. If not and if no relatives could be found she would be legally categorised as dying, 'instate', in which case everything of value would go to the British crown. Mr Amis also told me the repair to the window would be carried out tomorrow. The frame was to be replaced in its entirety. A conservation order had been the cause of the delay. It had taken him a while to find a firm who still made the old type of wooden window frame.

While I was chatting to Steven, I informed him that I had spoken to Simon Greenberg at a Golders Green synagogue about a funeral, though there was nothing to suggest she was ever an active member of the community. I was waiting for a call back from him once he had been able to chat to the senior rabbi. We ended the conversation at this point and went our separate ways. I had just put the phone down when it rang again. It was Steven Amis again. He had forgotten to ask me about the key. I said I still had it. He asked me if I'd give it to one of the men who arrived tomorrow. I said okay.

"Oh, just a second," he said just as I was about to put the phone down. "My memory isn't what it used to be."

"Why is that?" I enquired.

"Earlier today, I received a telephone call from a man with a German accent."

"Okay. What about?" I enquired.

"About getting access to Ms Grabowski's things."

"Oh right," I said.

"I told him he'd have to give us some ID to say he was a family member. Before we'd entertain allowing him to take anything. Do you recall meeting this chap?"

"As it happens, I do. She used to be visited by a chap who spoke German. A large portly chap. Perhaps late seventies or so. I told the police about him."

"Did you ever see this chap with Ms Grabowski?"

"A couple of times."

"When?"

"Months ago. Stepping out of the house together. I don't have a clue who he is, but I'd seen him a couple of times in the past year or so."

"What's he like?"

"To look at?"

"Yes."

"He's about six feet two tall. Twenty stones. Hairless head. Hands like buckets. Round, well lined and creased face. I saw him at the door to the flat just after her death. He even tried the door then asked me if I had a key. That's when I told him he'd be better off speaking to you."

"He asked me for the right to look through her possessions. I told him not without legal authorisation."

I didn't say anything for a second, then said. "Him asking me about a key gave me the cobble-wobbles. I mean he was pretty adamant." I stalled for a second. "I wonder if he was the chap behind the break-in?" I added.

"I was thinking the same thing," Amis said.

"He wasn't the one I saw. But it doesn't mean to say he wasn't behind it." I went on to inform him about the car I had seen parked on the cul-de-sac. It was the old-style Mercedes. "I wonder if there is a connection?" I enquired.

Mr Amis didn't know what to think. Like me, he could only speculate that there was a connection between him and the chap I saw climbing out of the window. It was now getting a bit too hairy for words. It was at this point that I thought about the wooden box containing the list of names and the photographs.

"Tell me," I said. "Did the chap make any reference to a specific item?"

He thought about it for a second. "No. Nothing specific. What like?"

"Like the paintings on the walls." In that moment I knew that I had made an error. My mistake pounded in my chest. I had inadvertently revealed that I had been inside the flat. I had previously told him I'd never been further than the doorway. He didn't appear to instantly recall our previous conversation. I sought of a way to end the conversation before I really dropped myself in it, or before he twigged that I knew more about the contents than I had let on.

"I'll ensure I give the key to one of the chaps who arrive in the morning. I'll ask him to ensure it gets back to you. Oh, just a second, my wife is calling me from the kitchen I have to go. I'll speak to you later. Bye."

He said 'goodbye' and ended the call. I dropped the receiver into the cradle and drew in a deep sigh of breath. The revelation that the German man was looking for something in the flat was a game changer. Was it the box containing the sheets and the photographs? Was it the blue envelopes containing the letters? One or the other? Or both?

Chapter Ten

Tuesday 13th June

Mr Amis was good to his word. The very next morning at a quarter past seven a large white van pulled up in front of the house. It was a removals van. It had the logo of a removal company on the side, above the words: 'Wembley A1 Removals.' I watched two men, both wearing khaki overalls, climb out of the cabin. They went to the back, opened a pair of swing doors and dropped a ramp. Two other men, also wearing overalls, emerged out into the light. I had considered storing some furniture in a facility in Wembley when Leah and I were in between moves, five years ago. They weren't cheap.

This morning, I was up at six. I hadn't been able to sleep. Though, right now as I took in a gulp of coffee, I did feel my eyelids drooping.

One of the chaps came up the steps, went through the front door and came inside. He had been given a key to the front door. I could hear his heavy booted feet on the staircase. Twenty seconds later there was a knock at the door to my flat. I opened it to a smiling face. He said his name was Terry something or other, I didn't catch his surname, not that it had any importance. He asked me for the key to flat number 1. I was happy to give it to him. It was out of my hands for good. I never wanted it in the first place. I could hear voices from below of the other three men discussing how they were going to get every single item out of the flat in six hours. The van was a large size. They just might get everything inside, but six hours. I was sceptical, but I don't know why was I bothered.

I was glad to get rid of the key. It had hung around my neck like a millstone. Terry thanked me and said he would hand it personally to Mr Amis. I said 'fine' and thanked him. Wembley was only a couple of miles from here. At least the operatives wouldn't have to travel far once they got everything out.

I departed for work at seven-forty-five. I accompanied Leah to the school where she was based. It wasn't far from here. Close to the north-west tip of Hampstead Heath. I carried on walking the short distance to Golders Green railway station for first leg of my journey to work, the second leg was a tube from Kings Cross to Westferry.

My day at work went without any trials or tribulations. Again, I heard some talk about the possibility of redundancies to reduce costs. If they got rid of some of the senior execs, they'd save money. Most of them did bugger all for their inflated salaries and expense accounts. It was always those at the middle management level who got it in the neck. I was sick and tired of it. I earned an annual salary of close to £80,000 with bonuses on top, and a share option scheme. Leah earned about £23,000 a year as a dyslexia specialist. We were very much comfortable, but not always. We still had to pay bills and find the £1,000 a month for the rent. My wife only worked part-time, term time only, so she had plenty of free time, but it wasn't as simple as that. She was still required to prepare for her teaching commitments. She had been considering going into private practice as a consultant especially to a number of fee-paying schools in this area. She might make more money than her current salary, but there was the work-life balance to consider. The Golders Green, Finchley and Hampstead triangle was well-to-do. There were some big homes in these parts and a lot of money.

As I had not been at home all day, by the time I got home at six-thirty, I assumed that the removal men had completed the task of taking everything out of the flat. Plus, the maintenance crew had replaced the window frame. As I couldn't hear a thing on my return, I assumed it had all been completed.

Wednesday 14th June

Wednesday soon came around. Today, I had to visit the office of 'Translation Services' in Bloomsbury to collect the transcripts of the five letters. I assumed they had completed the task. I had not heard from them to say otherwise. I was looking forward to reading the content. It would be interesting to gauge if they shed any light on Greta's previous life and experiences in a concentration camp. There was no guarantee they would. Perhaps she had taken them from out of a drawer, or whatever, in the camp commandment's office in the hours before the fall. Apparently, Henrich Himmler, himself, the head honcho of the SS, at the time, had negotiated the surrender of the camp to the allied forces. That still didn't stop him being a war criminal. Within a day or two of the liberation the British 11th armoured corps had bulldozed thousands of corpses into pits, then erased the barracks from the face of the earth in a firestorm. A fitting end to such a terrible place. Perhaps the lists were the names of fellow inmates and she kept them as a personal reminder. Though that seemed a tad farfetched. Even in the fog of war. For she must have been traumatised by what she had seen with her own eyes. Consider that she was only twenty-seven or twenty-eight years of age in 1945. How do you deal with the trauma?

    Yesterday, I had asked to take Wednesday afternoon off as annual leave. I did get six weeks, thirty days in total. The company had a staff of about sixty, ranging from the senior execs to office juniors and students taking a year out on a sandwich degree course. I sort of thought my job was safe with the current calibre of graduates coming through the system, though I couldn't be cocksure.

I left the office at a shade after one-thirty. Thirty minutes later than I had planned. I took a cab from outside of Westferry dockland station, across the five or six miles of central London and arrived on Judd Street at five to two. I briskly walked down the street, turned into the side street and entered the offices of 'Translation Services.'

I presented myself at the counter and was served by the same lady I had spoken to on Monday. She went into the office and returned a minute later holding a stiff backed A4 size manila envelope. I felt the urge to open the envelope and read the first of the translated letters, but instead I showed some decorum and controlled my eagerness. I could read them at my leisure once I was home. I popped the stiff envelope into my document holder, then I paid the £180.00 fee in nine, crisp twenty-pound notes.

When I had received a receipt, I stepped out of the office, onto the street and made my way towards Euston Road. I did contemplate dropping into a pub for a beer and a sandwich, but elected to carry walking towards Kings Cross station from where I could catch a northern line tube train to Golders Green. It was nearly the middle of the month. Getting on for four weeks after the discovery of Ms Grabowski's body. I liked London in the summer, but not when it got really, really hot, humid and sticky. Today was manageable.

On this afternoon I was home for three-fifteen. I'd missed the rush-hour which usually commenced at about three-thirty until six-thirty. It tended to put at least another forty-five minutes on my journey home.

Chapter Eleven

The moment I got home, I recalled I had agreed with Leah that I would start the evening meal, so although I was keen to get into the letters, I first went into the kitchen. We always had salmon steaks on a Wednesday. Today was no different. I got the salad ready and took the mayo-garlic sauce from out of the fridge. It was a simple meal. I took the steaks from the fridge, opened a drawer and took out a roll of tinfoil. I ripped off four segments, brushed a little oil on the fish, then wrapped them in the tinfoil. I put them on a baking tray, turned on the oven, opened the door and slide the tray onto the top shelf. I added a drizzle of oil to the salad, tossed it, and added a few sliced tomatoes. Leah would be home at six, therefore the salmon should be about cooked on a low heat.

Now that I had started the preparation for the evening meal I went back into the lounge, took my document holder, unzipped it open and extracted the stiff manila envelope.

Before I could open the envelope to take out the transcripts the landline telephone rang. "What the...," I said to myself outloud. I assumed it would be Leah asking me if I was home and to remind me to put the salmon into the oven. I sighed, then jumped up off the sofa. "I've done'em," I said. I reached out, grasped the ringing receiver and lifted it out of the cradle.

"Yes," I half snapped down the line. There was a silence, though I thought I detected a presence at the other end of the line. A tinny rattle reached my ears.

"We've got your wife," said a far-off voice.

I was knocked back a touch. "What?" I enquired.

"We've got your wife," the voice repeated in the same tone and cadence.

"What? What do you mean?" I was having trouble understanding simple English. I was dazed and confused.

"We've…got…your…wife," said the caller, inserting a second between each word. Probably even longer. I thought the speaker had an accent. It sounded like a French accent. Definitely European. German, possibly. But it sounded more Mediterranean. I was dumfounded by the exchange.

"What do you mean?" I asked again.

"We want the contents of the box. We know you've got it."

"What box?" I was on auto pilot, just responding aimlessly to what the caller was saying. I had gone from a high to a low in less than a millisecond. From joy to despair. But it was more than that. My cognizance kicked in a touch. "You've got my wife? Where?" I asked.

No answer. My chest felt like a punctured sack. As if all the air had been forced out of my lungs and they were about to collapse. My heartbeat seemed to have been plugged into the mains. The hairs on the back of neck were standing on end stiff. Like the stiff leather studs on an old-fashioned pair of rugby boots.

"My wife?" I asked as if puzzled by the combination of words.

"That's right." The accent, the slight over pronunciation of the words. As if someone was trying to be too precise. To speak perfect English. It didn't sound like the man I had spoken to at the door of Ms Grabowski's flat. It wasn't him. The voice sounded thirty to forty years younger. The command of English was far better.

"What do you want?" I asked.

"The wooden box."

"What wooden box?"

"The one you take."

My heart was beating profusely. I didn't know what to do or whether I wanted to visit the toilet, have a shave, or a haircut. My life had been turned upside down in a heartbeat.

"Where is she?" I asked.

"She here."

I now thought I detected more of a German accent. The speaker's pretence to speak English like a local had slipped. A new voice came down the line.

"Alan," I hardly recognised my own name or Leah's voice come tumbling down the line. "Give them what they want," she said.

The speaker must have been pulled from her hand.

"We want the chest. The wood box," said the voice.

"Or else."

"Or else? Or else what?" I wished I hadn't said it like that.

"We hurt her." I heard a thud followed by a shout. The sound seemed to be more manufactured than anything else, but I wasn't sure. "We give you one hour. We call back in one hour to arrange to you to give us the chest." There was a click and the line went dead.

"Wait," I shouted, but it was too late. The caller had gone. I couldn't do anything but gaze at the telephone for what seemed like thirty seconds, but was nowhere as long as that. They, whoever they were, had my wife. They wanted the box and the contents I had taken from under the bed. How in God's name did they know I had it?

A series of questions began to rifle through my head like a barrage of incoming projectiles. Had someone seen me take it from out of the flat? That was unlikely, but I couldn't be sure. Then I remembered the chap who had entered the office of 'Translation Services' after me. Had he seen me and heard me discussing what I required translating? Was he one of those who had broken into the flat? Then I wondered about Steven Amis. Had he informed them that the box wasn't one of the items the removal men had taken out of the flat? Then it hit me like a sledgehammer. The chaps who had emptied the flat could have been bribed to find a chest. Had they been paid by someone to lookout for the wooden chest and give it to them? But it wasn't in the flat. Not on the list of items they had taken out. So, whoever had paid them, knew I had a key and assumed I had taken the chest.

    I stepped back to the edge of the sofa and sat down in the seat I had vacated. My mind was still in a state of flux. Scrambled. Scores of thoughts were going through my mind. The synapses in my brain were opening and closing like a myriad of doors opening, then slamming closed in a fierce force-nine gale.

    What if I called DI Cillian Doyle? Told him that my wife had been abducted. Oddly enough the kidnappers hadn't advised me not to call the cops. Did they think I wouldn't consider doing that? Or they just forgot to mention it. I still had DI Doyle's card in my jeans pocket. I sat back into the soft backrest and crossed my legs. I glanced down at the stiff cardboard envelope and took out the first of the letters. The transcribed words were on a plain, white A4 size sheet. I held it in my hands and read what was written on it:

*** *** ***

April 1942

Dear (the name was blanked out)
I am writing to express my deep love for you. Times have been hard here in (blanked out). My commandant is a good Nazi believer, and is a firm believer that the nation will be triumphant, and the Reich will deliver for all.
I am getting good food here with plenty of nourishment. I hope you are too. I pray for the victory of the party over the bolshevist, communist scum and those who the Fuhrer wants to banish from our lands.

All my colleague and friends are good people and believe in the strength of the Nazi party, the cause, and the leadership of our glorious leader and that final victory will be ours.

I couldn't read anymore. My mind was numb. I couldn't take in the words or make any sense of them. It was all gobbledygook. On the spare of the moment, I jumped up off the sofa, went to the table and grasped my mobile phone. I tapped the figure 9 into the face, then the second 9. Before I hit the third 9, I turned off the phone. My head was in a spin. Almost as if an invisible mist had invaded my mind. I returned to the sofa, picked up the white sheet and carried on reading the text.

…. For the glory of our national socialism against those pigs the bolshevists and the tyranny of the British and their lackey friends. This is why we must continue to fight for what is right and reverse the cruelty placed upon us.

The Fuhrer is right. We couldn't continue to live with their rules and whims. The White German race are not their slaves. When the day the Fuhrer is triumphant will be the day we are released. We shall continue to carry out his orders to rid ourselves of the enemy within. The Jews. The German race is the master race.

We have believers here, and I learn that our comrades are excelling on all fronts and victory for our glorious Reich is close. So long and goodbye. Until I written again. My Love and kisses.

That was it. The name of the writer was blanked out, along the senders' address. I had stopped taking in the words a few sentences ago. However, from the gist I did take in it sounded like someone who was a keen supporter of the war and the Reich.

Perhaps, Greta had taken them from the camp commander office or from a prison guard. Perhaps they were love letters, but there wasn't much evidence of love. Maybe a male to a male, or, vice-versa, a female to a female. I didn't know and perhaps more to the point at this time in my life I didn't much care.

It was getting on for twenty minutes since the call from the mystery person to tell me my wife had been abducted, and they wanted the wooden chest containing the lists of names in return for her coming home. I debated in my mind what to do. I didn't have any choice. Her safe return was my first and only priority. I once again considered contacting DI Doyle or DI Arnold, then I recalled the caller had said I had one hour to decide what to do. At that moment I decided to wait for the second call to tell them I was willing to give them the chest, so long as they guaranteed Leah's safe return. Then I realised they had not asked about the letters. Only the content of the chest. The lists and the photographs. Maybe they didn't know that the letters existed or perhaps they didn't care. I decided to tough it out, to wait for the call. I wouldn't call the police. I honestly don't know if I was being stupid or what. I would contact the police as soon as Leah was free. Then I had an idea. I got up off the sofa, went out of the room, stepped across the corridor and entered the second bedroom. I made straight for a storage unit, opened the double doors, reached up to the top shelf and took a hardback case containing my Pentax camera. I brought it back into the lounge. As I came into the room, I could smell the fragrance of the salmon cooking in the oven. I had just opened the kitchen door when the alarm on the unit went off. I turned off the oven, then pulled the hatch open to let a wave of hot air escape. Armed with the camera I went back into the lounge. My head was racing. Mostly away from me. I recalled that I had placed the chest at the bottom of the same storage unit, so I had to go back into the bedroom.

When I was back in the lounge, I opened the chest and took everything out, then went to the table we used as a dining table, come drop for newspapers and other things. I arranged the fifty sheets out in rows and columns, from left to right, from top to bottom, then the photos in four rows of six across.

I opened the camera case, took it out and turned it on. I leant over the sheets, put the viewfinder to my eye and began to take individual snaps of the sheets, going from left to right, from top to bottom. Because I knew I didn't have a lot of film I only took photos of six of the sheets, but I did get all the twenty-four photographs of the people in the black and white images. When I was happy I had enough I put the sheets and the photographs back into the chest and closed the lid. I remembered to turn off the camera and put it back into the case.

Chapter Twelve

It was now nearly one hour since I had spoken to one of the abductors. The time was getting on for five-thirty. Outside, I could hear birds chirping, despite it not being that warm outside. Low cloud had it overcast and a bit grey. Chipper was in his basket. He hadn't been well for a day or so, but he seemed to be getting better.

A further ten minutes elapsed. The hour had lengthened by more than two minutes, but I wasn't panicking. I knew they would call back. Sure, enough one minute later the telephone rang. I went to it and scooped up the receiver.

"Hello,"

"Well?" asked the voice.

"You can have the chest. No problem. Just bring my wife home."

"You've not called the police?" It was the same person. The same accent.

"No."

"If we see the police then it's off."

"I haven't called the police. I just want my wife back. Safe."

There was a silent pause before he responded. "Okay, then. Now you listen very carefully. We'll make it as simple as possible. We have no desire to hurt your wife." I didn't reply. "Now listen. Walk out of your home and go to the end of the street. There'll be someone waiting there for you. On the corner. Give the box container to him. He'll look inside. When he's happy that everything is there, he'll make a phone call. A car with your wife in it will be close by. It will be there in less than one minute."

"Okay," I said.

"You repeat instruction."

"I walk to the top of the street with the chest. I give it to someone standing on the corner. He will look inside, then make a phone call. I'll wait for a car with my wife in it."

"That's right. Now be on top of street in two minute." The caller then terminated the conversation and he was gone.

I didn't dawdle. I grasped the box and held it in my hands. Hastily, I left the flat, not either bothering to lock the front door. I left Chipper dozing in his basket. I went down the staircase and out of the front door and into the grey light of the early evening. The time was about a quarter to six. There was very little traffic on Cleardown Gardens, but I could hear the zoom of cars on the busy, nearby North Circular, just half a mile from here.

The cul-de-sac was quiet. Not one soul was around. Cars were parked nose to tail tight into the kerb. Up ahead I could see the smart detached home on the stretch of the road ahead. I headed along Park View by the side of a white painted brick wall for thirty yards to the top of the street. As I neared the corner a boy racer in a souped up Corvette came by in a hurry. Ten yards from the turn of the corner I felt a cold draught cover me, then I saw the figure standing on the turn of the pavement, almost on the edge of the kerb. He was six feet tall. Wearing green military type pants and a green waxy jacket. A solidly built sort. Dark hair cut short to his head. A slightly oily complexion. He had a sharp featured face. A long nose and deep eyes. He had a look of the street about him. The black gloves on his hands gave him the appearance of a killer. He turned to see me approaching him. His eyes went to the chest I was carrying. I kind of thrust it towards him, as if to say, 'here it is, take it off me, let me get my wife back and let's put an end to this stupidity'.

Rather than take it from me he motioned for me to keep it level with my chest. I did exactly as he motioned. He stepped forward a pace, opened the lid and peered inside. His gloved hand went inside. He could see the fifty sheets of names and the black and white photographs. He took the sheets and carefully lifted them out. I could hardly see him over the top of the lid, but he was just a foot away. I could smell the whiff of aftershave on his skin. He didn't utter a word. He took hold of the box and gently coaxed it out of my grasp, then he stepped back a pace, bent his knees, reached down and placed the chest on the floor. His eyes went from side to side, as if he thought he was going to be jumped on by a bunch of coppers. He raised his head and looked at me in the eye, but there was no expression on his face. He had a nondescript killer's look in his eyes, then he gave me a half smile, but still no words. I watched him reach into an inside jacket pocket, for a split-second I thought he was going pull out a tiny pistol. It was a mobile phone, which he put to his mouth and said a single word, which I didn't catch. He didn't say another word, but then motioned for me to spin around to face the brick wall, which I did without protest. He scooped the chest up off the floor, turned and walked away from me along Cleardown Gardens. It crossed my mind that I would have an awful lot of explaining to do to my wife. Seconds passed before I heard the engine of a car coming towards me from my left. I was still facing the brick wall. I turned my head slightly to my right to see the man with the chest walking away along the pavement, from me at a quick pace. The car stopped, on the opposite corner of the cul-de-sac. I could hear a door opening and someone getting out. The door closed with a solid thump, and the car drove away at speed. I turned to my left to see Leah standing on the corner of the street, opposite me. She looked shattered. I immediately ran across the road to the opposite pavement where she was standing. It didn't cross my mind to look at the car as it drove away. I was more concerned about my wife.

As I reached her, I wrapped my arms around her shoulders and pulled her close to me. I felt a great weight leaving my shoulders.

"What the fuck was all that about?" she asked in typical Leah understatement. Her eyes looked reddened, but she had not been crying. She was far stronger than me. I held her like I had done when I had first fallen in love with her. Ten years ago. I pulled her close. After a few short moments we walked back home without saying a word. I had my arm wrapped around her, all the way to the front door.

When we got back into the flat, I poured her a very large G&T. We headed for the sofa. For the next ten minutes I told her everything. How I had searched the flat. How with Chipper's help I had found the wooden chest. I showed her the envelopes containing the old and barely readable letters.

She was not happy on several points. Who could blame her? One, because I hadn't told her. I could more than see her point of view. It was a betrayal of a kind. She was more sad, than livid with me. She demanded that I contact the police. I didn't have a leg to stand on. I knew I had to contact DI Doyle to report the abduction. I simply couldn't let it go unreported. I tried to dissuade her by saying it could lead to more trouble than it was worth. But she was rightly adamant. If I wasn't going to call the police, she was. After all, it was her who had been bungled into a car outside of the school gates, not me. It was her who had been blind-folded then driven to an unfamiliar place.

I located DI Doyle's contact card in the back pocket of my jeans. I didn't want to call him, but refusing to do so would have been the straw that broke the camel's back. There was no way I wanted to lose her. She told me that the same dark-complexioned man I had given the chest to, approached her outside the gates to the school. He had told her he was from Interpol and that he wanted to ask her some questions about Ms Grabowski. A car had rolled up, by her side, the door was opened, and she was pushed inside. That is when the blindfold was placed over her eyes. They drove around for a while, then went to a car park, about ten minutes from here. Thankfully, she hadn't been physically hurt on the outside, but she was hurting emotionally inside, and that was just as bad. I could understand that. It might take her a while to get over it, but she was a strong individual.

Common sense dictated that I had to call the police. I took my mobile phone, found the number on the card and prodded the numbers into the number pad. I got through to DI Cillian Doyle after a thirty second gap of dead air.

"DI Doyle," he said.

"It's Alan Grovenor," I replied. That was my full name. I made a note of the time. It was five, fifty-two.

"Yes, Mr Grovenor. How can I help you," DI Doyle enquired.

"Would you be able to come to my place right away?" I asked. "Immediately. Like now." He didn't reply. "My wife was kidnapped this evening," I added. My voice was even and in control. I wasn't panicking. He must have assumed she was okay. I could hear him take a sharp intake of breath.

"Was?" he asked in an appropriately candid tone.

"Yes. She's home now. Those who took her released her about ten minutes ago."

"Ten?" he asked, perhaps surprised it had taken me this long to call him.

"Yes."

He must have been wondering what the hell was going on here. Who could blame him? "By whom?" he asked, suspecting I knew the answer.

"By those who I assume broke into Ms Grabowski's flat."

"Is she okay?"

"Shook up," I replied.

"Just shook up?"

"She wasn't hurt, but obviously she's upset and shook-up." I had to stop using that word. It sounded as if I didn't care. That wasn't true. I did care.

"How long was she held?" he asked.

"About a couple of hours."

"Why was she held?"

"That's what I want to see you about."

"Okay. Any idea where she was kept?"

"No. They bundled her into that old Mercedes, I told you about. They blindfolded her." I could sense that he wanted to ask a dozen questions, but might not get a clear answer, and didn't want to continue the conversation over the telephone.

"I'll be there in twenty minutes," he said. "I'll swing by DI Arnold and ask her to accompany me. We'll get there as soon as possible."

"Thanks," I said, then ended the call. Relief flowed through my veins. I was glad I had made the call. At least they could protect us from now on, if it came to the need for around the clock protection, which I hadn't discounted. Although I had given the chest to them, I still had the photographs of five of the sheets and all twenty-four photographs on my camera.

I went into the bedroom to tell my wife. Chipper was by her side. She was laid on the bed dozing. I told her the police would be here shortly.

Chapter Thirteen

"What the hell happened?" was DI Cillian Doyle's first question as soon as he entered my home. DI Arnold had gone into the bedroom to speak to my wife and to comfort her. I repeated what I had told him over the telephone.

He, DI Doyle, asked me when all this had occurred. I gave him a day-by-day rundown of events, from me entering the flat on the first occasion, then going back for the second longer look and finding the chest, containing the sheets and the photos, under the bed, and the letters. I showed him the five letters that had been translated by the people in Bloomsbury. The original language was Hungarian.

As he poured his eyes over the letters, he didn't say a great deal. Perhaps, he didn't know what to make of it. Or he was keeping his powder dry and his cards close to his chest. I suspected if it was either of them, it was the former. Still, I couldn't be certain he didn't know more than he was letting on.

He asked me for Steven Amis's telephone number, which I was happy to give him. Like me he thought there was a good chance that those who had broken into the flat, were the same people who wanted the chest. Perhaps it was what they were looking for. I agreed with him. I was losing the plot to a degree. I couldn't remember the date of the break-in, though I knew that today was still Wednesday 14th of June 2000.

It was all merging into one. Paradoxically; perhaps, I felt very relieved to be sharing this with the police because they provided an element of protection. I could feel the pressure lifting off my shoulders. I offered him a glass of something strong, but he said he was on duty, a coffee would be fine, so I went into the kitchen to make a pot, taking the time to give Chipper some food. The salmon steaks could be reheated for later.

After ten minutes, DI Arnold joined both DI Doyle and myself in the lounge, first reporting that my wife was feeling better and had just nodded off. Leah was as strong as an ox, she would soon get over the trauma. Or so I hoped. She was a school teacher and therefore resolute. She had had to face some stiff tasks in her career, but perhaps nothing as crazy as this. She had given DI Arnold a full description of the events that had taken place.

DI Doyle filled his colleague in on the things I had told him. Doyle asked me to show them the remaining, untranslated letters which I had little option, but to do. I also revealed that I had taken photographs of six on the sheets and all the old black and white photos of the people in the dark uniform jackets glaring at the camera. He requested to see them. I had little option but to share them with him. I went into the bedroom and got the camera case.

He wanted me to download the images from my camera, to a laptop, then onto a memory stick. That took about five minutes to set up and do. Both the DIs viewed the sheets listing the long line of names, then the black and white mugshots. They had no idea what the lists represented or who the names could have been. We speculated that Greta Grabowski had, indeed, taken the sheets with her when she was liberated from Bergen-Belsen in 1945. Or one of the camp commandant's underlings had given them to her, fifty-five years before. If that was the case, we asked each other why she kept them instead of handing them over to those investigating the Nazi's crimes? It didn't add-up. And if it didn't add-up, then there was another reason.

DI Arnold, asked me for a description of the man I had handed the chest to. I described him as best as I could. It was, for me, the same man I had seen climbing out of the window. Sadly, I hadn't been concentrating and had not got a look at the car number plate. There couldn't have been many old-style Mercedes models around, but again, I didn't know for sure. Perhaps, the discovery of the number plate would lead to the identity of those who had seized my wife from outside of the school gates.

DI Arnold suggested that two members of the local community-based bobby team would take the time to visit us to see how we were coping. I thought that the police were not taking it as seriously as they should have been, but perhaps that feeling was my emotions getting the better of me.

The DIs stayed until about seven-fifteen. DI Doyle took the stick, containing the lists of names and the photographs, with him, plus the five translated letters. He didn't ask for the other nineteen letters I had told him about. Maybe he had forgotten I had mentioned them, or perhaps he didn't think they were of major importance.

Leah and I the salmon at about eight. I took Chipper out for a swift fifteen-minute walk on the park to the rear of our home. We stayed up until late. She appeared to be getting over her ordeal, but it could have been still building up inside her. Waiting to come to the surface and blow like a boiling kettle. I was surprised to a degree that she hadn't really laid into me. Perhaps that was still to come when all the emotion inside her would come tumbling out. Who could blame her if she really hammered into me?

Thursday 15th June

The following morning – Thursday – I left home for work at eight. Leah called into the school to tell them she wasn't feeling well and therefore would not be there today, but would be in tomorrow. She only worked part-time, three days of the week: Monday, Thursday, and Friday. She occasionally did a stint on a Wednesday evening when she provided extra tuition for children with dyslexia issues in schools in the wider Finchley, Hampstead, Hendon and Church End districts. All within the control of Brent education authority.

When I got home that evening, Leah said she was feeling a lot better. She had even taken Chipper out for a stroll in the park at the back of the house.

Over the course of the following two days, we didn't do a lot. Neither did we hear from the police. If and when we went out it was together. Leah was a little tired and withdrawn, but overall getting over it. We talked about a holiday in August. Perhaps we'd make that trip to the Algarve we'd talked about on a few occasions.

Sunday 18th June

On Sunday at about ten in the morning we got a knock at the front door. It was PC Ravinder Chatto and his colleague WPC Tina Sprake, coming to pay us a visit. Nothing much more than a courtesy call. They checked that we were both okay, hung about for ten minutes, then left. They didn't ask many questions, other than about our health, then they were gone. It would appear that all the investigation work would be carried out by their plain-clothes colleagues, which I guessed was par for the course. I never thought that the uniform branch would get too deeply involved. After all, they were more interested in finding missing children, attending road traffic accidents, looking for vandals, and looking out for persons of interest. More reactionary, than proactive. I wasn't an expert in police procedural matters.

The weekend was soon over. We'd spent most of the time in quiet reflection. I guess Leah still loved me because she hadn't threatened to leave me. We counted our lucky stars that she had not been badly hurt. No one had threatened to break in to our flat. Then it really would have got hairy, not that I was trying to put a damper on her ordeal. I hadn't questioned her much about what she had seen. I had asked her who was in the car, but she had been blindfolded right up to the moment of release. She thought there were three of them. One in the back with her, one driver and one in the front passenger seat. There had been no conversation, so she had no idea if they were German or whoever. But they did have non-British accents.

Monday 19th June

On Monday morning, I was back at Heathcote & Hamilton for eight-thirty. Leah went to the school. The day drifted by without any mishap. I was home for six-thirty. Leah had gotten home at five. That evening I took Chipper for a walk between eight and nine.

Leah had become restless. She told me she wanted to move to somewhere new. Away from here. I thought that a change of scenery would do us both the world of good. So, I was in agreement with the idea. However, what I didn't want was the upheaval of finding a new place to live and the moving of our bits and pieces. Her contract was with the local school authority. If we moved far away say to someplace nearer to my place of work, then she might have to break the contract. Therefore, she might have to find a new authority, or go into private practice as she said she might do. Or end her career, but that made little sense. She said she liked doing what she did, so why not carry on? Talk about moving wasn't dropped, but ending her career was. At least sanity had prevailed. By the end of Tuesday talk about moving had decreased to the point where it was only mentioned once or twice.

Wednesday 21st June

On Wednesday, whilst I was sitting at my desk, in my place of employment, I received a call from DI Doyle to my own personal mobile phone. The phone I used to contact customers and clients, if I was out of the office, was a work phone. I never used it for personal communication.

He told me he had handed over the stick I had given him to colleagues and they were examining the items. As yet, they hadn't been able to establish what the lists were, or who the photographs were of.

I took the opportunity to reiterate that Ms Grabowski must have somehow got hold of them at the fall of the camp in March 1945. He agreed that this was the likely outcome. Why she would choose to keep them was another issue, altogether. A victim of Nazi terror was hardly likely to want to keep them, rather than hand them over to the allies and those searching for Nazi murderers. The possibilities were endless. We must have chatted for ten minutes before I was disturbed by a colleague coming in to see me on a work matter. Before Doyle and I ended our conversation he quickly asked me about my wife. I said she was fine, bearing up well, and succeeding in coping with the aftermath. It was now nearly, exactly one week since she had been snatched.

Thursday 22nd June

On Thursday morning, I accompanied Leah to the school gates, like a guardian taking a child to school. She would be home early today and promised to take Chipper for a walk in the park. I carried on to Golders Green overland station for the train going into Kings Cross.

I had just gotten to work for 9am when my phone rang. It was Simon Greenberg, the chap from the local Golders Green synagogue. I had forgotten all about him to a large degree. I greeted his re-emergence like a call from a friend I hadn't seen or spoken to in a while. It had been, I calculated, nine days since I had last spoken to him. Actually, in truth it was ten. I had virtually forgotten the content of our last conversation.

"Oh, that's right. I contacted you to ask if someone by the name of Greta Grabowski was a person who attended the synagogue," I said reminding myself.

"That's correct," he confirmed.

I waited for his next words, but there was a gap of dead air between us. "Is she someone you know?" I asked.

"No," he replied in earnest. "I've asked the chief rabbi and several of the people who attend on a regular basis and over the past twenty-five years. No one is familiar with that name."

I don't know if I was surprised or not. "Maybe, she stopped attending some time ago," I said.

"But, no one knows that name."

"Oh, right. Okay," was my underwhelming response. "I thought I'd once heard that she was a regular attendee, but maybe I misheard the words. Or perhaps it was a different synagogue. It's possible, I suppose. Perhaps, she went to a different one."

He agreed with me. "It's in connection to her recent passing, isn't it?"

"That's right," I said. "She had lived in Golders Green for the past thirty years. I'm led to believe by the chap from the property management company that she was an active member of the Jewish community. But perhaps not, hey. Unless she was known by another name."

"Can you describe her?" Greenberg asked.

I thought of a response for ten seconds. "Slight lady. Golden hair. Blue eyes. Always slim and lithe. Tended to wear black rimmed glasses with big lenses. Walked with a cane. Liked to wear big bauble jewellery now and again. Seemed to like to wear mustard-coloured cardigans or in a yellow shade. I only really knew her for a couple of years. Though I didn't know her well, or anything."

"What was her background. Her origin. Do you know?" he asked.

"According to what Mr Amis told me, he's the chap from the property company, she came to England in 1947 from Holland. Got citizenship in 1951. She was from Austria. She survived Dachau, then Bergen-Belsen because she could play the piano and the violin and used to entertain the big wigs in the camp. That's what might have saved her from the gas chamber."

I could hear Greenberg make a tuneless whistle sound. "That's amazing," he said. "I would have recalled that story if I had heard it before."

"It's documented in a 'Jewish Chronicle' article I found on the internet. Under Greta Grabowski from Vienna, Austria," I said. "She was born in 1917," I added.

There was a silence. "No. I don't recognise anyone of that name. I'll ask again."

"Please do," I said. "I'd really appreciate it if you could find anyone who might know her. To think I was above her for two years, but I'm only just beginning to understand who she was. I mean someone who went through what she went through in her life."

"I see."

"Tell me do you have any members who are from Austria?"

"Austria?"

"Yes."

"We have a pretty wide bunch here. We have Russian Jews. German, and Hungarian emigres who escaped from east Europe in the 1950s and before the war to make a new life here in England."

Mention of the word Hungarian got me thinking. I still required nineteen letters translating. I paused for a moment. "Do you know people who can speak Hungarian?" I asked.

"Yes, there are several. Is there any reason why you ask?"

"Wow. That's a bit of luck," I said in an upbeat, bubbly tone.

"What? What's so lucky about that?"

"I wonder if someone will be able to do me a favour?"

"What's that?"

"I have a few letters Ms Grabowski left behind."

"What letters?"

"I'm not sure. But I'd like them to be translated." Greenberg was silent. "I'd pay," I added.

"Do you have any idea where she got them from?" he enquired, suddenly interested.

"All I can think is that she took them from the office of a senior guard at Bergen- Belsen."

"Do they have any date?"

"I think they're from 1942 right up to 1945."

"How many?"

"Nineteen to be precise."

"And they're in Hungarian?"

"That's right."

"Well, I can ask," said Greenberg.

"Thanks. I'd really appreciate that."

"Why do you want to know what's written on them?" he asked.

I thought it was a good question, but I had an answer. "I'd like to learn more about her life. A true history." Then I hit on an idea. "Once they're done. I'd like you to have them as a reminder of the evil your people endured."

He didn't reply straight away. "That sounds fine," he said after a few long beats.

I suspect he didn't really know how to respond to what I had just said. I continued. "Though, the ones that I have read sound as if they are more sympathetic to the Nazi cause. Which leads me to think they came from a senior person at the camp." He didn't reply. "How can I get them to you?" I enquired.

"You can drop them into the synagogue at any time tomorrow evening. I'll be here from say seven-thirty."

He asked me for my full name, once again, which I gave him, then I asked him for directions just in case I got lost on the way. We arranged a meeting tomorrow in the early evening. Right on half past seven. I bade him farewell and we ended the conversation with a shared 'goodbye, until tomorrow'.

Chapter Fourteen

Friday 23rd June

It was Friday. Nine days since I had given the chest to the chap on the corner of the street. Nearly five weeks after the discovery of Ms Grabowski's body. Eleven days since I had taken the five letters to 'Translation Services' in Bloomsbury. Only one of which I had read at length.

It all sounded crazy, like a story I had read, but never believed it could be true. If it was a movie script I would have questioned the sanity of the screenwriter. My wife being bungled into a car. Strange characters hanging around on street corners. Photographs of people wearing Nazi uniform looking up glumly into the camera. A living history. Now gone. Though only fifty-five years ago.

During my day at work, I finished off a premium quote for a valued client then got on with some other tasks. Before I departed for the day, I helped myself to a wad of clear plastic document wallets from the stationery cupboard and slipped them into my document holder.

I took a tube from Westferry station into the centre of town, then the northern line to Golders Green. I was entering my home at ten past six. Before I did anything else, I retrieved all nineteen letters and carefully placed each individual sheet of writing paper into one of the clear plastic wallets so as not to damage them in transit. Of course, DI Doyle had five of them, but these nineteen would more than provide an adequate picture of what the letter writer was saying and perhaps suggest who he or she was writing to. Assuming there was only one recipient. I didn't know if that was or wasn't the case.

I placed all the plastic wallets into my document holder. Before I had completed the task, Leah came home and the pair of us went into the kitchen to make a quick evening meal. Nothing more than a Spanish omelette with salad and a tasty dressing.

At a time just after seven-fifteen, I told my wife I was taking Chipper for a walk. I got his lead from off the coat pegs and called his name. He came bounding towards me wagging his tail. 'Time for a walk,' I uttered at him. I clipped the lead to his body harness, took my document holder under my arm and off we went. The main synagogue was only ten minutes away on Temple Fortune. On a side street whose name escaped me. Not that far from the Jewish cemetery and the crematorium.

I was there in seven minutes. It was a solid, red brick building, that resembled a social centre rather than anything else. I strolled along the side street, through a gated rail fence entrance and onto the forecourt, tugging Chipper with me. It now had the look of a former school building with a tall glass panel façade. Single story. I aimed for the glass encased double door entrance on the right. The time was just hitting seven-thirty. I entered through the door and into a shaded foyer.

A chap, who I'd guess was in his late forties, was standing there to greet me. He was wearing a loose fitting light brown jacket and trousers. A striped tie over a plain white shirt. I noticed the skull cap perched on the crown of his head and the silver rimmed spectacles over his eyes. He was portly, but not overweight. He had a stout build and must have been close to my height, five nine or so. He had thick lips. A goatee beard was neatly trimmed and travelled down to cover the bottom of his chin. He did look very Jewish.

He observed Chipper and me. He didn't have a smile on his face, more of a down to business frown. Could it be that he didn't like the idea of a dog in his office? I immediately attached Chipper's lead to the door handle, so he couldn't move far away from the front entrance.

"Mr Greenberg?" I asked and glanced from side to side, noticing the glass cabinet attached on the wall that contained several prayer books and several other religious items.

"You must be Mr Grovenor?"

"Yes. We talked yesterday on the telephone. I've brought the letters I referred to," then gestured to the document holder wedged under my arm. He came towards me the couple of feet, extending his right hand. I took it and we shared a brief handshake as a greeting. He was quite a solid looking chap. His grin had become more of a rictus smile.

"Follow me, please." He led me across a wood parquet-pattern floor, through a single door and straight into an office, about ten feet square at a guess. There was a plain mushroom coloured carpet on the floor, a desk and a couple of chairs. The top of the desk was adorned with a gold painted traditional seven-branch menorah brass candleholder. A decorative plate, with words, which I assumed must have been Hebrew or Yiddish, glazed around the rim.

He guided me to a round back comfy seat at the other side of the desk. He plumped down into a dark leather swivel office chair at his side. I noticed a peach like fragrance in the air. I reeked of Old Spice. I rested my weary bones in the seat and opened my jacket to reveal my work shirt and tie. I put the document holder on my knees. I saw the picture frame on the wall behind him. It contained a photograph of a man who must have been the chief rabbi of Great Britain or wherever. I was conscious that I couldn't stay too long as I had left Chipper by the door and he might soon become restless and start to bark.

He must have seen me looking at the photograph in the frame and turned his head to face it. "That is the Senior Rabbi. Mohsen Bervazski. I'm the community liaison officer." It sounded like a part-time role. I nodded my head and smiled.

"The letters," he said, then paused. I thought he was going to say something else, but didn't.

"I found them in Ms Grabowski's flat." He didn't reply. "I'd like to know what they say. Not because I'm prying or anything, but because they could tell me who she was. And shed any light if she's got any family left. I understand she may have left some money. Perhaps the church can benefit." I didn't know why I had said that, but I had.

He smiled at me, then simply nodded his head like a wise old sage. "I can ask Mister Nagy to look at the letters. He will be able to translate them. Are they long?" he enquired.

"No. Just two sheets of back-to-back text. I guess the writer used both sides to save paper. After all it was the 1940s. Some of them are very creased and a little flimsy after all this time, but by and large still intact. It would appear that some of the key information was censored.

"How very interesting," he said. "May I have a look at them?"

"Of course."

I opened my document holder and began to extract them, two at a time. The light in the ceiling reflected in the glossy, slippery plastic covers. "These are them," I said as I reached over to the edge of the desk to lay the wallets down flat. I noticed the desk tidy and the single telephone unit. I tried to ensure the wallets wouldn't slide off the desk. They had a green shade which contrasted nicely with the blue of the paper.

Greenberg extended his neck to look at the wallets, but didn't take one. "So, Ms Greta Grabowski lived underneath you?" he asked.

"Yes. We, that's me and my wife. We've been there for two- and a-bit years, but I understand she had lived there for thirty. Right from 1970…Before I was born," I added. "From what I know she came here in 1947, after living in Holland. Because of the conditions in that country. I guess." I knew I had to stop saying the word, guess. It sounded cheesy and clumsy at the same time. "She had the ground floor flat since 1970. Where she resided before that is anyone's guess."

"Did she speak with an Austrian accent?"

"She had an accent, but I couldn't tell you if it was Austrian. Maybe. We initially thought it was German, but it may be that she was from Vienna, or someplace like that, possibly even Salzburg. I'm speculating that she was in one of the camps in the east and south, Dachau possibly, but she was transferred to Bergen-Belsen as the Russians advanced across German territory. I understand that many people went the same route as the Nazis tried to hide the camps and their crimes."

"That is my understanding too," said Greenberg. "So, Ms Grabowski was in Bergen-Belsen at the end of the war?"

"That's what I gather. I think she may have taken the letters from a guard, or whoever. But I guess, we'll never know for sure. I had a list of names, fifty sheets thick, but I've no longer got them."

"Why?"

I didn't want to tell him about my wife being abducted, so I told him I had returned them as they didn't belong to me. I don't know if he believed me. If that was the case, and I had return them, why had I chosen the keep the letters?

He sat forward so he leaned over the desk. "Leave them with me, Mr Grovenor," he said, then ran the tip of his fingers over the smooth plastic sheets. "I'll ask Mr Nagy if he can read them and translate the words into English."

"Thank you. I'd be willing to pay him."

"I don't think that will be necessary. I'm sure he will happily do the task for free. He's a very community spirited chap."

"Excellent," I said.

"But I can't promise it will be quick. I mean it could take him several weeks to read all those and get every word correct."

"Of course," I said. "I'm in no massive rush. He can take as long as he likes." I was secretly wishing that he could get them done sooner rather than later. Still as he had asked for no fee I was in no position to be demanding a swift turnaround.

Mr Greenberg rose to his feet. I slipped my document holder under my arm and stood up. He led me out of the office and into the foyer. I had almost forgotten about Chipper. He was laid out across the floor, his eyes closed as if he was asleep. He looked dead to the world. The loop of his lead was still wrapped around the door handle.

The last thing Mr Greenberg said was that he would get back in touch with me when Mr Nagy had completed the task. I said thanks, then we shared a handshake and I was out of there. I was suitably impressed with Mr Greenberg. He had come across as a kind, agreeable sort of chap. The time was just after ten to eight.

Chapter Fifteen

Friday 14th July

   Three weeks had passed since I had visited Mr Greenberg in his office. Even though it was only twenty-three days since the longest day of the year I could feel the nights slowly drawing in. That thought made me feel depressed. Both Leah and I were looking forward to our ten-night break in the Algarve in August. We had already booked Chipper into a nearby dog retreat for the period. We had, by and large, moved on from the events of Wednesday 14th June and put them to the back of our minds. Though they were still there. The property management company had been to renovate the flat below and to install new modern appliances, especially in the kitchen. The interior had been decorated from top to bottom and new carpets laid.

      It was now also exactly thirty days since I had last heard from DI Doyle and DI Arnold. I assumed their colleagues were still examining the letters and the six sheets of lists and the photographs I had given them on the memory stick. I thought their failure to contact me was a little bit disrespectful and symptomatic of a laissez-faire attitude. Though I could be wrong on that score. Could it be that they did know what the lists represented and who the photographs were of, but they were reluctant to share any information with me. Perhaps their reticence to contact me was a reflection that they had no idea who had abducted my wife. Perhaps those responsible had left the country and were in Europe or even further afield.

      What the wait and the gap did give us was a reduction in stress. Leah had been experiencing some angst, that increased then plateaued out again. She said she had felt the stress coming back to make her feel isolated and vulnerable. It was a kind of delayed action to what had happened to her.

We sought our doctor's advice. She advised Leah to reduce her hours at her place of work. Our summer break was only a couple of weeks away so that married in well. We decided to tough it out. We had not thought anymore about moving away. Well not to the stage of contacting estate agents and the like.

Wednesday 19th July
It was a few days later when I finally heard from Simon Greenberg. He, at first apologised for the length of time it had taken Mr Nagy to translate the letters. The delay was partly due to a sudden death in the Nagy family. I commiserated with him, though I didn't know Mr Nagy from a hole in the ground. I was only just getting over that when Simon Greenberg dropped a bomb of enormous potential that sent things cartwheeling and spiralling off in an altogether different direction. He told me that the letters appeared to be from one Nazi camp guard to another. Love letters. From a male to a female. I wasn't hit for six by this disclosure, but it did register a four. That wasn't the bombshell. That was still to come.

"I'd like you to come in and meet a chap I know," said Greenberg, right out of the blue. "He's an authority on such matters."

"What matters?" I asked.

"Searching for escaped Nazis and those who have evaded justice."

I was knocked back, several paces, by the implication in his voice. "I'm not with you. What do you mean?" I enquired.

"This chap belongs to an organisation that researches and searches for Nazis who have evaded detection."

"What's his name?"

"Michael Rosen."

"What does he do?"

"Investigates crimes by the Nazis, against all people. Looks for those who escaped. He's a Nazi hunter."

I was astonished by this sudden interjection. I knew people like that existed in the 1950s, 1960s and the 1970s. Nazi hunters like the renowned Simon Wiesenthal. Today was the middle of July 2000. I didn't think people still searched for second world war criminals. Fifty-five years after the end of the conflict, when many of those who escaped justice would have passed away some years ago.

I remember watching a story about the top Nazi, Adolph Reichmann, the architect of the final solution, on tv. It was a drama. He was captured by Israeli Mossad agents in Argentina, in 1964, then surreptitiously transferred to Israel to face justice for his crimes against humanity. There were many others, less well-known figures who had escaped from their day of atonement in a court of law.

"Why would this chap want to meet me?" I asked.

"Because the letters are from one male SS prison guard to his SS guard female lover who has never been indicted in a court of law."

"Oh," I said in a kind of aftershock to such a statement. "So, who are the letters from?" I asked.

"Probably from a Hungarian man called Pavel Raskovic."

"Who's he?" I enquired.

"He was a senior prison guard at Dachau."

"Are you saying he was never captured?"

"No. He was brought to justice."

"He's the letter writer?"

"So, it would appear."

"To whom?"

"Agneta Brigit."

"Who?"

He repeated the name slowly for my benefit. "Ag-net-a Brig-it."

"Does he know why Greta Grabowski had the letters?"

"He doesn't know for sure. He can only speculate."

"Speculate what?" I enquired.

"That Greta Grabowski is really a Hungarian called Agneta Brigit."

His words hit me like the bright, glowing lights on a speeding freight train emerging out of the dark arch of a tunnel right before my eyes. "What?" I asked in almost zombified one-word question.

He took in a deep breath. I could almost hear and see his lungs expanding as he took an intake of oxygen into his chest.

"That Greta Grabowski is really someone called Agneta Brigit. A Hungarian who worked for the SS as a female prison guard in Dachau, then Bergen-Belsen."

I could hardly get my head around what he was saying. Though it was slowly sinking through my mind like a lead weight the end of a fine, gossamer strand.

"The lists," I said. "That could account for why she never handed them into the authorities."

"What lists?" he asked.

"The lists in the wooden chest."

"What chest?"

That's when I had little alternative but to tell Simon Greenberg about the wooden chest I had found, in the flat below, under the bed. The one containing fifty sheets with forty names on each. I also informed him about the photographs.

"Have you got them?" he asked.

"Not with me. No."

I swiftly brought him up to speed about the abduction of my wife and the terms for her safe return. In doing so I told him about the German man appearing at her door. I described the man. Detailing his six feet two frame, his bulk, his pug nose and his bulbous eyes. I told him about the break-in to the flat and who I had witnessed climbing out of the window.

Greenberg asked me if I would be willing to meet Michael Rosen. I said okay. I agreed to meet him. We set a date for two days from now. Friday the 21st at 8pm at the same location I had visited Greenberg. It was settled in less than a minute. Then I told him I had five photos of the sheets on my laptop, along with the twenty-four photographs. He asked me if I would be willing to show them to Michael Rosen. I said: 'Fine, not a problem.' Though I did add in the proviso that I was not to be named, because I didn't want my name in any investigation report, as it might get back to my employers, one day. They might question me about why I had gotten into such an investigation, when we had many German clients. We ended the call at this point.

I was stunned by the sudden seismic turn of events. Gobsmacked was more appropriate. That the lady who lived below us could have been Agneta Brigit, a Hungarian born, SS prison guard, not Greta Grabowski.

I refrained from sharing this revelation with my wife. She had been on at me to drop it from a great height. I told her I would. Now I was planning to meet with a Nazi war criminal hunter. I had no idea if he was famous or not. I was totally unprepared for that sudden and abrupt switch. What I couldn't understand was why an escaped SS prison guard would want to keep lists of names and old black and white photographs of people who may have been concentration camp guards. Not if she was trying to hide her true identity? It was a question I had been asking myself repeatedly, but now it was in a new context. I concluded that the men who had broken into the flat were looking for the chest. They must have known she had it. Then they bribed the chaps who had come here to empty the flat and paid them to give them the box, but it wasn't in there. Therefore, they must have put two and two together and realised that I had it. Plus, I did have a key to the flat. Terry, the head of the gang emptying the flat, would have told them that. I had given the key to him to give to Mr Amis. I'm not sure why I suspected Terry was the source, but that was the only conclusion I could come up with.

Chapter Sixteen

Friday 21ˢᵗ July

   Tomorrow was the commencement of another weekend. I was home for 4pm on this Friday evening. I had a couple of hours owing to me, so I took them for an early getaway. When I arrived home, I retrieved my laptop and popped it into a shoulder bag, or in other words, a rucksack.
        That evening I left home at seven forty-five to walk the short distance to the synagogue to meet with Simon Greenberg and Michael Rosen. I was using Chipper as my excuse to get out.

 Michael Rosen wasn't how I had imagined a Nazi war hunter to be. I had seen a tall, big, larger than life character in my mind's eye. When I actually met him, he was a little underwhelming. Quite frankly I was disappointed. But I don't know why I was disappointed. He was close to forty-five years of age. About five, six tall and beanpole thin. He had the look of someone who very seldom let his hair down. His hair was thin and fair and didn't have much bounce in it. He wasn't wearing a fine suit and a dickie-bow tie. He was casual in drainpipe trousers, and a green turtle neck jumper. He looked like a tv weatherman, appropriately attired for dress down Friday, on some regional station. Simon introduced him to me. We shared a handshake, then the three of us, Rosen, Simon Greenberg and I sat around a circular table in the centre of the room. The table was an addition to the last time I had been in this room, almost one month before. I slipped the rucksack off my shoulder, opened it and extracted my Toshiba laptop. I had left Chipper out in the foyer with his lead secure to the front door handle. All the letters I had given to Simon were on the table, still inside their plastic wallets, along with a transcription of the words.

"I can hardly believe it." I said, as I was settling into my seat. Greenberg was on my left. Michael Rosen was to my right. I was the one in the middle, but sat around a circular table we were all in the middle. They watched me, turn on the laptop and raise the screen.

"Believe it?" Rosen asked in a question.

"That the lady I knew as Ms Grabowski could be someone else. Agneta Brigit a Nazi female concentration camp guard. How did you conclude that?" I asked.

"A number of reasons," said Rosen. He was British. His accent had a plummy, educated, Oxford University scholar, edge to it. The ruff of his turtle neck jumper was riding high, nearly covering the arch of his chin. I waited for him to continue talking and a follow-up of the reasons.

"Agneta Brigit was known to have escaped from Bergen-Belsen in the days before British soldiers overran it. She was traced to Holland, but the trace soon ran cold. We think that she disguised herself as a Jewish inmate from Bergen. It's known she knew the real Greta Grabowski and may have taken her identity, after first killing her. She even had a tattoo stencilled on her arm. The exact same numbers on Greta's arm."

I made a 'brrr' sound with my lips and blew out a sigh. "Wow," I said. "It's almost too incredible for words. I mean. Who would kill someone, then assume their identify?"

"Someone who was devious, and wanted to escape punishment for their crime," said Greenberg.

Rosen cocked his head to a side. "Believe me. It's not the first time we've heard of such a story. It was quite common for guards to disguise themselves in Jewish clothing in order to blend into the crowd and portray themselves as victims of the German Reich. Not villains of the Reich. They even stole the identifies of some of those they butchered at the end. Some of the guards and the capos, those who cooperated with the Nazis, were caught. Some were executed. But many of them escaped, especially the female guards. Of the five hundred or so at Bergen-Belsen its calculated that less than half were caught. Some of whom said they were just following orders."

"As if that was an excuse," I said. Both of them chose not to comment. "So Agneta Brigit may have taken her identity?"

"Yes. They were similar in looks. Same age. Same height. Weight. Same Slavic look. Same blonde hair. Brigit was Hungarian. Greta was Austrian. There may have only been born say a couple of hundred miles apart from each other."

I was getting a lesson in the realities of the end of the war. That perhaps half of the female guards at Bergen-Belsen had gotten away. By the time the Brits arrived on 15th March 1945, some of the guards had melted into the throng. No one knew for sure. The camp commander, Josef Kramer was still there at the end. He admitted his crimes for which he was executed by hanging in December 1945. When, by the time Rosen had finished the history lesson, I couldn't say anything. I was too saddened to talk.

"Tell me about the break-in at the house," Rosen asked.

I told him. Then we moved to my wife's abduction. And when I was made to hand over the box containing the sheets and the photos. That's when I mentioned the copies I had made.

Rosen said he wanted to view them. I found the relevant file in my laptop memory. Opened it, raised the screen and showed them the six sheets, then the twenty-four photographs. I remembered that Chipper was outside. I asked to be excused for a second. I went out to check on him. When

I returned, I could see that the pair of them were eagerly examining the lists of names.

Rosen told me he thought the names were not lists of inmates, but the names of female prison guards, who had served at both Dachau and Bergen-Belsen. The insignia at the top was the trademark logo of the SS guards. The first column was the name, followed by an age in the form of two digits. Next was the town or city or district of their birth, the country of birth. The fourth column, the one I hadn't been able to understand, was their rank. I was amazed to discover that there were as many as twelve ranks. Ranging from a high of *'chief overseer'*, to the lowest, which was a plain, common-everyday *'overseer'*. The fifth column was the name of the camps they had served in. The final column was the X. Rosen suggested that this column indicated whether they had been captured, arrested, executed or died a natural death, or both.

We then moved to the photographs, not before Rosen wanted to find the name of Agneta Brigit on the list. We found it on the fourth sheet. About a quarter of the way down from the top. The final column was blank. There was no X against her name!

Agneta Brigit was born in Budapest, Hungary in 1917. She served the German Reich in Dachau, then Bergen-Belsen as a SS female prison guard. 'Oh, my good Lord,' I said to myself. There she was on the list of names. The list of the guilty. Next, we turned to the photographs. The images I had taken were okay, considering the originals weren't the best. The features on the faces could be just about made out. We scanned though the twenty-four. Rosen said he had found Brigit's photo and pointed to it. She looked to be in her mid-twenties. A nice face, but for the stiff stare across her eyes and lips she would have been attractive. Her wavy hair was down in a kind of 1940s pageboy style. Perhaps, made famous by a Hollywood actress of the time. Under her prison-guard tunic she wore a brownshirt buttoned up to her throat. I peered at the image looking back at me. It could, feasibly, have been the lady who lived below me in flat number 1. A face from sixty years before I had met her. Her eyes were dazzling and sparkling. Slender nose. Thin lips. The right arm of the jacket had the common Nazi insignia on it. There was no denying who she was. Unless, the photos were made up, which was very unlikely.

Once again, I considered why she had kept the lists in the box. Could it be that she had kept them out of posterity? A souvenir to remind her of all the gay times at Dachau, then Bergen? I felt sick to the stomach.

Rosen shifted his position and took my attention away from the photograph. He asked me about the German fellow I had encountered outside of the flat. I described him as best as I could. "Late 70s or early 80s. Large chap. Brusque features. Small round, almost bulbous eyes in a face of the rosy pink flesh. Large shaved head, tanned, round chrome dome."

"That could be Otto Dietmar," he said.

"Who?" I asked.

"Otto Dietmar."

"Who's he?"

"He's part of the Nazi protection clan. Their role is to protect former prison guards from being exposed for what they were."

"How do you know?" I asked.

"They call themselves the Brotherhood of Volunteers. Protectors of those who did their duty for their country, and their Nazi beliefs."

I thought it was an absurd name. Brotherhood of Volunteers. It sounded like an old, rubbish punk rock band. I repeated it under my breath in abhorrence.

"That's correct. They are a protection league. Their sole aim is to protect the clan from being uncovered for what they are. Nazi murderers. To imprison anyone who didn't believe with their Nazi ideology.

"The holocaust wasn't just about the Jewish people," Greenberg advised. "It was also about silencing those who challenged the Nazi political thinking. Along with gypsies, travellers, homosexuals, and communists."

I took in a deep breath. "This Otto chap. How come he's still walking the streets?" I asked.

"Because he's being protected," said Rosen.

"By whom?"

"The gang. The clan of the Brotherhood."

"It's almost too crazy for words. It's a mad world we inhabit," I uttered.

"It will have been Otto Dietmar and his followers who would have kidnapped your wife. They are the protective arm of the clan."

I sat back in my seat and took in a deep breath.

Greenberg cleared his throat. "If you saw him again, would you be able to recognise him?"

"Who?"

"Otto Dietmar," said Rosen.

"Yes, for sure…. Him and the younger one," I added after a minor beat. "I still don't understand why they haven't been taken out." Rosen widened his eyes and pursed his lips. Greenberg did likewise. "Do you know where these people are?" I asked.

"Who? The members of the clan." I nodded my head. "All over Germany. We know that Otto Dietmar is in Hamburg."

"Hamburg?"

"That's right." I didn't respond. "If you saw him again. Would you be able to recognise him?" Rosen asked, despite Greenberg asking the same question five seconds before.

"Yes, for sure" I repeated. I was wondering where this conversion was heading and where it would end.

"If we find him, you'd be able to tell the British police he was the one responsible for abducting your wife and that might lead to Interpol arresting him on an international warrant." He seemed to know what he was talking about.

"That's true," I said. "Tell me. Where are we heading with this?" I enquired straight out.

"Help us to identify the person was Otto Dietmar. Who was helping Agneta Brigit to escape from justice."

"Oh right," I said. I now knew the direction of travel for sure.

"They were supplying her with financial support. I bet if you check her bank statements all the money came from an account originating in Hamburg, Germany."

"Her flat wouldn't be cheap," I said to back him up.

"If we find him. We'll find them. The clan of the Brotherhood. Can you help us?" Rosen asked openly.

I waited for a few long moments before I replied. "I don't know," I said, hesitantly. "It's sounds a little dangerous to me."

They agreed with me and didn't attempt to soft soap me. I wondered why they couldn't show me a phototroph of Otto Dietmar for me to confirm it was him. Perhaps it wasn't strong enough evidence. They required a face-to-face identification.

"Have a think about it," Rosen encouraged. "We'd all go to Hamburg, find him and you've got the evidence it was him."

"Have you got an address?" I enquired.

"Yes. We have a good idea where he'll be."

I had never visited Hamburg. I'd been to both Munich and Frankfurt with my job, but never to Hamburg. At this moment in time, I didn't know where to turn. It was a city I had never shown any interest in visiting. I guess it was just a large port city. A bit like Rotterdam. When I went there for a weekend break, five years ago, it was a big disappointment. Hamburg might be the same.

That evening I got home for nine o'clock. I had promised Rosen and Greenberg I would seriously consider a proposal to travel to Hamburg with Michael Rosen and a so far unnamed third man to try to find Otto Dietmar and ID him as the man I had seen with Agneta Brigit.

Leah asked me what had taken so long to walk Chipper into a nearby park. I said I'd diverted to another location. A place on the other side of Golders Green. A wood called, rather simply; Big Wood. I think she believed me.

Lying to my wife wasn't something I was used to doing and something I was loathed to do. I did it with a heavy heart. I felt like admitting all, but I couldn't tell her I was thinking of going to Hamburg with a stranger and a third man I had never met. In order to identity the man I have seen outside the flat and whom I believed was responsible for her abduction. It was too mad for words. She would have gone ballistic.

Chapter Seventeen

Friday 4th August

After meeting with Michael Rosen and Simon Greenberg on two more occasions I was persuaded to accompany Rosen and a man called Chaim Begg to Hamburg. I had never been introduced to Begg. He was also a Nazi hunter. Perhaps he had a higher profile than Rosen in Nazi hunting circles.

There, in Hamburg, I would hopefully, positively identify Dietmar as the man I had seen. I might also find the chap with the short black hair. The one with the dark, olive complexion. The chap I had handed the chest to.

Before the Hamburg trip, first, Leah and I were going to Portugal next week, for ten days of lazing on the beach, enjoying the sunshine, drinking too much port and having a great time. I wouldn't be available to travel to Hamburg until the first week in September. This was because I had to cover for staff holidays for the last two weeks of August.

I informed Leah that my employer had asked me to go to Hamburg in September as part of the package they, Heathcote & Hamilton, were presenting to a new client based in that city. I would be gone for only three days, or about sixty hours or so.

Michael Rosen had made all the travel arrangements for the Hamburg trip. Booking three rooms in a four-star hotel in the central St. Georg district for three people, for three nights. All the travel arrangements had been made and paid for. I didn't have to hand over a penny. The plane would leave from London Gatwick, destined for Hamburg on Friday, 8th of September. We'd be back on Monday morning. The objective of the trip was to eyeball Otto Dietmar and for me to confirm it was him. The man I had witnessed at the door and seen with Agneta Brigit on a few occasions. Agneta Brigit, one of the so-called 'Bastards of Bergen-Belsen' for their appalling behaviour towards the Jewish inmates and the other poor unfortunates who found themselves imprisoned there.

Following the first meeting with Rosen I had carried out some homework of my own, particularly about Bergen-Belsen and its infamous female guards. I was relieved in a way to discover that there had never been any deaths by gas in Bergen. However, it was estimated that has many as 70,000 people had lost their lives in the camp. Mainly due to disease and starvation. One of the female guards, Irma Grese, said she was just following orders, and relied on this defence at her trial. Did Agneta Brigit just follow orders? That didn't make her immune from a charge of murder and genocide. There were other notorious Nazi female guards, such as: Ilse Koch, Maria Mandel, Herta Bothe, and Elizabeth Volkenrath. Their participation in crimes against humanity were well documented.

According to what I read, there were as many as 20,000 Russian POWs in the camp when it was liberated in 1945. The Nazis were hoping to swap them for German POWs and to trade many of the Jewish inmates for their own men held by the allies sweeping across Germany from west to east. None of that had occurred. That meant many prisoners died of starvation or exhaustion due to hard labour.

Despite everything that was going on, Leah and I were determined to enjoy our ten-day visit to the Algarve. It wasn't the first time we had been to Faro. We had travelled there once before ten years ago when we were a courting couple. At that time, we both had two more years of university to do, then we were going out into the wider yonder world.

With little money, we had to bum it around for three weeks. Sometimes sleeping on someone's floor or on the beach. This time we were staying, all inclusive, in a four-star hotel. We had so many happy memories of the first time we had been here, we'd go back to the same haunts and recalled that time with great fondness. We were back home by the middle of August. Back to work and back into the nine to five.

    The final two weeks of August petered out and before I knew it was September and the trip to Hamburg was upon me.

Chapter Eighteen

Friday 8th September.

It was on this day, a Friday in the second week of the month, when Michael Rosen, Chaim Begg, and I set off for the trip to Hamburg.

Chaim Begg was more like the image of a Nazi hunter I had envisaged in my mind's eye. I first met him in Gatwick Airport. He was a large, rounded individual in more than one sense. He stood about six feet tall. Big build and he possessed a shock of grey-white hair that was bushy and thick. He was, at a guess, fifty-five years of age, though it was tricky to be precise on such things. He spoke with a kind of a mid-Atlantic accent as if he spent a lot of his time travelling between the UK and North America. His dress sense was practical. Baggy trousers and a simple office style jacket, shirt and tie. His portly stature suggested that he liked good food and no doubt plenty of drink as well. His moustache was nearly trimmed. He wore tinted silver rimmed spectacles that gave him a shifty appearance.

I had visited both Munich and Frankfurt on business, but never to northern Germany. The nearest I had been to Hamburg was probably a weekend trip to Copenhagen, three years ago. At a guess, this city was about two hundred miles to the south of the Danish capital.

My return from my holiday to the Algarve seemed like twenty-one weeks ago, not twenty-one days. I was still getting over the sunburn.

The Gatwick to Hamburg flight arrived right on time at 8pm. Once through immigration, we took a courtesy bus from outside the terminal to a car hire depot where we collected a rental car for the weekend. It had to be back on Monday morning. We had a flight back to Gatwick at 11am that day.

From the hire car depot, we drove the five to six miles from the airport, in the busy Friday night traffic, along a busy, urban three lane road, into the centre of the city. I didn't appreciate just how big a city Hamburg was. I was in for a shock when I discovered the population was near to the two and a half million mark. Making it the second biggest city in Germany after Berlin and one of the largest cities in the European Union that was not a capital city, though I wasn't sure about that fact.

The evening was a little overcast and it looked as if we had just dodged a heavy shower. Our luggage, which we had brought for a short stay, was in the boot. I'd admit that I was feeling a little pensive about the trip. I hardly knew Michael Rosen and I didn't know Chaim Begg at all. So, I was bound to be wondering where and when it would end.

The hotel we were staying in was four stars, touching four and a half. It was in a location in the central district of St Georg. It was to the south-east of the centre and close to the attractive and delightful Alster Lake area.

On the drive into the centre of the city, I was taken by the large number of fine baroque and renaissance style wedding cake like buildings, along with the myriad of tight, busy streets and the buzz of activity. Hamburg was a port city and had a wide number of active docks and miles of red-brick warehouses. It didn't have the feel of a rundown city. It was far more cosmopolitan, than say the likes of Liverpool or Bristol in the UK. As the docklands had been visited by the allies on many occasions during the final year of the war a huge area had been destroyed in the blitz delivered by British Wellington bombers and American B52s. In the aftermath of the war, the city planners were given plenty of empty land to work with.

The hotel, we were staying in, was on Kirchenallee, in an area close to a main railway station. It was a former law court building, now converted into a fine four-star accommodation. It had five floors, railed mesh balconies in front of high, round top windows, a colonnade façade and a short green tile parapet like roof with several loft windows along the length.

Before we had left London, Rosen had come up with a plan of action. The objective was to find and identify not only Otto Dietmar, but any other members of the clan who formed the Brotherhood. Those who protected any Nazi guards who had evaded justice from the courts for their actions during the imprisonment of people who didn't fit the Nazi's idea of Aryan race ideals. Though in truth, in the year 2000, there couldn't have been many of them still alive. Most of those at the senior levels had been traced and dealt with, but many of the junior officers have evaded capture.

Chaim Begg was a British-American Nazi hunter. It was Begg who provided the last known address for Otto Dietmar. He said he had it on good authority that he was in an area called Altona. A large metropolitan district to the west of the central area. It was believed that Dietmar did use a number of disguises and aliases. How sophisticated these were was not known. It could be that he used a hairpiece to cover his distinctive bald head. It was the new breed of clan members who were also of interest to the hunters.

Despite the late arrival on that first night, the three of us set out in the hire car to find the address. Altona was a big area covering a sizable slice of real estate in the western half of the city. It had fourteen satellite districts such as: Altona-Allstradt, Nord, Lurup, Rissen, and Sulldorf, plus others. They, when combined, took up a chunk of land north of the River Elbe, going about seven miles to the west and several miles north-west to the edge of the urban build-up. Most of the buildings in the neighbourhood seemed to be five or six floor high tenement blocks of flats that appeared to be everywhere. Though there were some pockets of housing estates with either terrace, semidetached or detached properties, along with business parks, light industry factory units, and the like.

Begg had an address for Otto Dietmar on Gertrudestrasse. It was believed he, Dietmar, lived alone in a one-bedroom flat. Begg never told me where he had got this information from. As the car driven by Rosen made it onto Gertrudestrasse, I was beginning to regret ever agreeing to come here, but here I was in an unfamiliar city in a part of Germany I didn't know. I was not only lying to my wife, but getting involved in some dodgy dealings. All to see if I could identify Dietmar as the man I had seen at the door to the flat. Or the man I had seen climbing out of the window. Those who had abducted my wife.

Gertrudestrasse was a decent stretch of road, perhaps a quarter or a third of a mile long, maybe even pushing half a mile. There was a combination of relatively low maintenance, four-floor, tenement type housing, small to medium business parks, parades of shops and railway sidings in a grid setting.

On the right-hand side of the road there was an almost continuous line of tenements of the same red-brown brick design. Opposite, across a four-lane commuter route, two lanes in each direction, was a line of detached homes, behind a long, predominately yellow painted metal partition. The road was busy with lines of traffic. A thin, central median ran down the middle of the road.

On this side, the right, the front of the tenement blocks were all the same. Blocks of eight flats, two on each floor, to a flat roof covered with flues and satellite dishes. One central door in the middle appeared to be the only way in and out. The facade was slightly jagged in that at the end of each block of eight flats there was a wall slanting out at a fifteen-degree angle. A narrow verge ran between the road and a wide path, then a wider patch of tree and bush lined grass to the front of the block. Down both sides of the road were parking bays full of stationary vehicles. We drove past a large neon advertisement for Mercedes cars glowing bright in the gloom. There must have been in excess of eighty, single door entrances along the length. Making six hundred and forty individual flats in total. Trees were planted at equal distances along the length in order to provide some greenery. With the onset of autumn perhaps six weeks away it wouldn't be too long before the leaves started to turn a golden brown.

The address we had for Otto Dietmar, was flat 7 at 220 Gertrudestrasse. Surely, we wouldn't find him at home, sitting in a rocking chair, smoking a cigar. Rosen pointed out the signs on the end of tall poles that were the rundown of the numbers in blocks of forty. 761 to 800, then 721 to 760 and so forth. I asked Begg how he knew Dietmar was at that address.

"Contacts," he replied, but that's all he would reveal, just that one word. I didn't pursue it.

It wasn't too long before were at the start of the 300 block, then the 200's starting with 281 to 320. I noticed that the windows were in perfect unison. Colourful blinds or curtains were drawn. Electric lights behind the windows were beaming bright. There were a few walkers on the path, a couple with dogs, but not many. The time was getting on for 11pm and it was possible to see a large moon in the sky.

We soon went by the 201 to 240 block. The block containing flat 220 was in middle of the next set of five, eight flat blocks. As there were two flats on each floor - one at the front, one at the back - it was possible that his place didn't face the front.

We couldn't pull up into the parking bays because they were all full. Rosen had to carry on to a traffic-light controlled, four-way junction, and the end of Gertrudestrasse, where it continued beyond the junction.

"A pretty ordinary looking place," I said to cut the silence. It was. Not that a Nazi sympathiser would reside in a countryside mansion. It was an ordinary tenement in a long line of similar ordinary structures. I had noticed a side street almost level to the 201 to 240 block. It was close to the entrance to the segment containing flat 220. It might give us a place from where to observe the front of the building. I mentioned it to Begg and he agreed. I wasn't convinced we would find Dietmar any time soon. At the upcoming junction there was no way we could do a U turn, therefore Rosen had to turn right onto a new road. After one hundred yards he was able to get off the road, go down a side street then back around again to face Gertrudestrasse, with the tenements now on the left-hand side. He headed down the road on the other side, through the traffic lights, before turning into the side street I had pointed out a couple of minutes before. He pulled up, did a three-point turn and turned to face the front of the block, drove on for twenty yards, then pulled into the kerbside at the end of the road. The entrance to the block 217 to 224 was about forty yards across the expanse of Gertrudestrasse. It was seventeen minutes past eleven on a night that was dark, but for the illumination of the streetlight's and those on the buildings in the vicinity.

We remained in the car. Just looking onto the road. The traffic was still busy, after all it was an active road on a Friday night. I felt a little conspicuous, after all three men sitting in a car was bound to be noted by someone. Someone was sure to call the police. I voiced my concern. Both of them agreed with me. We left the area five minutes later and returned back into St Georg and the hotel on Kircheanalle.

At just gone midnight Rosen requested we have a pow-wow in the hotel's foyer so we could plan our next course of action.

Chapter Nineteen

Saturday 9th September

I called home on Saturday, at just after 9am, 8am UK time, and spoke to my wife. She was fine. She asked me how things were going in Hamburg. I said 'okay'. The hotel was good and last night's meal had been excellent. I did wonder if she knew what I was really doing here. But she never asked me to explain the real reason why I was here. I felt like telling her, but that would have been a massive betrayal. I knew I was wrong, I should have told her, but I lacked the moral courage to do so.

    She had some news of her own. Last night she had met a young couple looking at flat number 1. They were roughly the same age as us. They liked the flat but had several others to see. It wasn't a done deal. Apparently, they were a Spanish couple. Daniel and Lyla Ortiz. He was a doctor on a long contract to do some research at a medical institution in London, she was a Pilates instructor. Leah and I talked for twenty minutes then I had to ring off when I heard a knock at the door.

    It was Michael Rosen. The second day of surveillance was about to get underway. The three of us, Rosen, Begg, and I had some breakfast in the downstairs dining room, then at half past ten we were out and back on Gertrudestrasse for eleven o'clock, watching over the front of the tenement block. It was a better day than yesterday, warmer, the wind had dropped, and the sky had turned brighter. Whilst we were not basking in wall-to-wall sunshine it was okay. I had dispensed with my fleece jacket for something more appropriate. A zip front sports jacket. I still couldn't get over the feeling that this task was bound to fail. There was zero evidence to say that Otto Dietmar lived in the block across the road. He could have moved out some time ago. I had no idea. From my pitch on the street corner, I did observe several people leaving the 217 to 224 block, but not him. The traffic moved along the road in a constant parade of metal. Those long, Euro style, bendy buses came by every few minutes, plus delivery trucks, vans and service vehicles. A couple of emergency service vehicles came by in a hurry. Sirens wailing. Lights flashing. Every big, bustling city had every type of vehicle. Hamburg was no exception. I felt as if the place had a German preciseness about it, a go-getting work-ethic and a beating energy.

It was getting on for one p.m., when I took a call from Rosen, suggesting that we swap positions. I agreed. I was in the centre of the three of us. Rosen was further down the road, by the traffic lights, Begg was in the other direction. We were, all three of us, hoping to see Otto Dietmar.

I moved to a position nearer to the traffic lights. Rosen took my spot. I had fast come to the conclusion that this was the worst surveillance team in the history of surveillance. I had been told that there were no exit points at the back of the building. I was beginning to doubt that. Apparently, at the rear, there was a cinder walkway along the banks of a contributory of the River Elbe. A series of metal bridges led across to the other side.

It was at a time like this when I wished that I still smoked. I mean me standing here doing nothing, smoking a cig would be cool and make me look like some perfect example of a surveillance agent in practice.

We stayed in the locality for the next few hours right throughout the day. Just lazily watching the traffic and the activity. We swapped positions every two hours.

I was back in my original spot opposite the block for 7pm up to the 9pm shift. It was becoming chilly. By seven-fifteen, I wished I'd put my fleece on. In the next ten minutes, I did observe a couple of individuals come out of the 217 to 224 block, but two of them were young, the other was a female. My legs were starting to ache and my back hurt from the continuous standing. I felt like jacking it in, telling those two to do one, I was going back the hotel to pack and go home. I knew there was a 11pm flight to Stanstead. I wanted to be on it.

It had just gone twenty past seven. I was about to take my phone to call Rosen and Begg when a security light above the door to the block of flats came on. From this distance, about thirty yards, I saw the front door open and someone step outside. Despite the distance I could see it was a figure who resembled the person of interest. Otto Dietmar. It looked like the man I had seen outside of the door to flat 1. The chap who had tried the door. His large, round, rotund shape was a dead giveaway. He walked to the end of the path with a limp, as if he had a muscle injury of some kind. He paused, then appeared to put his hand into a pocket to extract a packet of cigarettes, take one and light it with a lighter. Then he turned to his right and made off towards the traffic lights at a slow relaxed gait. He had donned a flat cap over his distinctive shaved head. He was wearing a thick black wool type jacket and what resembled blue jeans or plain trousers. The jacket had a thick collar. I watched him walk about ten yards, then suddenly the penny dropped, and I remembered that I had better follow him. I felt into my trouser pocket to feel a few Euro notes, just in case I needed to call a taxi or whatever.

His hand went up to his mouth to take the cigarette from his lips. I hastily walked up the path on my side, opposite him, and headed towards the busy four-way junction. The traffic lights, on a high and wide metal frame over the junction, were on green. The cap looked like one of those imitation leather caps with a stiff peak. In a mix of excitement and panic I had forgotten to call Rosen. It was only when I reached the top of the junction that I took the phone out of my pocket and made the call to Rosen to tell him to look out for Dietmar. I had him in my eyeline.

"Stay with him," Rosen advised. He sounded as shocked as I that he had emerged into the night.

I said 'okay'. Not really knowing what I was supposed to say. In the next few yards, I was at the pedestrian crossing, and stepping across the dual carriageway. A line of paused cars, with their engines revving, in the two lanes. Overhead the night was drawing in rapidly. I was conscious of my surroundings, the noises and the smells. A tall, white stone, office block building in the distance was prominent against the background of the darkening sky. The H sign for a hospital, called Albertinen, was attached to the end of the tall pole. Some of the vehicles now had their headlights on, and there was plenty of movement. I swiftly crossed the road to the other side. Getting there before the walk sign turned from green to red. Otto Dietmar had turned right at the crossing and was walking along a road called Colotentrasse. It was much narrower, and less busy, than Gertrudestrasse. We walked onward over a smooth pavement, then over a bridge that took traffic and pedestrians over the River Elbe contributory.

The evening was busy. I looked around for Rosen and Begg, but they were not in my line of vision. On the other side of the road, there was a forecourt, containing a large convenience store, several fast-food outlets and other businesses. What might have been a health centre and a fitness club. There were these, intermittently placed, ten feet tall advertisements in those moving displays, about every twenty yards along the roadside, covering travel to a sunny destination, a Pizza express delivery service, and a medical centre. After fifty yards Dietmar turned right onto a narrow, tree lined road that seemed to dip down towards an overhead bridge, about three hundred yards, in the distance. I followed him, keeping a good thirty yards behind. As we got closer to the overhead bridge I could see the distinctive S-Bahn sign attached to the side of a brick building directly underneath the railway line crossing. I glanced behind, but I couldn't see either of those two. I was feeling a little pensive, and a bit on edge, but I don't know why. There was nothing to suggest Dietmar had eyeballed me. I had no idea where he was going to take me. The surroundings were quite open, not that squashed in, and not too intimidating.

My mobile phone rang. I answered it on the third ring. It was Chaim Begg. "How close are you?" he asked.

"About thirty yards behind him," I replied.

"Don't lose him," he warned. I didn't reply to that.

"Where are you?" I asked.

"Behind you. Stay on him."

I carried on walking down the descent towards the overhead bridge and the S-Bahn station. Above the bridge I could make out the canopy roof of a station at the platforms.

As Dietmar dropped into the dark and came level with the building that housed the station he stepped off the walkway and went out of view. I quickly increased my pace. I was soon at the bridge and moved down into the area under the railway track. I turned to face a stone staircase that ascended up onto the station concourse. I took the fourteen, or so, stone steps, to the summit, went through a swing door and stepped onto the concourse. There was a brightly lit, tight foyer that contained ticket machines and wall displays showing both the S-Bahn and U-Bahn network maps. There wasn't a soul near to me. I glanced through a grill-like metal gate and could see a line of about ten commuters standing to the left, under lights, beaming down from the overhead canopy, overlooking the rails. I had no idea if Dietmar was one of them. That was until I moved forward, looked through the grill and caught a glimpse of him. He was standing slightly to one side and partially hidden by of one of the thick concrete posts that held up the canopy roof. A tannoy message came out of the speaker. Probably advising those waiting that the next train was approaching. I aimed for one of the ticket machines, withdrew a few Euro notes, and sought to discover how to buy a ticket for a single journey. I brought up the English language instructions on a console, followed them to the letter and purchased a ticket for a single ride. Chaim Begg and Rosen were nowhere to be seen. I did feel a little exposed and let down. Nevertheless, I threaded the ticket into the slot at the barrier, pushed through it and walked onto the platform. I was at the Bahrenfeld station, on the S1 line. On the other side was the platform for trains going in an easterly direction. I was going west. Across the rails there was a metal chain link fence that backed onto a block of residential homes. A score or more satellite dishes were visible in the growing gloom. Plus, the lights behind the windows. I stayed at this bottom end of the platform. A thick yellow band on the floor was a warning for commuters not to step beyond the line until the train had come to a halt. All around me there where notices in German. No information in English. Still, I could understand one or two words coming out of the PA. I could just about make out a thin line of commuters standing along the platform. Otto Dietmar was one of them. A tv monitor above the platform was flashing the name of the next station. My hand was wrapped around the mobile phone in my pocket, hoping that it wouldn't suddenly spring into life and draw attention to me standing here on my jack jones. Otto was on his own. Hopefully, Begg and Rosen were not far away. As I looked to my right, the front of a train, its headlights beaming, appeared about thirty yards down the track. In these strange surroundings, I did feel a little vulnerable, but nobody had given me a second look. A breeze wafted through my hair. A voice came out of the tannoy. I didn't understand a word. The train came along the platform. It had an all-red livery and a slanted front. The common DB logo was prominent just below the cab windscreen. Lights inside the carriage were bright and reflecting on the platform. It suddenly crossed my mind that it was now more than three and a half months since I had seen Otto Dietmar in close-up and only for less than half a minute, therefore it was unlikely that he would recognise me now. Still, I had to play it cool. I didn't have a disguise, but why would he think it would be me?

    A squeal of brakes brought me out of my thoughts. The engine noise deceased, and the five-carriage train glided to a halt. When it had come to a complete stop a bell sounded and the doors began to slide open. I chanced a peek to my right to see Otto Dietmar enter the middle carriage at the first door. In order to get behind him, I darted along the platform for ten metres. I hoped I didn't draw any glances from any of the other travellers. I didn't.

    I stepped into the same, middle carriage but at the other end to him. The carriage was sparsely populated. Close to twenty people were spread across a space that could easily accommodate eighty. They were sitting on blue backed seats. The set-up was four banks of two seats, facing the direction of travel, then two banks of four, followed by a further set of seats, on both sides of a centre aisle. A panel in the ceiling was showing the route map and the next station. I got the feeling that the Hamburg S-Bahn was very efficient and modern for the year 2000.

Chapter Twenty

Otto Dietmar had made himself comfortable in the second seat of a row in the direction of travel and nestled up close to the window. I stayed well behind him, about twenty rows back, and sat down in the first of the vacant seats. I had a clear unrestricted view of his back. The train stayed stationary for all of twenty to thirty seconds, then a bell sounded, the doors automatically slid closed, the motor revved, and the train set off. It was soon out of the cover of the station canopy and out into the open. Trackside lights were now bright. The sky was turning dark with every passing second, though patches of radiant blue sky were still visible in-between clumps of dark. We zoomed past the back garden of a line of buildings on the right-hand side. An open football field on the left. We were going along at about twenty to thirty miles an hour towards the next station on the line, which I had no idea of, or how quickly we would arrive there. The ride was smooth with minimal buffeting. We zoomed over a bridge spanning a busy road. The streetlights and the headlights of the cars were now piercing. I could feel the phone in my pocket. Frankly, I didn't want to attempt to contact either of those two and alert anyone to the fact that I was speaking English.

  The train entered a dark tunnel and sped through it for around one hundred yards then it was back into the open. The wheels rattled over a set of points or a loose rail. I don't know why but I had memories of being on a Munich over ground train in a similar surrounding. It was another minute before the train began to slow as it appeared to be about to enter and stop at the next station. It entered under the canopy roof of the station and we were along the platform in twenty seconds. The train came to a halt. A couple of passengers got up. The doors opened. They got off and a group of about ten got on. Dietmar remained in his seat.

Four of the new passengers sat between myself and him, therefore blocking my view, but only moderately. The light in the carriage was now reflecting in the glass window and distorting the view out. The train soon set off. We were now in a mixed urban and parkland setting. A mixture of building types. Blocks of tall, four or five stories high, maisonettes. Local authority, match-box type housing estates. Perhaps for a migrant community and the less privileged. I had a feeling we were heading deep into the western suburbs.

We went onward for ten minutes at a good rattling pace. The group of newbies had broken out into loud chatterbox voices and their laughter was becoming boisterous. It was say another four miles before the speed began to drop as we approached the next station. The station destination flashed in the panel in the ceiling. The speed decreased from forty to ten miles an hour in less than five seconds and a pre-recorded voice came over the public address.

The next stop was Klein Frottbeck. Dietmar didn't move. One person got on, nobody got off. The train was soon on the move again. We were going deeper into the widely spread western suburbs. Hochkamp was next on the list of stops. We were there in about eight minutes. A few more passengers got on here and a few more got off. Outside, it was now dark, though the graffiti on the partition between the track and the housing was visible under the trackside floodlights.

Five minutes later we entered the next station. The train reduced speed as it slipped by the platform on my side of the carriage. The driver or conductor or whoever announced the name of the station. I didn't catch the name. I kept my eyes on Dietmar, that's when I observed him struggling to get to his feet, after all, he wasn't a fit young guy. He must have been touching eighty years of age. He turned away from me and headed the few yards to the same exit point he had entered through.

I responded by getting to my feet and stepped onto the aisle. The carriage jolted from side to side. I had to take a firm hold of the rail at the back of the seats to keep my balance. The group of four who had got on, joined me at the exit. I sneaked a glance forward to see Dietmar was at the exit, waiting for the door to open.

The train eased to a stop, the doors opened and we all stepped forward, onto the platform with the thick painted yellow line running a couple of feet from the edge. A name board told me we were at Blankenese station.

The sign for the Ausgang/Exit was up a set of a dozen or so stone steps to a concourse, then out through an opening and onto the street. I took the steps behind the majority of travellers. Otto Dietmar was on the last step, about to step onto the concourse. I had no idea where I would end up.

I made it onto the last step, and turned to my right, stepped through a brightly illuminated hallway, through an arched opening and out onto the darkened street. I could feel the chill envelope over me, but I couldn't hear much in terms of traffic or activity. It would seem to suggest we were in a quiet neighbourhood of west Altona.

I saw Dietmar turn out of the entrance and go to his left. I followed about ten to twelve yards behind. It was a tight narrow street with a thin pathway and big shiny headed cobbles on the road. I glanced back to see a wall partition blocking the way, so it was a dead-end street. The group of four young people were in between me and Otto Dietmar.

The wall of the line of buildings along both the sides had a yellow shade to the plasterwork. Up ahead was a junction, about, at a guess, thirty yards ahead. There was a quiet hush of sound. The surroundings were tight and hemmed in. The phone in my pocket suddenly sprang to life. I took it and put the mouthpiece to my lips.

"Yes?" I enquired.

It was Chaim Begg. He wanted to know where I was.

"I've just come out of a S-Bahn station…Blankenese, I think. I'm going along a narrow one-way street."

"Where's Dietmar?" he asked.

"About twenty yards ahead of me."

"Where are you?" I enquired.

"We got lost. We're on a train behind you."

Oh great, I thought. I was on my own. In an unfamiliar city in an equally strange part of town with old buildings along cobble stone streets in the middle of setting that had a 1960s feel to it. It looked like a part of town that might be in line for demolition in the next couple of years.

"St…wit…."

"What?" I waited for a reply. But it didn't come. It took me all of two seconds to realise the connection was breaking up. It must have been the tight hemmed in streets that prevented a clear signal. I glanced upward at the dark sky; the wisps of moonlight were just starting to make a presence. Ahead of me, the group of four suddenly diverted off to cross to the right-hand side of the cobble street.

We were nearly at the end. Dietmar had just turned a corner and was stepping out of view. I was about, give or take, twenty feet behind him. I hesitated slightly and reduced my pace. I was nervy and on edge, but there was no one close to me. Maybe that's why I felt edgy. I came to the top of the street, then paused to glance round the corner to make sure there was no one there. The path was only a couple of feet wide, then the gutter and the heads of the cobble stones on the street. A light high up on the wall at my side was reflecting on them. I turned the corner and went left. The street ahead of me was narrow, with high, cracked and chipped plaster covered walls on either side, so it was bathed in shadow. I could just see a figure in front of me. It must have been Dietmar in the gloom. I edged forward passing darkened doorways, then an alleyway. I continued on for a few yards, and walked past another darkened doorway. That's when I saw, out of the corner of my eye, the dark clad figure come out of the shadow. I felt his weight come down onto my back. My legs buckled from underneath me. My knees folded like a pack of cards and I fell to the floor with a thump. It didn't take long to work out that I had been jumped on by a figure lurking in the doorway. I couldn't react. A combination of his weight and mine took me down to the hard concrete floor and I whacked my right-side pelvis against the edge of the path. I was powerless. I cried out, but it was no use. I could feel the bulk of my attacker on my back. All his weight was pressing down on me. I was not conscious of any thoughts, just one of an inability to do anything and not knowing how to react. I couldn't. He was on top of me, pressing down onto my back so I was pinned to the floor. I had never been a fighter. I wasn't big or strong enough. For some crazy reason I had a vision of being like a turtle trapped in a net with my hands stretched out in front of me, and my legs likewise. I could feel the warmth of my attacker's breath on my neck. Then I was aware that there was more than one of them. That actually there were two of them. I was petrified. Paradoxically I wasn't frightened. Were these the same men who had snatched my wife off the street in Golders Green? My eyes went to the right to see that my head was level with the cobble street. The cracks in between the cobbles were deep and filled with cracked cement. I heard a few words above me in German, then I felt a hand grab the back of my jacket. I feared that I was about to be beaten to a bloody pulp, or worse.

Chapter Twenty-One

Miraculously, perhaps, I wasn't kicked on the floor. Instead, I was hauled up off the ground by these two men and put onto my feet. Was this in order that they could punch me about the head and body? I automatically went into a defensive mode and tucked my face into my chest and brought my arms up to protect the sides and the top of my head. I thought I was about to be beaten, but it didn't happen. The next thing I felt was the pair of them, taking my arms and pulling them down to my side. I looked from side-to-side in an effort to see the faces of my attackers, believing that I was about to see the face of the dark-complexioned chap, but it was too dark. I couldn't see either of their features in a clear light. They each took a secure grip of my arms. I could hear a shout from some distance away echo in the space. It probably had nothing to do with this incident. I could feel the pain in my pelvis go all the way up to the top of my ribcage. It came to me in a kind of delayed reaction. I cried 'oouch' and pushed my head back as it cut into me.

Now that I was under control, the men took my arms. Instead of beating me to death they forced me to walk between them. We cut over the narrow pavement, walking in the same direction I had been going. They had said nothing. I had zero idea of where we were heading, then thought perhaps they were looking for a quiet spot to execute me and dump my body. I tried to pull my arms free, but they were far too strong and powerful for me to break away.

"Relax," one of them said in clear English, "and, for God's sake, stop struggling."

I was forced along the path. Our pace increasing with every step. Despite the gloom I could see that the cobble street curved ahead in a left to right marginal dog-leg turn.

There was no light but for the pale-yellow paint on the plaster covered walls.

"Schnell...schnell," one of them said and they forced me to walk quicker. I tried to feel for the phone in my jacket pocket, but it felt empty. All I could assume was that the phone had fallen out when I hit the ground. After another thirty yards I was aware that we were about to step across a street on the left. On the corner of the street there was a light in a long window that curved, about forty-five degrees, around the turn. Above it there was an unlit noticeboard with a few words in German on it, but I couldn't make out what they said. We walked past the window. Before I knew it, I was being forced into a darken doorway, through it, down a short alleyway, then into a space, inside the building and into a room. The space was illuminated by a number of burning candles stuck into the necks of tall bottles. The flames were flickering and twisting so the resulting light was reflecting up the stone wall and the ceiling. It was a smallish room, perhaps twelve feet square. The floor was just plain concrete slabs and the walls were bare flaking plaster. There was a wooden bench by a square table, then a few round wooden stools. A low ceiling, with protruding beams running across it, gave it a claustrophobia feel. There was a dirty, old looking net curtain over the long window, thicker dralon or cotton curtains at the side were wide open. Then I saw the small bar counter and behind that the empty shelf that perhaps once held bottles of wine, beer or whatever. The shelf was flanked by two large Bavarian drinking steins. Maybe it was a secret drinking den.

  The two chaps still had a tight hold of my arms, but didn't move me. Seconds past before I could hear voices behind a door adjacent to the bar. It opened, and two men appeared. That's when I saw Otto Dietmar emerge out of the dark and into the light. He had removed the cap, so his prominent shaved head was visible. I could only assume that I was about to be interrogated. Visions of some black uniformed Gestapo officer filled my mind. I now feared more than ever that I was about to be stabbed, beaten, shot or whatever. That my existence on this planet was about to come to a premature end. But I didn't protest. As soon as they appeared and came in, that's when I was taken to the bench by the table and forced to sit down. Was I about to be tried for my crimes?

The two men took a few steps into the room and faced me. The one on Dietmar's left side was younger than him. He had neatly styled grey hair. Very German looking, but he could have been British. The candle flames in the bottles, twisting and reflecting, gave the surroundings a very ambient and a surreal feel. The shadow of the figures reflected on the wall, like a scene in some cult, arthouse occult movie. As if it was in a way all stage managed and manufactured to create a weird ending to a weird tale. The two men who had lifted me off the street, backed away to leave me sitting by myself.

"What is it you want with me?" Otto Dietmar asked, looking direct at me. His heavy Germanic accent made some of the words difficult to understand, but he got the gist of the question out there. It wasn't put in an aggressive tone of voice.

I repeated the question to myself, under my breath. I had better get the right answer, I thought. All four of them were standing tall, looking down at me, expecting an answer. Almost as if I was in a court of law and this was a trial.

"The list of names for starters," I said in a rather stupid brazen tone of voice. The room had a slight hollow echoey effect. I could see Dietmar glance sideways to the man at his side.

"What list of name?" he asked.

"The list of names Agneta Brigit had in her flat. You took them."

"Who?"

"Agneta Brigit. The list of names detailing the names of female Nazi prison guards in Bergen-Belsen."

I saw Otto Dietmar, the leader of the Brotherhood for the protection of former Nazi prison guards, give me a pinched look then a grin.

"You wrong," he said.

"Wrong? How?"

"What have they told you?"

"Who?"

"Those who bring you here to my home city. What they tell you?"

"Tell me?"

"Yes. What they told you?"

I didn't reply.

"Speak freely," said the man at Dietmar's side. "You have nothing to fear from us."

Dietmar stepped forward a pace. "The woman you say was Agneta Brigit was Greta Grabowski," said Dietmar. "I know for fact," he added.

"No." I shook my head. "She was called Agneta Brigit. She was in Dachau, then Bergen-Belsen prison as a camp guard." I was being cocksure, maybe a bit too much. I was doing the right thing, showing them that I knew the truth.

"There's something you need to know," said the man on Dietmar's right. His English was very good.

"Such has?" I asked.

"We suspected that Greta Grabowski was Agneta Brigit, but we were never able to prove it. We could never prove her true identity. Which lead us to believe she was really Greta."

"What?" I asked. I was confused. "What are you getting at?"

"We receive a 'tip-off' as you Englanders say," said Otto. "That the lady in the house you live was really Agneta Brigit. Known to be a Nazi prison guard."

"But we never found a shred of evidence to back it up," said the chap at his side.

I was really confused. "Why?"

"Why what?"

"Why do you want to know if she is a former Nazi prison guard?"

The man to Otto's side moved forward and spread his arms. "Because we are Nazi hunters," he said.

I half grinned, chuckled and frowned at him at the same time. "No, that's not true. You're the Brotherhood. The clan who help to protect former prison guards." Now that I had revealed I knew who they were, I realised that my life could be in danger.

"No, you wrong," said Otto. "This organisation hunts Nazis down and brings them to justice."

"Just see our record," said one of the two chaps who had yanked me off the street.

I narrowed my eyes and cocked my mouth at him. I was bemused by his words. Dumfounded by their meaning.

"The people who brought you here are the protectors," said Otto.

"What?"

Dietmar repeated what he had already said, this time more slowly.

"Who?"

"You tell me. Who are they?"

"Michael Rosen and Chaim Begg," I replied.

"We don't know of anyone with that name. There are not known investigators with those names," said the man to Otto's side.

I blinked my eyes several times as if I was seeking to dispense a misty smog before my vision. "How?" I said, but I don't know why. Perhaps it was because I was confused. They were seeking to cast doubt in my mind. "Why would they persuade me to come to Hamburg to help them identify you?"

"So that they would prove something. That I did exist, but that in truth, I'm the wronged person here. They are the protectors," said Dietmar.

"Why?"

"Maybe they believe that she was a Nazi guard and were embarrassed that she live in their community. That she was about to be uncovered for whom she really was. But we are convinced she was not Brigit. She was really Greta Grabowski."

He seemed to have an answer to all my questions. But then I had a question to ask him. "How did you get a tip off?" I asked.

"Two and a half years ago there was a programme on tv here in Hamburg about Greta. It was a BBC programme. She said she was Greta born in Vienna in 1917 and that she had survived in two Nazi camps. It was made some years before. Someone here saw it, but thought Greta was really Agneta Brigit. She told us and asked us to look into it. We know that she live in London, so we made enquiries and learn that she is in Golders Gren, I think, you say. We find an address and we visit her to find out if she is really Agneta Brigit. But we conclude that she is Greta Grabowski."

"But the lists of names. You broke in to find them. When you realised I had them that's when you decided to abduct my wife."

"What list of names? And what abduct of wife?"

"If you didn't break-in, then who did?" I asked.

"They did."

"Who?"

"The people who call themselves Rosen and this Begg."

"No." I shook my head.

The man beside Dietmar stepped behind the bar. He reached down under the counter. I thought he might have been going for the gun with which to kill me. Instead of a gun he brought up a glass bottle and five shorts' glasses. It looked like a bottle of Schnapps. He unscrewed the cap from off the top of the bottle, then proceeded to pour five tots into the glasses. He handed one each to the two men, then one to Otto. He came to me and placed a glass on the table. I looked at the liquid. It had no colour, just like a clear colourless water like liquid. The flickering light from the candles reflected in the glass.

I was finding it very difficult to grasp the fundamentals of what was going on. Were these people on the level? These men were not protectors of Nazi camp guards, but actually hunters? I looked at Dietmar. "I observed you with Greta on a few occasions and that time about four months ago outside of the door. What were you doing there?"

"We were determine if she really was who she said she was, or if she was really Agneta Brigit. It took a while for us to investigate, because there are cases were Nazi guards took someone else identity in order to escape. If she was Brigit, she could have taken her identity and become Greta in order to escape. We were determine, after befriending her and speaking to her, she really was Greta Grabowski who had been capture by the Nazis in 1938 and taken to Dachau, then to Bergen-Belsen." He knew all the details. He continued to talk in a positive manner. "It was only after learning that she could entertain guards by playing the piano and violin that was she treated with respect and compassion."

"We patriotic, proud Germans have to account for what some of the German people did," said one of the two other fellows. Right out of left field.

'Wow,' my mouth fell open. I had not taken the glass of Snapp's. I was waiting for them to drink theirs first. "But the letters in Hungarian. The letters I found. From Pavel Raskovic to her, Agneta Brigit. Love letters."

"They might be fakes," said Dietmar.

"Fakes?" I asked. "Why?"

"They could have been written in the last few year and made to look old. It's not too difficult for someone with the expertise and the knowledge," said the unknown chap on Otto's left.

"It's an old trick the Gestapo first used many year ago to suggest a connection between two people," said Otto. "The people who break-in to the flat after her death. They could have left them to implicate her. Also, to convince you. To make it look as if she really was a Nazi prison guard. And they are serious about finding the people who protected her."

Could it be that Otto Dietmar and the men really were Nazi hunters and not protectors? I didn't know for sure, but there could have been something in what they said.

"Tell me this. Why did you try the door when I saw you. That time at the door?" I thought I had him here.

"Because I wanted to see for myself that she wasn't there. I didn't know who you were. I thought you might have been one of them."

The four chaps took their shot glasses and downed the contents, one after the other. I took the glass in front of me, lifted it to my mouth, smelt the content, then tipped the liquid down my throat. It wasn't much but it burned in my throat. It certainly didn't kill me. I looked at the four men in front of me from one to the other. I reckoned for the first time that they really might be telling the truth. That's when I felt into the deepest recess of my jacket and found my mobile phone. It hadn't fallen out. It had become trapped in the lining.

"Why if what you say is true, and I don't doubt you, why did they ask me to come here?" I asked.

"Because they hoped we would kill you or at least give you a severe beating. Then you would have been more inclined the drop the thing entirely," said the unknown man. He continued. "I think if we looked into her finances more closely, we'd see that the money she received was from London. Perhaps they thought she was Agneta and she didn't deny it, so they helped her financially. We can't be certain."

"What about the lists of names and the photographs."

"Perhaps, Greta Grabowski did take them at end of the war and kept them hidden. For a reason she only herself knew."

"Nobody in this organisation knew she had them. If we had, we would have wanted to take a look, to see if they would have been of great interest to us."

"So, those believing she was really Agneta took them?" I asked.

"These people called Rosen and Begg really believed she was Brigit and that you were close to revealing her, so they had to find a way to stop you from doing that, so they dreamed up the story about us being protectors. Then persuaded you to come here to find us. In effect they had to make you feel as though you were on the right lines."

I finally had a sense that they were pushing on an open-door They had no need to convince me, I was ninety-nine percent sure they were telling the truth. Maybe Rosen and Begg, if those were their real names, really were the baddies. After all they had left me high and dry. Hoping that

I would be killed or badly beaten, so I would be more inclined to drop it, forever.

"Where are you staying?" Dietmar asked. "And when do you return home?"

"At a place in St Georg and we arrive back home on Monday."

"I wouldn't think it would be sensible or wise for you to stay there or return on your own. We'll accompany you back to the hotel."

"There's a flight back to Stanstead at eleven tonight. I'd like to be on it."

The distinguished looking chap by Dietmar's side, stepped forward. "We can take you back to your hotel for you to collect your possessions, then take you to the airport. But only if you wish."

"Thanks," I said. "That's very kind of you." I looked at the two fair haired Germans in a new light, and realised neither of them looked like the dark-complexioned man I had seen escaping from out of the window. Or the man I had handed the chest to.

Chapter Twenty-Two

It was getting on for nine-thirty when I arrived back at the hotel in St. Georg. I hadn't heard from either Rosen or Begg, or whatever they really called themselves. That just about confirmed to me that Dietmar could have been telling the truth.

I was flanked by the two beefy men who had tackled me on the street. They had taken me in their BMW car from the place I had been frogmarched to, to the hotel. Otto Dietmar was in the back of the car, outside, waiting to take me to the airport. I was going to get the 11pm flight, German time. I had one hour to get there.

I first collected my things from my room, then I returned downstairs to check-out. At the desk I asked about Mr Rosen and Mr Begg. The person on the reception desk hadn't seen them all evening and there was no message for me. I didn't want to see them on the plane. That was the last thing I needed. I still couldn't get my head around their game. In fact, I was finding it hard to connect any of the dots. Either the real facts or the made-up ones. It was a puzzle; I would never solve. I now did think that Rosen and Begg were not who they said they were. I recalled asking Rosen how he knew where Otto Dietmar lived. He never gave me an answer. I think he said something about been given the address, but it didn't sound convincing at the time. Were they just as surprised as me to see Dietmar? Having no real knowledge that he was there.

I made it to the airport with a few minutes to spare and managed to get a seat. I had to pay for my own ticket. Neither Rosen or Begg were on the flight home.

Whilst waiting to board the plane I had put in a call to my wife to ask her if she was okay and to inform her that I was on my way to the airport. I would be home in the early hours of tomorrow - Sunday.

When I got home to Stanstead at half past twelve, UK time, I took a taxi all the way to my home in Golders Green. I was opening the door to my flat at quarter to two. Leah was still up, watching some movie on tv.

    She asked me why I was home much earlier than planned. I debated whether to tell her the truth about what I had got up to in Hamburg, but decided not to until perhaps a later date when she would be less inclined to fly off the handle. I told her we had got the business done earlier than expected. She didn't question me. She could see that I was tired and needed to sleep, though she wanted to know why I was walking with a slight limp. I told her I had banged into a door in the hotel. I don't think she believed me.

    She informed me that the Spanish couple Daniel and Layla Ortiz would be moving into the flat below us next week.

    "Any kids? I asked.

    "DINKYS," she replied.

    I chuckled. "Well, at least it's not an elderly spinster," I remarked, without really knowing why I had said that and in the way I had. I had nothing against elderly people. I would be one, one day.

Several days passed. It was the start of another week. I considered calling DI Doyle to speak to him and to tell him about the amazing turn of events of my trip to Hamburg, but I soon went off the idea. It would reveal my lies to my wife and reveal that I was an untrustworthy, mendacious person. Maybe they would take my claims about Nazi hunters and Nazi protectors with a massive grain of salt and with little sympathy.

After a few weeks of nothing happening, I asked Leah if it was about time we thought about moving to a new home closer to my place of work. After all, we had lived here for over two and a half years. Leah could find a job with say Tower Hamlets education authority or somewhere nearby. She would have none of it. She said she liked living above the Ortiz's. Actually, I think it was because she fancied him, after all he was a very good-looking chap. He did make some of the best burritos I had ever tasted. I said 'okay', we'd stay here for a couple of more years, until we lost the DINKY tag.

You know, I never did come across the likes of Michael Rosen or Chaim Begg ever again. I never did return to the synagogue, but when I called, four weeks after I had returned home, and asked to speak to Simon Greenberg, I was told that no such person with that name had ever worked there.

I was more confused than ever before. Perhaps I had dreamed up the entire story. It seemed almost too absurd to be true. At the end, I thought it was all a bit of an anti-climax. A bit abrupt. I mean, I could never decide which, if any, of the facts were actually true. I had lost the ability to know the truth some time before. My final thought was that I was never going to tempt fate ever again by pretending I really cared what a neighbour had or had not done or achieved. Or where he or she had been in their life.

However, park that thought. If Daniel Ortiz didn't stop eyeing up my wife, he would have to pay a price.

The End

About the author….

Neal Hardin lives in Hull, England. He is the author of several novels, novellas and short stories. His first published novel, 'The Go-To Guy' was published in March 2018, by Stairwell Books, based in York, England; and Norwalk, Connecticut, USA.
Before retiring in 2016, Neal worked in the Education sector for over 21 years. He enjoys travelling whenever possible. He has visited the United States and Canada on many occasions, along with Japan, China, Australia and other countries.
He follows his local football team and enjoys most sports and working out in the gym. He continues to write and enjoys the discipline of writing and constructing great stories.

Neal Hardin is also the author of…
Dallas After Dark
A Gangland Tale
The Four Fables
Moscow Calling
On the Edge
The Wish-List
A Titanic Story
The Taking of Flight 98
Perilous Traffic
Triple Intrigue
Soho Retro
A Trio of Tales
Saigon Boulevard
It's Murder in London

All these novels are available to purchase on Amazon
See me on Twitter   @HardinNealp